THE ADVENTURE OF THE MURDERED GYPSY

The Early Case Files of Sherlock Holmes
Case Two

Liese Sherwood-Fabre

978-1-952408-03-8

WHAT THEY ARE SAYING ABOUT "THE ADVENTURE OF THE MURDERED GYPSY"

Overall, [Dr.] Sherwood-Fabre's reimagining of the famous detective ably expands the possibilities of the Holmes canon. A multifaceted and convincing addition to Sherlockian lore.

—Kirkus Review

[Dr.] Sherwood-Fabre's attention to detail and vivid prose are on full display in this delightful look at the evolution of a young Sherlock Holmes.

—Book Life Prize

A classic in the making!

—Gemma Halliday, *New York Times* and *USA Today* Bestselling Author

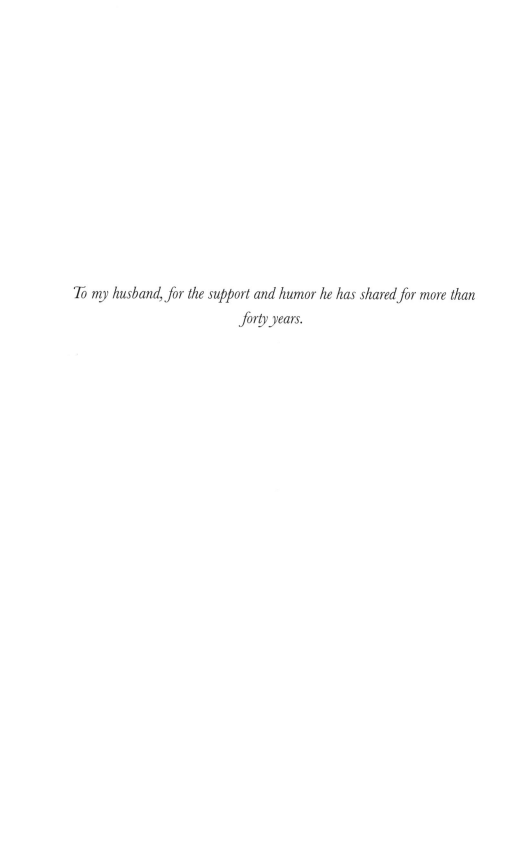

To my husband, for the support and humor he has shared for more than forty years.

CHAPTER ONE

Mother pivoted, swung her foot, and hit her opponent squarely on the jaw. The man landed on his back against the wooden floorboards with enough force to send tremors through the soles of my feet.

Mr. Moto raised himself onto one elbow and rubbed the side of his face with his other hand. "Very good."

Mother extended her hand to our *baritsu* instructor, but he waved it away. "I'm quite amazed," she said, "at the freedom of movement these Turkish trousers allow."

I couldn't argue with her statement. The blousy coverings permitted full use of her legs—something her skirts had never done. At the same time, I found them rather unsettling. Until she had introduced the garment for our lessons, I had not seen her lower extremities, and certainly not in motion. I also couldn't help but wonder what our instructor thought of her visible, albeit covered, limbs.

On the other hand, both he and I bared most of our legs. The traditional *baritsu* costume, or *gi*, consisted of a loose, long-sleeved white tunic that all but covered a pair of very short pants.

When he rose to his feet, I was struck again by our instructor's diminutive size. He matched my mother closely in height and weight, but I had learned at our first lesson his stature did not indicate his strength when it came to defending himself.

Of course, my mother was rather tall compared to many women in our village. Slim and dark-haired, I was told repeatedly how much I resembled her.

"Your turn, Master Sherlock."

By this time, I'd gotten used to his accent and enjoyed how he pronounced my name, roughening the *l* almost into an *r*.

I took the traditional opening stance, but before I could bow, Trevor entered, leaving my uncle's workshop open to the winter air. My seven-year-old cousin stood just inside, almost as if he were afraid to enter. The cold air rushed in, causing goose bumps to break out on my legs.

"I was told to come and get you. Cousin Mycroft is here."

"How wonderful," my mother said. "I know he'll want to freshen up from his trip, so we'll be there shortly. Sherlock was about to have a go at this new move. If you wish to stay and watch, you may. But please shut the door."

Once we were no longer exposed to the elements, I bowed to our trainer and prepared to imitate the kick my mother had just executed.

Trevor spoke up behind my back. "But Mother said you were to come directly and bring Uncle Ernest with you because a friend of his has come too."

I turned my back to Mr. Moto to ask my cousin to repeat the statement. In all my years, I couldn't recall a single time my quite, private uncle had received a visitor. Before I could voice this observation, my instructor swept his leg behind mine, flipping my feet out from under me and the rest of me toward the floor. The air rushed out of my lungs with a *whoosh*. I wasn't sure which hurt more, my back or my pride, when I heard Trevor giggle.

My instructor's face hovered over mine. "Are you all right, Master Sherlock?"

I nodded and accepted his hand to pull myself up.

Once righted, he pointed a finger at me. "Never turn your back on an opponent."

My cheeks burned from his reproach. While he might have overplayed his point, he was correct in demonstrating I had given him the advantage. I had no time to note this because Mother spoke again.

"A friend of Ernest's? That does put a different wrinkle on things." She tilted her head to one side, as if weighing this new information, and turned to Moto. "I'm afraid, then, we'll have to cut our lesson short today. Let's continue tomorrow, shall we?" She glanced at me. "Sherry, dear, please collect your uncle from the barn and join us in the parlor. We'll see you at dinner, Mr. Moto."

The man bowed low. "Until then."

Retrieving my pants from a nearby workbench, I pulled them on over my *gi*.

When I turned to go, Trevor asked, "Might I go with you?"

I hesitated in my response, seeking a socially acceptable excuse to avoid including him. To be honest, I found the boy annoying. I was, after all, six—about to be seven—years his senior, yet he insisted on following me everywhere. Since he'd arrived two days ago, whenever I turned around, I found him staring at me with wide eyes and a slight smile on his face.

Mother solved my quandary, although not in the fashion I'd hoped. "An excellent idea. Trevor's been asking to see the horses. This will give him an opportunity to do so."

With a sigh, I bowed once again to Moto and moved to the door, where I jammed my feet into my boots and wrapped a scarf about my neck. "Come on, then I need to change before dinner."

The boy's delight was obvious. He bounced next to me and kept up a running commentary as we made our way to the stables. He noted how cold it was, how we could see our breath, and didn't he resemble a dragon when he blew out through his nostrils, and how quiet it was here in the country. I considered pointing out the last was difficult to note with his persistent jabbering, but instead, let my mind wander, providing various grunts and other noncommittal noises while he nattered on. My ill humor was only partly related to his constant tagging along. Another portion reflected the humiliation I'd just experienced at the hands, or rather the feet, of Mr. Moto.

The majority, however, involved Mycroft's arrival. While he'd been away at university, I'd been able to relax in a way I found difficult when he was at home. His criticisms of my violin practicing; constant corrections to my French, German, and Latin pronunciations; and complaints about any noise I made that disturbed his thinking always kept me on guard. With his return, I would have to, once again, increase my caution. Not that I didn't like my brother. We had certainly developed a greater appreciation for each other when our family had solved a murder and freed my mother from gaol a bare three months ago. He simply wasn't the easiest person to get along with.

As we neared the barn, I stopped and turned to Trevor. "Can you repeat what you just said?"

"I said the woman visitor was very pretty."

Thankfully, I was no longer in the middle of a *baritsu* lesson because Moto would have kicked me onto my back for a second time as I stared dumbfounded at my cousin. Uncle Ernest's friend a woman? And pretty? I didn't recall Ernest ever mentioning a woman, other than once, and she had been the daughter of an Indian royal.

"Is she an Englishwoman?"

When he nodded, I quickened my pace. I had to get my uncle back to the house to see his female friend for myself.

Our footfalls echoed in the cavernous barn. Built for a much larger number of horses than we presently kept, many of its stalls were empty, but the current occupants responded to our calls with a chorus of whinnies and stamping in the darkness. Their pungent animal odor, mixed with that of hay and leather, grew stronger, and Trevor edged closer to me as we continued toward a lantern glowing near the structure's black center. When my uncle popped up from behind one stall door to the side of the light, Trevor gave a little yelp.

I chuckled at his fright. What would his reaction be when he found out what my uncle was doing in there?

Ernest's resemblance to my mother was striking. She once had told me it was the nose, which I had inherited as well. My experience had taught me the French were thinner and their faces more angular than the British. Our connection to the Vernet family was quite evident in all three of us. And of course, the graying moustache gave my uncle a distinguished look in spite of his often-distracted manner.

"Boys, so glad you're here," he said. "Come. I could use some help."

Trevor ran to the stall but stopped at its entrance. "Where's the horse?"

"No horse," Ernest said and held up a rectangular metal box. "Mice."

My cousin's eyes rounded as scratching and scurrying from inside the box indicated it held several live ones. "What are you doing with those?"

"Uncle Ernest uses them in his work," I said.

From Trevor's stare, I wasn't sure if he was curious or fearful of the contents, but I didn't have the patience to explain it to him at the time. More pressing matters had brought us here.

"We came to get you," I said. "You're to come to the house—"

"You have a visitor," Trevor said, breaking in. "Two, actually."

I turned to him. Two?

"A lady and a gentleman. Mother said you were to come at once."

"I have some things to finish up here," he said, glancing about the stall. "But I guess the mice will keep until I can come back to collect them. Let's set up the traps and then go back to the house."

He handed me another metal box and pointed to an empty stall midway between the center and the far door. "Put it in that one."

"I've never seen a mouse trap like that," my cousin said.

"It's my own invention." A broad smile split his face. "To capture them alive, you have to attract them but not harm them. The key is the entrance."

I turned the box for Trevor to see the hole.

"Put your hand in." When he hesitated, I added, "Don't worry. It's empty."

After another studied pause, he pushed his hand inside. A wire cone connected to the hole's entrance led inside the box. As a mouse (or in this case, my cousin's hand) slipped into the box, the cone closed in on itself, trapping the mouse inside. In Trevor's case, the wire constricted about his wrist. Upon realizing he was snared, Trevor tried to pull out his hand, but it held him fast.

"I'm stuck." Panic tinged his voice. "Get me out."

My uncle stepped up and patted the boy on his back. "Don't worry. It's actually based on a toy. A tube made out of straw. It's woven in such a fashion that when you put your fingers in each end of the tube and pull, it tightens just like the wire cone. But one has merely to push the contraption in the opposite direction…" He placed a finger inside the cone next to the boy's wrist and pushed it upward and toward the box's center. It widened enough for Trevor to extract his hand with a sigh of relief. "To be free of the contraption."

I checked his wrist. The wire had left slight imprints on the skin, but he was otherwise unmarked. "No harm done."

"It wasn't a very nice trick," he said, his lower lip pouting out.

Before I could respond, Ernest snickered. "How do you think he knew what would happen? I caught him the same way."

"Truly?"

Trevor glanced at me, and I dropped my gaze, too embarrassed for the second time within an hour to answer.

Ernest must have recognized my discomfort because he tugged on his overcoat's lapels and brushed off the larger bits of hay and changed the subject. "Let's leave the traps and return to the house. I shouldn't keep my visitors waiting. A man and a woman? I have no idea who."

My uncle's strides were too long for Trevor's much shorter legs. When we had gone no more than a quarter of the way to the house, the boy was a number of paces behind us. He called out, and my uncle instructed me to wait for him. By the time Trevor caught up to me, Ernest was far ahead of us.

"What does Uncle want with the mice?" he asked as we continued across the yard.

"To experiment with. We're cataloging the effects of various poisons."

"Are you trying to find the best one?"

"No. Although that might be a possible result. Imagine you were to find a dead—er, animal…"

I paused before completing the explanation, weighing my words. Aunt Iris probably wouldn't want me to talk about poisons killing animals, and certainly not people, the true explanation for the experiments. My father's younger sister had had trouble having children, and she doted on her only child almost to the point of suffocation. She kept him in a shift long after most boys no longer wore infant clothes. And she refused to cut his hair. If it hadn't been so curly, it would have reached farther than his shoulders. That she had allowed him to come to the workshop to get us was out of the ordinary. She rarely allowed him to be outside for fear of his catching a chill. Which meant her curiosity about Mycroft's companions outweighed any concerns she had regarding her son crossing the fifty yards between the house and the workshop.

In the end, I chose a rather mundane explanation for my uncle's work. "If you found a dead animal like a cow or sheep, you might want to know what it had eaten so you could protect others from eating the same thing. Noting whether they foamed at the mouth or stopped breathing because their throat constricted could tell you something."

"I had a puppy. Papa said it ate something that made it sick, and it died. Maybe if you'd been there, you could've saved it."

"Right now, we're still learning what the different poisons might be. But in the future, I suppose so."

"Papa bought me another puppy. His name is Speckles, 'cause he has spots on his back..."

This new monologue continued all the way to the house and wandered from puppies to horses to the train ride from London to speculating what we would be having for dinner. Never had I been more grateful for arriving at the house than when we stepped inside and were directly met by his mother.

Unfortunately for Aunt Iris, she took after the same side of the Holmes family as my father—stocky with a wide girth. At least she hadn't inherited his baldness. At the moment, she had pulled her dark hair away from her face, allowing the curls to descend down her back. All the same, the scowl she now gave me resembled my father's.

"There you are," Aunt Iris said, folding her arms across her ample bosom. "I was going to send someone out to look for you."

"Uncle Ernest wasn't in his workshop. He was in the barn. Did you know he's catching mice to poison them? I got my hand caught in a trap, but it didn't hurt. See?"

"Truly, Sherlock, I would hope you would keep a better watch over your younger cousin. What if he had injured himself in the trap or been bitten by mice? Heaven only knows what dreadful fever he could catch. And it would have been *your* fault." Her gaze traveled from my head to my boots while I removed my jacket, and she gave a harsh sniff. "What sort of shirt is that you have on?"

"My *baritsu* costume."

"I suppose you don't have time to change. Come along and meet your uncle's guests."

After hanging up my jacket on a peg and kicking off my boots, I followed a few paces behind her. Despite the distance, I could clearly catch her mutterings. "Violette in that indecent outfit of hers. The boy in pajamas. I don't know how we can keep the Holmes name from scandal with such goings-on."

Only Father's etiquette lessons and my recognition that her visit should be over shortly after the holidays kept me from responding to her complaints. If she understood what circumstances had driven my mother to decide she needed to be able to defend herself, she might have had more sympathy. One had only to confront a killer once to determine some training in self-defense was essential.

When we entered the parlor, my father, uncle, and a stranger I assumed to be one of our visitors rose to greet my aunt. I observed Mycroft was absent and assumed he had gone to his room to change for dinner. I shouldn't have been shocked or disappointed he hadn't waited for me to arrive. He would have placed a higher priority on dressing for dinner than greeting me.

Ernest gestured for me to step farther into the room.

"Come here. I want you to meet one of my oldest friends from—"

"India," I said, extending my hand to the lean, short gentleman with graying hair and beard standing quite erect by my uncle's side.

"How did you know?"

"Quite easily, actually. Despite the traveling clothes, your bearing indicates military service. Your dark skin speaks of years in the sun under harsh conditions. Given your friendship with my uncle, the most obvious location would be India."

"Ingenious," he said, and gave a crisp bow. "Colonel Herbert Williams at your service. And what can you tell me about my niece, Miss Meredith Cummings?"

I bowed to the young woman seated next to him and

observed her for a moment. Trevor had been correct: despite my limited experience with women outside our village, I had before me one of the most exquisite examples of feminine beauty I was ever to meet. A silver broach held the collar of her bright turquoise traveling dress closed at the bottom of a long, slender neck. A peacock feather crowned her hat, perched on dark hair, pulled back to expose a heart-shaped face. The ruddy color of her cheeks suggested exposure to elements not common to the English climate but served to complement the deep blue of her eyes. Her slightly hooked nose formed her only flaw, but it simply enhanced the overall effect.

Father's cough brought me out of my reverie.

I smiled and said, "Also shortly arrived from India and recently engaged, but no longer. The area around the finger a slightly lighter shade—"

"Oh," she said and drew her hand to her breast, covering it with the other.

Another cough—this time from my mother—told me I had overstepped convention again.

I bowed, knowing my face now burned a bright crimson. "Sorry. You asked, and I—"

"Quite all right," she said. "You have keen powers of observation."

"Thank you."

I stepped away, taking a spot beside the door, knowing I'd be sent to change directly.

"Colonel Williams, what brings you to the country this time of year?" Mother asked.

Before the man could answer, my uncle broke in. "Whatever the reason, I insist you stay here with us."

Father glanced at Mother. He had to be considering how full the household was already, and his other sister, Rose, and her family still hadn't arrived. Mother gave the slightest nod of her head. She must have already worked out the arrangements because her smile seemed genuine when Colonel Williams responded to her brother's offer.

"Thank you very much, Ernie. We could use a few days' rest before continuing on our way."

"Excellent," Ernest said and slapped the man on his arm. "Let's see to your luggage."

The colonel shifted his feet. "We're traveling rather… light at the moment. Most of the baggage was shipped on ahead. We have just two valises—"

"Only two?" Aunt Iris asked. "I can imagine a man traveling with such limited baggage, but surely Miss Meredith requires more than the contents of one valise?"

"I've found a large wardrobe a tedious burden, Mrs. Fitzhugh." Meredith turned to my mother. "I do, however, have a maid traveling with me and would appreciate it if you would be able to accommodate her as well. I believe she's currently with your housekeeper."

"A maid? Yes, of course." She rose. "If you'll excuse me, I must consult with Mrs. Simpson about her and preparing your rooms. Come with me, Sherlock. We both need to change before dinner."

"If you please," Meredith said, stopping my mother's forward movement. "Are those Turkish trousers? I've seen something similar while in India but have only read about their introduction here."

"They are indeed. While some consider it indecent for a woman to show her limbs"—her gaze drifted to her sister-in-law for a split second—"I daresay the fact that females have lower appendages should not be a shock to anyone."

"And you, Master Sherlock, are you wearing a *gi*?"

Meredith's keen knowledge of both my mother's and my dress surprised me. "Mother and I have been studying *baritsu*. How did you know?"

"In India, we are very familiar with Far Eastern culture. I have seen such costumes before."

"I have employed a master to teach us this form of Japanese physical culture. His drills require loose-fitting garments for movement." Mother smiled and glanced at those assembled. "You will all have a chance to meet him at dinner. He's gone to change, as both Sherlock and I must do if we are to dine on time. If you will excuse us, we'll see you again shortly."

Mother instructed me in a low voice as we ascended the stairs to our bedrooms on the second floor. "I'm afraid I'm going to have to ask you to sleep on the third floor with your cousin for a few days, so Miss Meredith might have your room."

I nodded, not at all surprised with this announcement. The moment Mother nodded her head at Father, I deduced her solution to the room arrangements. One had only to do the calculations to know we had too few bedrooms for the number of houseguests. And I, being the youngest, was the most natural choice to be sent to the nursery where Trevor was staying. While I had no philosophical objections to returning to my previous quarters, I did balk at sharing the room with Trevor. Only my inability to identify another option kept me silent. Perhaps after Mr. Moto left, I might be able to at least move to his room in the servants' quarters for some privacy? Until then, I would have to bide my time.

At the top of the stairs, Mother said, "Miss Meredith will probably want to freshen up as well. Take some clothes for now, and I'll have one of the maids transfer more to the third floor during dinner."

I sighed and crossed to my room to follow out her orders.

Once I'd changed and carried some items to the children's bedroom on the third floor, I almost ran into a woman when I exited the nursery. Tall and dark-skinned with long, black hair, she wore yards of saffron-colored fabric wrapped around her waist and twisted upward under a gray wool shawl in deference to our cold climate. But her eyes drew one in. They were rimmed in black with deep brown irises that darted back and forth as she gazed first at me, then about the hallway.

"I am so sorry," she said in a voice with tones that traveled up and down the scale in the most fascinating way. "I was looking for my mistress's room."

I pointed to the stairs. "It's down one floor. I can show you."

With a dip of her head, she followed me to the second floor and to my bedroom. An open valise and Meredith's bright traveling cloak both lay on the bed. Mother had guessed correctly she would want to change. But without her maid?

"Yes, this is the room," the woman said. "Thank you very much, Master…?"

"Sherlock," I said with a quick bow. "Sherlock Holmes."

Another dip of her head. "I will see to my mistress's unpacking then."

When she entered the room, I caught a hint of a spicy scent, reminiscent of Cook's cinnamon buns. My stomach growled, and I moved to the stairs to join everyone for dinner. After descending a few steps, my—Meredith's— bedroom door opened. I peeked up the stairs to see the maid step into the corridor and toward the servant stairs.

I wondered if she would need help finding her way to her quarters and was contemplating following her when Mrs. Simpson called to me from the first floor.

"Master Sherlock, dinner is served. They are waiting for you."

After a final glance in the maid's direction, I decided she would find it one way or another and made my way to the dining room.

Our family meals tended to be quiet affairs with polite conversation in the language of the day. In an effort for both Mycroft and me to become fluent in several languages, my parents insisted that table discussions occur in different tongues, depending on the day of the week. Usually, we would have spoken French for the evening, but in deference to our guests, English prevailed.

Uncle Ernest, often distracted and quiet, regardless of the topic, was more boisterous than I'd ever seen him. He and the colonel had a number of tales about life in India, to everyone's amusement.

My brother's behavior, on the other hand, was the exact opposite of our uncle's. Never had I seen him so taciturn. He barely greeted me, even though we hadn't seen each other since his arrival. In addition, he kept his head down, staring at his plate. Also out of character, he wasn't eating so much as pushing the roast beef about in the sauce. My brother never turned down second helpings, but today he hadn't even finished his first. Was he sick?

Halfway through the meal, I glanced at my mother to see if she had spotted his peculiar behavior. Her head was turned in the other direction, but I did catch Mycroft's gaze lift for a moment and land on Miss Meredith. When he caught my notice of his action, he returned to drawing patterns in the gravy with his fork, but I observed a dark crimson creep above his collar and form a bright spot on each cheek.

Was our guest's presence at the root of my brother's odd conduct?

A minute later, my suspicions were confirmed when she turned to me and said, "Your brother mentioned you will be going to Eton after the holidays."

Mycroft jerked in his chair as if someone had poked him, and had the question not made my own stomach contract, I might have laughed out loud at his response.

The very thought of returning to classes eliminated any remaining appetite. I'd only been in school a few weeks when my father had called me home because my mother had been accused of murder. During my time at Eton, I'd found the public-school experience most undesirable. I hadn't got along well with either the other students or our instructors.

I realized my contemplation of my future had gone on too long when she blinked at me, waiting for a response. I sought out the most positive aspect I could.

"I'm looking forward to joining the boxing team again."

"Boxing?" she asked.

"He's quite good, you know." Uncle Ernest spoke up from the other end of the table. "Taught him myself."

"But given his slim build, I thought it best to consider another method that would rely less on brute strength. And I wanted to learn as well. Hence, the *baritsu* lessons." Mother glanced at our quiet Japanese master. "I had read of the self-defense method and placed an advertisement in the London papers. Mr. Moto responded with quite excellent references. I'll be sorry to see the lessons end, but he already has another engagement."

"Not that she has need of such practices," my father said, practically interrupting her. "It's more for the physical drills. Good for the health, you know."

"Quite a bit different from our times back in India, eh, Herbert? Needed to be in tip-top shape for a reason. Always some skirmish or another we had to put down back then."

Our guest shifted in his chair but gave an indulgent smile to my uncle. "You were lucky to leave when you did, Ernie. The rebellion was—" He glanced about the table and wiped his mouth. "It changed everything, you know."

"How do you see the shift?" Mycroft asked, speaking up for the first time. "Surely the government has a better grasp of the politics in that country than the East India Company?"

Colonel Williams glanced about before responding. "You might think so, but you have to understand, the *Company* had worked there for centuries. The government, on the other hand, has a different focus. Not always the most harmonious of relationships."

"If I understand things correctly," I said, "it was exactly a lack of understanding of certain customs that created the problems in the first place."

"Quite right, but now other instabilities exist," Meredith said. "The Russians are moving to the west and north, the Chinese to the east—"

"Imperialists, the two," Mr. Moto said, speaking up for

the first time. All heads turned in his direction, and he raised his chin slightly to meet our gazes. "The Russians, the Chinese, they *desire* my country too."

Mycroft pointed his knife toward Father, obviously warming to the subject and overcoming whatever restraint he'd displayed to this point in the meal. "I've told you. The world is changing. While our focus has been on Europe, forces in other parts of the world are encroaching on various British holdings. We must be vigilant, spread our attentions wider."

"Well said." Colonel Williams rapped his knuckles on the table. "I'm quite impressed with your sense of world affairs. So good to see a young person with vision beyond what's happening in Oxford."

"He's always had an interest in world affairs." Mother straightened her back and glanced at Mycroft and me, bestowing a smile on each. "As you can see, both my sons are well-read."

Aunt Iris cleared her throat at this point, giving a warning signal similar to her brother's. "How would you compare the *weather* here to that in India. I trust you don't find it too cold?"

With my aunt's effort to keep conversations away from matters that might upset the feminine constitution, the topic drifted to the prospect of snow in the next few weeks.

Following dessert, the men moved to the library on the left, and the women, to the parlor on the right. I stood in the foyer and transferred my weight from one foot to the other, considering my options. While I enjoyed my mother's company, with my aunt's presence, I knew the conversation there would most likely focus on some sort of female gossip, which my mother would tolerate for etiquette's sake. And according to my father's standards, I was too young to join those in the library. Mycroft had only been afforded the privilege in the past year. Under normal circumstances, I would have gone to my room to pursue my own interests. But at the moment, I had no room of my own. At this hour, Trevor might still be awake, and I had no desire to answer his endless supply of questions. I needed an excuse to keep him from talking.

My music.

As part of Mother's plans for entertaining everyone when Father's other sister and her family arrived, I had been practicing with Constance, the daughter of our steward's assistant, on a number of songs for the season. If I could sneak my instrument from the schoolroom without my cousin seeing me, I might be able to slip away to my uncle's workshop to practice.

While the plan seemed simple in principle, its execution wasn't.

The moment I stepped onto the third-floor landing, Trevor ran into the hallway, followed by his governess.

"I've been waiting for you. I saved some of my cake, in case you want it."

"I just came up for my violin. I was going to practice—"

"Can I listen? I promise to be quiet."

"I was actually going to go to the workshop—"

"Mother said as long as I was with you or Miss Bowen, I could go outside."

I glanced at his governess, hoping she would assert her authority and require him to stay inside. Instead, she raised and dropped her shoulders. He probably tired her out as much as he did me.

"But you're in your nightclothes," I said, seeking some way out of this predicament. "And it's cold outside."

"I'll put on my boots and coat over them. My boots are still by the back door. I'll go get my coat."

He was off before I could protest again, Miss Bowen running after him with the admonishment to put on socks and button the coat. It seemed impossible to say no to the boy. Even the governess appeared to indulge him. For a moment, I wondered if it made more sense to remain upstairs and practice there, but at least the walk to the workshop might convince him to return to the house.

I stepped into the schoolroom to retrieve my violin case and glanced about, recalling the maid's presence in the area earlier. I observed no changes, but then, it was rather dark, the only light coming from the moon through the window. I picked up my case and returned to find Trevor now bundled in a coat, wool pants, and a scarf wrapped about his head.

"I still have on my nightshirt," he said, his voice muffled by the knitted wool. "I just put on my pants over them like you did with your *baritsu* costume."

His remark surprised me. Given his incessant talking, I'd

not been aware of any attention on his part. This observation of my attire indicated he was more aware of his surroundings than I'd given him credit.

The wind had picked up a bit and passed through the coat I'd donned at the back door. I prayed my cousin's wrap was warmer than mine. Aunt Iris would have my head if her "precious boy" caught a chill.

When we entered the workshop, I went straight to a table for a lantern. The moment light filled the space, Trevor gasped.

The workshop was a peculiar and, on the surface, quite disorganized space. Originally a barn, the high ceiling created a sense of openness, until one took in all the projects—in various stages of assembly, disassembly, or total abandonment—scattered about on numerous workbenches and storage crates. In the back, separated from the rest of the room by a folding screen, was a sitting area complete with some of my parents' discarded chairs, a low table, and a cot.

My cousin's interest, however, focused on the table at the edge of the lantern's ochre glow.

"Are those the mice? I didn't notice them when I was here earlier."

He rushed to the workbench, and I followed with the lantern. Several of the rodents scurried about in one wire cage. Other smaller cages housed single occupants, all on their sides and quite dead. A tag on each pen identified the plant my uncle had tested for poisoning. A notebook lay open, with detailed notes on the poison, dosage, and any symptoms.

"I told you we were doing experiments with them."

"But I didn't know they would *die*." He crouched a little to be able to study the dead ones at eye level. "I've never seen a dead thing before. At least not this close." He wrinkled his nose. "They're so *still*. Are they frozen?"

"It's called *rigor mortis*," I said and poked one with a pencil I found next to the notebook. "This one hasn't been dead too long. Maybe three hours or so."

After a moment more staring at the dead ones, he asked, "Shouldn't we throw them out?"

"Uncle Ernest wouldn't like it if we disturbed his things. Come this way. I'll practice in his sitting room."

Taking the lantern, I headed to the living area in the back. When he was deep in his experiments or other projects (he had a knack for developing weapons and explosives), my uncle might go days without returning to the house, preferring to catch sleep when he could on the cot. Trevor settled onto the settee while I arranged the lantern, fed some wood into the round stove near the wall, and tuned my violin. I decided to focus on one particularly difficult phrase in the Handel piece where the fingering was a bit tricky.

Trevor twitched as I started on the third attempt through the section. Only a few bars in, he said, "Is that all there is to it? It's rather short and boring, if you ask me."

"Please, I'm trying to concentrate." I pointed my bow to

the front part of the building. "Why don't you watch the mice? Just don't touch anything."

"How am I to watch them if there's no light?" he asked, putting his hands on his hips.

I glanced up to the ceiling rafters. "Light a candle. There's one on the table here."

"I'm not allowed to use matches."

With a sigh, I put down my instrument, set a candle on the workbench next to the mice with a little more force than needed, and lit it. "Now. Leave. Me. Alone."

The boy blinked rapidly a few times, but he bobbed his head without another word.

I stomped back and continued my practicing. Halfway through my first effort, Trevor was by my side.

"I told you not to interrupt me."

"But—"

"If you don't quit bothering me—"

"But the horses."

I paused. "What about them?"

"They're making quite a racket. There was a fire once in a carriage house not far from our home in London. A horse was caught inside. It made a terrible sound. Can't you hear them?"

Another pause as I listened. With the workshop now quiet, I could hear stomping and loud whinnying. While I doubted the barn was on fire, the disturbance was unusual.

I picked up the lantern. "Come along."

Stepping outside, I studied the structure. No flames were

visible. In fact, the darkened outline in the moonlight showed nothing out of the ordinary. With the horses still making a commotion, I crossed the wide space to the barn door at a fast clip and pulled it open without much thought. I shone the light into the building. Trevor caught up to me just as I illuminated a form on the barn floor.

A man lay face down in the straw-strewn earth.

My cousin drew in his breath.

"Is he…is he…dead?" he asked barely above a whisper.

I turned to him. Despite the lantern's amber hue, I could tell he'd paled at the scene before us.

"I'm sure he's just unconscious," I said. "But we need help. Run back to the house and tell my mother to please come to the barn with her medicine bag. There appears to be an injured man here."

He continued to stare into the building, his breathing rapid and shallow.

I stepped in front of him, blocking his view and spoke sharply. "Trevor. Go. Get. My. Mother."

This time, he focused on me and nodded, taking two steps backward before turning and running toward the house.

As soon as he was out of sight, I stepped into the barn, closing the door behind me. For whatever reason, the horses had calmed, and I could focus on the man. Taking slow, steady steps, I approached the prone figure with caution, as if I expected him to suddenly rise and speak to me. No movement came from the man, and my instincts told me he was no longer capable of any.

With a swallow, I placed my hand on the man's shoulder and gave it a little shake. No response. I placed my hand below his nose. No breath passed across my palm.

He was most certainly dead.

Having decided he was beyond hope, I studied the area about him, searching for any sign of how he died.

No blood was visible on him or the ground. Any additional search would require my moving him.

My stomach roiled. Living in the country, one often had opportunities to come across dead animals. I'd been hunting enough to have even caused the demise of more than one. But I'd never touched a dead *human*. Of course, I'd touched the man briefly, but to check if he were still alive. It was altogether a different situation knowing the man was no more. The vicar, I was certain, would feel compelled to say or do something to show some sort of respect for the man. I could conjure no such words, and I had only a few more moments before everyone would arrive and my opportunity to find any hint as to what had happened would disappear.

I touched the man's shoulder again and jerked it back as if burned. Even through the jacket, I could still feel the man's warmth, as if he were only asleep.

Licking my lips, I put my hands on his shoulder and forearm, took a deep breath, and pulled hard to turn him onto his side, to expose his face. I confirmed I didn't recognize the man. His odd pants were also quite visible. Much more colorful and loose than those worn by any of the laborers or others in the area.

Gypsy pants.

But a quick glance at his hands didn't suggest the nomadic tradesmen. The backs were too smooth. His collar in front was pulled—or pushed—down and revealed white skin underneath. Like Colonel Williams, he had been out in a sun stronger than that found in England but wasn't born with the olive-toned skin of the Romani. And while his face had a stubbly beard, it also lacked the length or fullness I associated with those who had passed through our village.

Whoever the man was, he wasn't as he appeared.

My next thought was to go through the man's pockets to see if their contents would provide some information. Blinking twice, I prepared to touch him again. I raised my hand but stopped as the sound of running feet—many more than just the pair of one person—approached the barn.

I spun about and stood next to the dead man to await the others.

To my surprise, Colonel Williams entered first. He stood just inside the entrance and stared around him, studying the darkened corners outside the circle of lantern light. Father, Mr. Moto, and Uncle Ernest followed him. The colonel's wary stance must have put them all on alert. Instead of rushing to the body, they formed a line across the door and studied the area as well.

Mycroft's absence was immediately apparent to me, but I decided he might have volunteered to stay with the women. With the exception of my mother, none of them came into the barn. Mother pushed through the men and knelt next to the body, placing her valise of medical supplies next to her.

After a very cursory inspection, she rocked back on her heels. "I had no need to bring my bag. He's quite dead."

"I'll send Simpson for the constable and the surgeon." Father turned to go in search of our steward.

"I don't see the need for the surgeon," Williams said. "If he's dead—"

Father spun back around to face our guest. "A death has occurred. As justice of the peace, I need to assure protocol is followed. I suppose I should also stay here to make sure nothing's disturbed."

He glanced about, I assumed to identify someplace to sit. Nothing immediately stood out to me other than the floor. The image of my proper father, dressed for dinner, sitting on the stable's dirt floor would've made me laugh had the situation not been so gruesome.

Rising, Mother said, "I'll bring some refreshment and join you, perhaps a blanket as well."

We all moved to the door, preparing to return to the house, when a scream compelled us outside and toward two struggling figures. Father had had the forethought of grabbing the lantern as he exited and now held it high to illuminate the area.

I wasn't the only one to gasp when we saw Miss Meredith's maid squirming in Mr. Simpson's arms.

"Caught her whilst she was running away," he said.

In the light, the saffron skirt of Miss Meredith's maid appeared less bright but still quite recognizable under a traveling cloak. While she continued to struggle in her captor's grasp, the cloak's hood fell back to reveal her head and face.

Uncle Ernest stared at her.

"Susheela?" he asked, barely above a whisper.

The woman froze, as did the rest of us.

The colonel was the first to move. He stepped to my uncle's side and placed a hand on his shoulder. "No, old friend," the soldier said. "Not Susheela. Her daughter."

Father's gaze shifted between my uncle and the woman before turning to Simpson. "Let go of the woman and take a horse from the barn to fetch the constable and Mr. Harvingsham. Do *not* go near the body you'll find there."

Simpson released his grip on the maid, but only after giving her a scowl. With a nod of his head to excuse himself, he trotted off to the barn as if the notion of a body there was an everyday occurrence.

"I suggest we all retire to the parlor. I'm sure the constable will want to speak to us," Mother said. "I'll ask Cook to prepare some tea for everyone."

Father nodded to us and turned back to the stables. The rest of us followed Mother toward the house—except for Uncle Ernest, who still seemed immobilized by the identity of Miss Meredith's maid.

The colonel turned and spoke to him. "Ernie, old boy, come along. I'll explain it inside."

At that order, my uncle shook himself as if waking from a dream. The colonel waved a hand to send the two ladies and Mr. Moto ahead. He, my uncle, and I followed behind them.

At the back door, I glanced over my shoulder to the structure that now sheltered the second dead person to be found on our property in so short a time and sighed. After the problems my family had had resolving the last murder, I wondered if Constable Gibbons and Mr. Harvingsham, the surgeon, would be up to the task of solving this current death.

CHAPTER TWO

When I entered, Mother stopped me as I passed. "I need your help for a moment. Come with me to the kitchen."

Outside of everyone's view, she stopped in the passageway leading to the kitchen and sent a maid to fetch Cook.

Turning to me, she said, "After the others are in the parlor, I'm going to ask you to help me carry things out to the barn. We know from experience that Gibbons and Harvingsham miss things. I want us to have some time to search before they arrive. Did you notice anything about the man before we reached you?"

"He's no gypsy."

She nodded, biting her lip. "And quite recently deceased. His body was still warm."

I forced aside a shudder as I recalled a similar observation when I touched him.

She cocked her head and shook it. "What I'm not sure of is the *cause*. I need a chance to study the man more closely—"

"Ma'am," Cook said, stepping toward us, "you sent for me?"

"I'm afraid there's been an…incident. In the barn. The constable's been called. He'll want to speak to our guests. Please have some tea brought to the parlor while we wait. But first prepare a basket with some tea and sandwiches and a blanket for me to take to Mr. Holmes while he waits in the barn."

Once Cook had left, Mother waved her hand toward the front of the house. "Let's learn more about the young woman Simpson caught outside. It's quite possible one of our guests knows more than we think."

My lips pulled tight into a line as the gravity of her remark came home. The hairs along my spine prickled from my neck to my tailbone. Three new guests arrived and now a dead man. Was one of them—or someone else under our roof—a murderer?

As I HAD DEDUCED, Mycroft had remained in the parlor with my aunt and Miss Meredith. He now shifted about in a chair, studying the toes of his polished boots and sneaking a peek at our young guest every once in a while. The three must have been informed of the discovery in the barn because Miss Meredith kept blinking as if keeping some sort of shock at bay, while Aunt Iris fanned herself.

"I'm so grateful I sent Trevor upstairs," she said. "Imagine finding that...that...*that* in the barn. Why the governess allowed him to leave at this hour and in this cold, I don't understand. The poor boy is truly shaken. I'm sure he'll have nightmares. I'm so glad Sherlock is sharing a room with him. The governess is to sit with him until Sherlock goes upstairs, which I suggest he should do immediately. He must be experiencing a similar shock."

I'd opened my mouth to point out I'd seen—and been through—worse. Not to mention being Trevor's nursemaid wasn't exactly my responsibility, but Mother broke in before I could.

"I appreciate your concern, Iris. But Sherlock was the one who found the b...man. Constable Gibbons will have questions for him, I'm sure. I don't see, though, why you would need to remain. You seem quite upset. I'll have Cook send you up something to calm you."

My aunt straightened her back, probably preparing for additional protest, but, after a pause, seemed to accept my mother's dismissal and excused herself.

After she left, my uncle turned to Colonel Williams and Miss Meredith's maid.

"First things, first. What is Susheela's daughter doing here? And why is she disguised as your niece's maid?"

"Please, sir, if I may. I am Chanda." The woman brought her two hands together. "My mother had been in touch with Colonel Williams, and after she met with an unfortunate accident—"

Ernest cut her off. "She's dead." A statement, not a question.

"I am sorry to share the news this way," she said, her eyes shimmering. "Let me assure you, she held you in her heart until her last breath. She was also loyal to your countrymen, and that is where our troubles began—"

"Who's this Susheela?" Mycroft asked.

"I-I knew her in India. A daughter of a maharaja. We were…" My uncle swallowed. "We were…" His voice trailed off, unable to complete the sentence.

Mother stepped to his side and placed a hand on his arm. "Dearest brother. Two shocks at once—the loss of a love and the arrival of her daughter."

My chest tightened, cutting off my breath. I knew of Susheela—not her name until now, just of her existence—and could tell how deep his loss ran even after all these years.

The colonel broke in, clearing his throat before taking over his friend's story. "Susheela had been married off to a prince near the western border some years ago. Recently, the Russians have been active in that region, trying to convince the maharajas to sign treaties with them. Chanda's father was one leaning toward supporting them. Susheela, at great risk to herself, sent word of the Russians' activities.

The prince learned of the betrayal and had her—" The colonel paused, glanced first at Chanda and then my uncle, and coughed before continuing. "She passed away."

"Loyal to the queen until the end," Chanda said. "Before she gave up her earthly vessel, she passed me a letter as proof of my father's betrayal. I managed to escape my home with it and share it with your countrymen. My life was at risk as well, and I feared remaining in the country. The colonel offered to help me leave India."

"Despite being a *rajkumari*, a princess, she humbled herself and posed as my maid to hide her identity," Meredith said, bidding the woman to sit next to her on a settee. When the two were side by side, she took her "maid's" hand and patted it. "When we arrived in England, we learned her departure had been discovered."

"We needed a safe place to hide until we could determine what to do next. I thought of you, Ernie," the colonel said. "I do hope you won't share this with the authorities. No need for those outside this room to know our true purpose here."

Mother studied her brother and our guests for a moment and frowned. "I'm afraid I must tell Mr. Holmes, but I think I can convince him that, for everyone's safety, it is best to keep Miss Chanda's identity private for the moment." With a final glance at our guests, she continued. "I'm going to carry some things to Mr. Holmes. Sherlock, Mycroft, if you will please assist me with—"

"Might I stay?" Mycroft asked. His rather abrupt

response was followed by a scarlet hue creeping up his neck. "I can see to some refreshments—"

"I've already made those arrangements, but I suppose if you wish…" Her voice trailed off as Mycroft glanced across the room in Miss Meredith's direction and then quickly away. Mother's mouth turned up just a little—something I doubted anyone outside of the family would have detected. "If you'll excuse us, then, we'll see to Mr. Holmes's comfort."

As soon as we entered the barn, Father strode forward, blocking us from entering farther. Without thought, I took a step back, putting my mother between him and me.

"Mrs. Holmes, I must insist Sherlock be sent back to the house. This is hardly the place for him."

"It is exactly the place," Mother said, crossing her arms across her chest. "We need to know what he saw and heard to direct our investigation before the constable arrives. This man is not as he appears, and neither are Ernest's guests."

Father's mouth dropped open as Mother shared what the colonel had told us.

After Mother finished, however, he straightened his spine and said, "For everyone's safety, I suppose we can keep Chanda's identity from Gibbons—at least temporarily. I don't see how something that happened in India would be relevant here. Similarly, we aren't going to get involved in Gibbons's business. As a justice of the peace, I can't allow it. We don't need the constable to accuse anyone in the family of obstructing justice or, worse, murder."

My stomach lurched. Would Gibbons accuse *me*? After all, I did find the gypsy. Similar circumstances were the basis of my mother's arrest for the murder of the midwife.

"All the more reason for us to determine what he knew and saw before the constable arrives," she said, meeting her husband's gaze with a steady one of her own.

Holding my breath, I observed my parents. Rarely did they confront each other in such an open conflict of wills. Father, however, was the first to sigh and shake his head.

"I suppose we could at least establish what we know to ensure Gibbons doesn't make a mess of things."

"Sherlock," she said, turning to me, "tell us what happened."

"Where do you want me to start?" I asked.

"Let's begin with where you were," he said.

Easy enough.

"Uncle Ernest's workshop. I'd gone out there with Trevor. To practice my Christmas pieces."

Father nodded and asked, "And what called you to the stables?"

With the proper prompt, I was able to quickly summarize Trevor's role in alerting me to the noise in the barn and our investigation of it.

"You saw no one, heard nothing on the way here?"

I shook my head in response.

He turned his attention to my mother. "Were you able to observe anything when you examined the man?"

"I saw nothing to suggest what caused his death. I don't

suspect poison. We've identified telltale signs from Ernest's experiments with mice. I saw no spittle or signs of a seizure."

Father turned, I assumed to conduct an additional reconnaissance of the area. He'd barely made it to the gate of the first stall when the door opened, letting in a blast of air that stirred the hay strewn about the floor. All three of us watched Mr. Harvingsham, the village surgeon, push the door closed and face us.

"Good evening," he said with a slight bow. He slapped his gloved hands together before speaking again. "I met Simpson on the road. I was coming back from visiting the Bemchleys. The elder Bemchley has a bad cough. Could be pneumonia. In any case, the man said I was to go straight to your house. Mrs. Simpson sent me out here. Do you have a sick hor—?"

He stopped midsentence when Mother and I parted for him to see the man on the floor.

"Good lord, who's that? Was he kicked by an animal?"

"From what we can tell, no," Father said, his mouth pulling down. "Which is why we sent for you, to determine if the coroner must be called in."

At the word "coroner," Mr. Harvingsham's mouth turned down, as if recognizing the gravity of the matter.

"In that case, I'll get to it." He stepped forward, then stopped before passing me and Mother. "I would think the procedure might be too harsh for... Wouldn't this best be conducted in private?"

Mother's mouth flattened to a straight line at the surgeon's reference to our presence. As much as I'd wanted to remain and hear what he found, one glance at Father's pointed gaze indicated Mother and I were no longer welcome.

Somehow, Mother managed to push her lips into a smile and held out the basket with the food and blankets she had brought with her. "I'm not sure how relevant these are with Mr. Harvingsham arriving so quickly, but I'll leave them for you regardless. We'll see you back at the house, Mr. Holmes. Good evening, Mr. Harvingsham."

As we trudged back to the house, Mother muttered more to herself than to me, "Good thing I had a chance to examine the man earlier. At least I'll know what he gets wrong."

The ensuing hour involved sitting in a rather awkward silence, the time marked by the ticking clock on the mantel and the tea growing cold, as it remained untouched in most of the cups. Mother made no attempt to engage the others in conversation, her silence most likely reflecting her review of what she had observed in her brief examination of the dead man or stewing over her exile from the barn. Mycroft, never the greatest conversationalist, remained withdrawn, his attention on his shoes. Even Uncle Ernest, so boisterous at the dinner table when conversing with his friend, remained subdued.

About half an hour after the surgeon's arrival, Constable Gibbons appeared and was sent straight to the barn. If I hadn't been as curious as my mother about the observations of the three men out there, I might have begged off and gone to the third floor. Trevor's incessant questions might have proved a relief from the parlor's stifling atmosphere.

When a pair of footfalls finally echoed outside the parlor, the entire room seemed to straighten to attention. All heads turned in unison to the door when Father entered, followed by the constable.

"Gibbons, you know my family," Father said in the same grave voice he used when he presided over his court.

After my father presented the others in the room, Gibbons glanced about and said, "Normally, I would speak to each of you individually, learn your whereabouts when the boy found the b—man. But Mr. Holmes has assured me you were all inside, except for the boy here and you."

His gaze fell on Chanda. She raised her chin, as if daring him to question her. Instead, he turned to face me.

"I need to ask you some questions, since you found, er… him. I'm to use Mr. Holmes's office."

I took a step toward the door but stopped when Mother spoke up.

"I insist his father and I be present when you interrogate Sherlock."

My stomach squeezed at the word "interrogate," and I was grateful dinner had passed a few hours ago. *Interview* or even *question* didn't carry the harshness of *interrogate*. *Was* he considering me a suspect? How could he? As a boy of thirteen, I could hardly murder a grown man. A wave of fear swept through me, and it was all I could do to keep my knees from knocking.

"She's right," Father said. "As an officer of the court, I've observed countless witness interviews. This isn't any different."

"But he's your son." Gibbons peered at me, then my mother and finally at my father where he stood off to the left. Throwing up his arms, he said, "Fine. Let's all interview him, shall we? It's rounding toward midnight, and I would like a few hours of sleep before morning."

Father's office reflected his position as country squire. Wood paneling gave it a dark, solemn air. The large desk was centered in front of a many-paned window at the far wall. The Holmes family crest adorned the middle pane. My father's two additions to the room were the display cases holding his insect collection along the right wall and the stacks of papers in orderly columns on the desk. The left wall held a fireplace with several armchairs arranged around it. When Trevor called the men to the barn, they must have left their cigars in the ashtrays. The smoke and aroma still hung in the air, although none still burned.

When we stepped in, Gibbons glanced about and pointed to one of the chairs in front of the fireplace. I took the seat and my parents arranged themselves one on each side of me. The constable stood between me and the fireplace and pulled out a pad and pencil.

"Let's start at the beginning. Where were you before you went to the barn?"

"My uncle's workshop."

From there he asked me about what had compelled me to go to the stables, how I had found the man, if I had touched him, and what I had done while waiting for the others. After a good thirty minutes of this back and forth, he finally waved a hand, shooing me from the room.

When I stood to leave, he turned to my mother. "I would like to have a word with Squire Holmes alone, if you please."

I could almost hear my mother's spine stiffen. For the second time this evening, she'd been dismissed from any discussion about the dead man.

Father must have noticed her resentment because he said, "I'll speak with you right after this."

I followed her out, my distaste for the constable and pity for my mother both growing greater. While my mother had no standing when it came to the investigation of this crime, or any other, she was well-read in human anatomy and had heard my father discuss the cases appearing before him for more than twenty years. To be sent out like her son, the schoolboy, was certainly a slap in the face.

As we exited the office, Ernest stuck his head out of the parlor door. "Violette, everyone is asking how much longer. They are all getting quite tired."

"I'm afraid I have no indications from the constable about his plans. Perhaps he will—"

Before she could complete the thought, Gibbons and Father joined us in the hallway. Gibbons crossed into the parlor and spoke to all assembled. "I believe I have all the information I need for now. I'll be coming back in the morning when everyone is fresh."

"Surely you can share some information with us?" Mycroft asked. "For example, who is he?"

"All we can say for certain is he's not from around here. Neither Squire Holmes nor Mr. Harvingsham recognize him. He was dressed like a gypsy—maybe part of the group that arrived a few days ago and are camping near the village. But he's not one of them. All the wrong color for that. It could be a disguise he's using to hide among them. I'll check that out." He cleared his throat and glanced at my father. "On the off chance one of you might know him after you get a good look at him, Squire Holmes has agreed to allow you all, guests and servants, to view the face. Now if you consider your stomach too delicate for such a task, stay inside. Some of my men will be bringing him 'round to a wagon. We'll be checking with the gypsies on the way to the village to see if they claim him."

I considered crying off, using the excuse that I'd already had a chance to do more than *glance* at the man and knew I didn't recognize him. When none offered to leave, not even Miss Meredith, I paused before speaking up. Why would a young lady be willing to view the man? At that point, I decided to stay and focus on the reaction of the others.

After a moment, Gibbons waved his arm toward the parlor door. "Follow me."

We regathered in an awkward semicircle on the house's front drive, around the cart, waiting for the corpse's arrival. To get a view of all the guests' reactions to the man's face, I chose a place at the end farthest from the wagon. One of the constable's officers sat on its front seat, holding the horses' reins tightly as they stamped their feet on the drive's stony surface and snorted foggy clouds from their nostrils. After a moment, we all turned toward the sound of shuffling footsteps as four officers came around the barn side of the house carrying a canvas litter with a blanket-covered form weighing it down.

As the men reached our group, Gibbons ordered them to stop and bobbed his head to one side. His man lifted the blanket, and the constable held a lantern close to illuminate the face. I quickly studied the expressions of each of the assembled as he did so. To my disappointment, none of them gasped or drew back in horror. The only movement any of them made was a shake of their head, indicating no knowledge of his identity.

I checked to see if Mother had observed what I had. To my surprise, I found her still on the steps leading to the front door, her attention focused elsewhere. Following her gaze, I saw a figure in a window of the schoolroom on the third floor. Before I could make out the form, the curtain dropped. Other than the silhouette being too tall for Trevor, I wasn't even certain whether it was a man or woman.

The constable's loud sigh called me back to the dead man, and he signaled his men to load the stretcher onto the wagon.

Once the task was finished, he turned to address us. "I'll be back to speak to each of you. For the time being, I will request you remain here until we determine none of you is involved."

"But I have obligations," Mr. Moto said, alarm in his voice.

His protest took me by surprise. As inscrutable as the Asians are reputed to be, this man's darting gaze—to the constable, to the wagon now lumbering toward the road, and back—and stiff back suggested concern beyond staying an extra day or two at Underbyrne.

"I'm afraid you'll have to adjust your obligations," Gibbons said, his voice tinged with a bit of contempt.

The rest of our guests all seemed to display an unease similar to my *baritsu* instructor's. The colonel, however, stepped forward, pulling himself to full attention and peering at the constable as if he were a new recruit.

"For what purpose? None of us was in the barn. You aren't suggesting we will be held here against our will?"

The constable straightened his back as well, and I feared the two might come to blows. I released my breath when Father spoke in a calm, formal manner.

"It shouldn't be for long. This has been a trying evening for all of us. I suggest we all retire. Things will appear different tomorrow, in the light of day." Father waved his hand toward the entrance and directed all to pass inside.

Allowing the adults to pass first, I took up the rear. Father had remained just inside the foyer, and as I passed him, he put a hand on my arm to pull me aside, next to my brother and mother.

Both he and Mother were watching our guests ascend the stairs to the bedrooms, and I took a cue from them. In the stronger light of the foyer and with my uncle and the colonel for comparison, I realized Miss Meredith stood as tall as the men—something not apparent when she'd been seated. In contrast, Chanda created a much more diminutive figure. About halfway up the stairs, the smaller woman paused and glanced at the front door. As if in a trance, she clutched at her chest before shuddering and resuming her ascent.

Mother made a small sound in the back of her throat, and my stomach tightened. What had the woman's action told my mother? After each bedroom door opened and shut upstairs, Mother tipped her head toward the office, and we followed her there, my father quietly locking us in.

Mycroft was the first to take a seat, settling into one of the chairs by the fire.

I studied him for a moment as he stared into the flames dancing about the logs. He seemed more relaxed now that it was just the four of us, but still, he remained distant, preoccupied in a manner I'd never observed before.

"I wanted to speak with you to warn you all not to inter- ject yourself in this investigation," Father said.

"I don't see how we can avoid it," Mother said, running her hands down the front of her skirt. "Once again, a murder has been discovered on our property, and once again, someone in the household will be accused of the crime. The scandal—"

"Need not concern us this time. Gibbons has assured me he'll not be arresting anyone in the family. His theory at the moment is the man had some sort of falling out with those in the gypsy camp. The man couldn't have been part of their tribe and most likely had been paying them to hide out in their company. Gibbons figures he was some fugitive and will send his description to other parishes. He thinks the man was deposited in the barn to throw suspicion away from the camp."

"No," Mother said, shaking her head. "He was murdered nearby and only a little bit before Sherlock found him. He was still warm. In the middle of winter."

"Gibbons figures he was wrapped in a blanket or two to hide him. He found no sign of a struggle."

"Did Harvingsham note he was strangled? I examined his eyes when I checked for signs of life. There were small hemorrhages, indicating strangulation. After the man expired, the killer could have swept the floor around the body. Easy enough to remove any footprints or scuff marks."

"I asked Harvingsham about strangulation, but he said

there were no marks about the neck. He was most likely poisoned."

Another sniff. "Check with Ernest. We have yet to find a poison capable of causing the petechiae I observed."

"Let it go, Mrs. Holmes," Father said with a sigh. "The constable and surgeon are satisfied the man was attacked elsewhere and brought here. We are able to account for the whereabouts of all in the household. They could not be involved. I see no reason for us to be further concerned with the matter."

While Mother had made quite compelling arguments regarding Gibbons's and Harvingsham's conclusions, Father had made it clear the Holmes family had "no horse in the race," as Mr. Simpson would say. All the same, she'd aroused my curiosity, and I wouldn't be able to let it go any more than I was certain my mother could.

I needed some place to think.

The schoolroom.

Because I had been banished to the third floor anyway, I had to make no excuse for continuing up the stairs when we all filed out of the office. Bypassing the nursery, I continued to the next room.

Taking a seat at the teacher's desk, I opened a drawer to remove some paper before recalling Trevor and Miss Bowen used the room as well. No need to have them find a record of my thoughts. I took out a slate instead. Easier to erase.

I rolled the piece of chalk in my hand, its dusty

fragrance coating my palm while the board's clean surface mocked me. What to write?

I remembered Mother's thoughts when our family had sought to identify who was behind the village midwife's death, to consider the problem logically. Like a mathematics equation where one identified the known and unknown elements.

One set of knowns were all those present at the time of the gypsy's death. After listing my family, I moved on to the servants and, lastly, our guests. My writing gathered speed as I felt I was accomplishing something.

Next, common denominators.

Location seemed relevant, so I rearranged the list as to where they were when the gypsy had been attacked.

Trevor and I had been in my uncle's workshop, the women in the parlor, the men in the library, and the servants going about their business, which I identified as best I could.

Before I could consider another classification, someone spoke from the classroom doorway.

"Why are you practicing your letters at this hour?" Trevor asked.

He rubbed his eye with his fist and moved to the desk to glance over my shoulder.

I shifted the slate to the other side and asked, "Why are you still up? Aunt Iris and Miss Bowen are going to be very cross with you."

"I tried to sleep, but when I close my eyes…"

The scolding I prepared to give him stuck in my throat

when I observed he was unable to finish his sentence. As much as I had tried to keep him from viewing the man in the barn, I knew I hadn't succeeded. The nightmares I had experienced after being held at rifle-point only a few months ago had haunted me for weeks. Thank goodness for the laudanum that kept them at bay when they became too severe.

He took a deep breath and set his gaze on me. "I think I might be able to sleep if there were *someone* with me. But Miss Bowen left when she thought I was asleep."

"I can't go to bed until I finish what I'm doing."

The list would be on my mind until I did.

"Why's my name there?" he asked, pointing over my shoulder.

"It's a list of where everyone was when you heard the commotion in the barn."

He rubbed his chin in a movement that reminded me of Mycroft. "Who is Chanda?"

"Miss Meredith's Indian maid. She would have been with the other servants in their upstairs quarters."

"No she wasn't. When I told everyone to go to the barn, Uncle Siger told Mummy to stay in the house, and she took me upstairs to my bedroom and scolded Miss Bowen for letting me go outside. On the way, I saw that foreign woman run toward the kitchen from the greenhouse."

"You're certain it was her? And she came from the greenhouse?"

"She had on a gray coat, but I saw her yellow dress

underneath it. And there's nothing else down the hall that way, is there?"

I stared at him, and he blinked back. He was more observant than I'd thought. He'd accurately described what the woman had been wearing when Mr. Simpson had caught her outside the barn. I noted his information on the slate.

When I raised my head, he beamed at me. "I helped you?"

"Yes. Thank you. Anything else you can remember? Maybe about the noise from the barn?"

He screwed up his face, pushing his mouth to one side in deep concentration before shaking his head. "Just that the horses were all making a lot of noise, whinnying and stamping their feet."

I sighed. Except for Chanda's whereabouts, I wasn't sure I'd gained any new insights. Adding her reaction on the stairs, I felt there was more to her story than she had shared to this point, but what?

As much as I wanted to share my thoughts with Mother, Father's prohibition on further exploration of the issue made it clear we were not to interfere with an official investigation.

I gave a final sigh and wiped the slate clean. Any further effort on my part was only going to frustrate me and possibly be accused of obstructing justice. Better to forget it and leave it to the professionals, regardless of my or Mother's concerns about their conclusions to date.

"Let's go to bed," I said, rising from the chair. It'd been a trying evening, and I was suddenly quite weary.

A wide smile spread across his face. "I think I shall be able to sleep with you in the room."

The nursery was quite large and furnished with three narrow beds, a table for playing and eating, a bookcase, and a chest for toys. Coals glowed a deep crimson behind the fireplace screen, and the heavy drapes shut out the night's cold.

After changing into my nightshirt, I crawled under the covers, and Trevor gave a sleepy "good night" from the next bed.

"I'm so glad you're with me," he said with a yawn. "All the noises in the corridor are quite terrifying."

My eyes popped open. I turned to ask him what he meant, but his steady breathing told me I was too late. He must have fallen asleep right after that remark, and I had no desire to wake him and deal with his questions once again. Better to let sleeping chatterboxes lie.

That, however, didn't stop me from lying awake, listening for movement outside the room. At some point, my eyelids grew heavy, and I dropped off myself. If anyone did pass the bedroom, I missed them.

CHAPTER THREE

When I went down to breakfast the next morning, only Colonel Williams was at the table. He hid behind a newspaper, acknowledging my presence with a single grunt.

Despite our rather uneven sleep, Trevor rose too early as far as I was concerned and had tried to get me to stay and breakfast with him. I'd excused myself, explaining I was expected downstairs, but promised I would return and play a game with him.

"Has everyone else eaten?" I asked and took a plate from the dishes on the sideboard.

My uncle's friend now lowered his paper to fix his gaze on me. "I don't know about everyone, but your parents and aunt were here. Your aunt said something about visiting some neighbors, old friends I believe. Your mother went to the greenhouse, and your father is meeting with your steward. Ernie hasn't come down yet."

For a guest, I found the man more informed of the household's goings-on than I expected. He had, however, missed a few.

"And my brother? Miss Meredith?"

"I haven't seen Mycroft. My niece requested breakfast be sent to her room. Something about a headache."

I frowned. More than a mere creature of habit, Mycroft was steadfast in his routines. I'd never known him to skip a meal. If he hadn't arrived for breakfast by the time I finished, I vowed to visit him and confirm he was all right.

Taking a seat, I checked the headlines on the paper Williams held in front of him. "I see Mr. Dickens is still across the pond."

"What?" The man bent the newspaper over and checked the front page. "Oh. Yes. Dickens."

"Have you read any of his works?" I asked before he could hide behind the paper again.

"Don't really have much time for such drivel," he said and raised the gazette only to fold it down. "Military history is my passion."

"Then you've read *L'art de la guerre*."

The man's two bushy eyebrows formed a V over his nose. "By some Frenchman?"

"The Japanese general Sun Tzu penned it, and it was translated into French almost a hundred years ago. I understand Napoleon studied it."

"Didn't seem to do him much good, did it? We taught him a lesson at Waterloo."

"Wellington's tactic was actually warned of by Sun Tzu —not to engage the enemy on a territory they know better than you. I'm afraid Napoleon failed to recall that."

He gave a little *hurrumph*. "Where did you learn all this?"

"Uncle Ernest. Mother thought it was important Mycroft and I learn military strategy, and so Uncle Ernest had us study various battles." I decided not to mention the part of how we would line up lead soldiers as a way of studying formations or how Mycroft always insisted on being the victorious army.

The V deepened in the man's forehead. "Your uncle teaching military strategy. That's—" He appeared to catch himself before saying something inappropriate.

I was forming a question about his obvious disapproval of my uncle's ability when he rose.

"I suppose I should check on Meredith. I'll leave you to your breakfast." He pulled a page from the newspaper, folded it, and stuffed it into his breast pocket.

Once I was alone, I drew the paper toward me, still intrigued by the article on Dickens's visit to America. As I did so, the interior pages spilled onto the floor. The chair's arm dug into my ribs when I leaned over to pick up the papers. Only when I settled back into my chair did I notice not all were from *The Times*. Rather, one page was an advertisement listing from *The London Gazette*.

After a glance toward the door, I studied the announcements, from individuals selling various items to legal notices. The colonel must have left the page behind by mistake. Why would he feel the need to hide it behind the other paper? And what had led him to keep part of it?

My curiosity piqued, I took note of the date and missing page numbers and reassembled the papers. Afterward, I went in search of Mrs. Simpson to request she send the stable boy to get another copy of *The London Gazette.*

On the way back from the kitchen, I considered my options for the rest of the morning. Forced inactivity played with my thoughts, causing an unnerving disquiet. I found myself calmer when *doing* something. But what?

While I was considering the possibilities, Trevor spoke behind me. "There you are. I've been waiting for you." With my back to him, I sighed and then composed myself before turning around. His brow puckered when he continued. "I finished my breakfast ever so long ago, and I've been very patient. Miss Bowen gave me permission to search for you."

More likely, he'd tried Miss Bowen's patience to the point she'd suggested the boy seek me out. The colonel's reading material had pushed my promise to play with my cousin from my mind. I shrugged. Social convention required me to fulfill my promise, and it would solve the issue of what I was to do with myself.

"Right. Let's go to the nursery. Do you know how to play chess?"

When we arrived at the third floor, Miss Bowen was

nowhere in sight, but I found a board in the schoolroom and set it on the table.

We had just set up the pieces when Trevor stared over my shoulder and said, "Hello."

Expecting to see his governess, my mouth dropped open when I discovered Constance Straton instead. The oldest daughter of our assistant steward and I had become close friends in the past few months. But at the moment, her crossed arms informed me I'd done something wrong.

I gasped as the reason hit me and leapt to my feet, knocking over the board as I did so. "It's Friday, isn't it?"

She gave a tight nod, her lips pressed together in a thin line. Her stare shifted to the chessboard. "It seems you have somethin' more interestin' to do."

"No. I was just—" A quick glance at Trevor's turned-down mouth suggested my next words might evoke a similar response from him.

Turning to Trevor, I planned to explain how I had a standing appointment with Constance to practice the pieces Mother wanted us to play for Christmas entertainment— not to mention the girl's instruction in reading and writing. His downcast eyes, however, froze the words in my throat. I saw no way to proceed without causing a scene from one of the two.

An upended pawn still on the chess table rolled onto the floor, its landing breaking the silence and affording me a few precious moments to think. I stooped to pick it up as well as others already on the floor. With my head bowed, I braved a glance toward the doorway. She remained in place, arms crossed and foot tapping.

The last pawn retrieved, I struggled for a plan to appease both or at least stall for more time. I straightened up and placed it on the board. Turning to my cousin, I said, "Trevor, this is my friend Miss Constance. Miss Constance, my cousin Trevor."

I shifted on my feet, the awkwardness in the room pressing upon me.

Apparently oblivious to the resentment Constance displayed, Trevor gave her a bow. "I'm pleased to make your acquaintance." Before she could respond, he added, "You're very pretty."

Although such a remark fell outside the bounds of etiquette, I agreed with his assessment. Her auburn hair and freckles were quite endearing, and his remark seemed to have set well with her. Two bright spots appeared on her cheeks, and a smile played at her lips. At that, my dilemma was settled.

Facing Trevor, I spoke in the calmest voice I could muster. "I know I promised you a chess game, but Constance came over to practice. She's going to sing, and I'm going to accompany her on the violin. We'll have our match later."

To my surprise, he didn't protest but asked instead, "Can I listen?"

"I'm afraid you'll find it boring, like last night. We'll be stopping and starting." The mention of last night's practice caused me to draw in my breath. My violin and music were still in my uncle's workshop. I turned to Constance. "I need to get my things from the workshop. Do you want to wait here while I get them, or do you want to come with me?"

"Stay here," Trevor said before she could answer. "We can play a game while we wait."

"I don't know chess," she said, glancing at the board. "But I do know another game called 'hot and cold.' I'll explain it to you while Sherlock's gone."

With a nod from Constance to send me on my way, I rushed down the two flights of stairs and on to the workshop. As I entered the house on my return, Mrs. Simpson called to me.

"The boy is back with the paper you requested," she said, holding out a copy of the *Gazette*.

My fingers itched to open it and study the pages missing from the other copy, but I knew Constance was waiting for me and probably at the end of her patience with Trevor. I stuffed the folded paper under my arm and returned to the schoolroom.

To my surprise, she and my cousin were giggling when I entered.

"I like this game hot and cold," Trevor said. "You see, you hide something—we used this pencil—and then the other person has to find it by you telling them if they are hot or cold."

"I used to play it with my mum," Constance said.

Her voice dropped, and she became quiet. The

reminder of the loss of her mother less than half a year ago slumped her shoulders. She put up a strong front most of the time, but I knew the burden of helping care for her younger brothers and sisters was a lot for my friend. I sought to change the subject and distract her from her memories.

"What piece should we practice first?"

She raised her gaze to mine, and a small smile formed. "I haven't tole you yet. The vicar has asked me to sing at church on Sunday."

"That's wonderful. Which piece? 'Adeste Fideles'?" When she nodded, I said, "Then we should practice it first."

I set down my case, music, and the newspaper on one of the school desks nearby. For a second, I paused and stared at the *Gazette*, the temptation to study the advertisements returning. Constance sang a scale as Mother had taught her, to warm her voice, and I knew I had no time at the moment to indulge my curiosity. With a great deal of effort, I retrieved my violin and turned my back to the paper on the desk. The rehearsal went well for the first run-through. At the end, Trevor applauded, and another set of clapping hands sounded in the threshold.

"Please excuse the intrusion," Miss Bowen said with a broad smile. "I heard the music and had to come. You have excellent pitch and a very clear voice."

"She's singing in church on Sunday," Trevor said.

"I'm so glad you'll be sharing your gift," she said. "I'll be there for certain. At the moment, however, Trevor, it's time for your nap. Let's leave these two to their rehearsal."

My cousin turned to me with a wide-eyed plea for an invitation to stay. When I responded with a quick raising and lowering of my shoulders, he dragged his feet after his governess. After they left, Constance shut the door and faced me.

I swallowed, fearing whatever she felt she needed to discuss with me in private. Her crossed arms signaled I was about to receive her displeasure about something.

"Sometimes," she said, glaring at me, "I think I'm not important to you."

That remark raised my chin, as I took offense at the observation. I had no doubt of how I valued her. She seemed to be asking for reassurance, so I gave it to her. "Of course you're important."

She relaxed slightly, and I congratulated myself for providing the response desired, and then added, "I'd appear rather silly playing my violin without your singing."

Her jaw dropped, and she blinked rapidly. What had I said to bring her to the point of tears?

"Constance, are you all right?"

She turned her back to me, but I could tell from her straight spine she was fighting off some emotion. Anger? Sorrow? Something else? And was I the cause?

"Please, tell me if I did something. Whatever it is, I apologize."

She took a shuddering breath, and when she turned back to me, her countenance was composed, but her voice had a detached tone to it. "Let's do it again, shall we?"

We proceeded to run through the first piece again and then continued with a second, but I found her performance, while adequate, offered less enthusiasm than she'd displayed on the first attempt.

I also found my own attention straying, my gaze drifting from my music to the periodical lying on the table near my elbow. When I hit my fifth wrong note, my friend stopped and threw up her hands.

"What is so fascinatin' about that bloody paper?"

My face grew hot as I searched for an explanation that didn't make it appear that Colonel Williams's behavior was more important to me than she. When I didn't answer right away, she marched to the table and studied the front page.

"Colonel Williams, my uncle's friend, was reading this, and I—"

She pointed to a word in the headline. "What's that say?"

With a teaching moment apparent, I asked, "Can you sound it out?"

"This ain't no lesson time," she said, rolling her eyes toward the ceiling.

Her syntax and diction, much improved when she sang, always reverted whenever she grew upset, and at the moment, her huffing warned me to tread carefully and not irritate her further. To avoid exacerbating the tension between us, I chose the briefest answer possible.

"Catastrophe."

She studied the paper again and asked, "Where's the *f*?"

"Sometimes, words use *ph* instead of *f,* remember?"

"That makes not a whit of sense. Why not just write it the way it sounds?"

I shrugged. She had a point. But if she thought English was hard, I didn't even want to explain German or Latin to her.

"It just is," I said without much enthusiasm.

Her shoulders slumped, and she blinked several times. "You must think me terribly stupid."

Once again, all the bravado was gone from her voice, and I feared she was going to cry. This time, however, I had an answer ready and enthusiastic. "Never. You are one of the cleverest people I've ever met. What you know about lifting, taking things without anyone knowing, is beyond superior."

"Is that all you think of me? That I'm a good thief?"

The sharp edge of her voice warned me her anger was back. I had somehow offended her once more, but how, I had no idea. "Of course not. You also sing quite well. And you're good with children. Playing with Trevor like that—"

"I'm not that good. Otherwise, that Emily Gibson wouldn't be takin' care of 'em so much. She's with 'em right now."

"Isn't she—?"

"She works in the kitchen," she said with a nod. "She's always comin' over to the house. Bringin' things left over from your supper."

The tone of her voice had an edge that told me she didn't approve of the effort.

"You don't like what she brings? I can see about—"

"It's not *what* she brings. It's *her* bringin' it."

I didn't know much about our cook's helper beyond her name, but she appeared to be a hard worker, always busy whenever I passed through the kitchen. Feeling I should at least defend my parents' choice in employees, I said, "She seems nice to me."

"She's not goin' after your father. Always laughin' at his jokes, smilin' at him all the time, oohin' and aahin' over the children, tryin' to get 'em to like her too."

I paused. The laughing, smiling, was that…*flirting*?

"You mean she wants…she's thinking of—?"

Tears now shimmered in her eyes again, and her chin quivered as she spoke. "My mama barely cold in her grave, and that…that *hay bag* settin' her sights on him, gettin' him to forget about her…and us." The tears now spilled over and slid down her cheeks. "And you're goin' to do the same thing too. Forget all about me."

"How could I forget you? You're my friend."

"That's what you say now, but you're headin' off to that Eatin' place. There's gots to be girls there. Lots prettier and smarter than me."

"Constance, it's a *boys'* school. Only boys. The only females there are the house dames and some of the servants. They're all old. Older than my mother."

She sniffed and swiped at her cheeks. When she raised

her gaze to meet mine, I could see how the tears had damp-ened her lashes, forming them into tiny points. A small smile, however, graced her lips. "You mean it's not like the school the vicar runs? For boys and girls?"

With the help of his wife, the Reverend Adams opened a Sunday school to provide the village children with some basic instruction. He made pleas for books and funds on a regular basis during services, but I had only a vague understanding of how it operated. All the same, I knew it was quite different from what waited for me after the holidays.

"Eton isn't a Sunday school. But even if there were girls there, it wouldn't matter. I could never forget you."

"I'm goin' to make sure of that. Your mother has already said I can writes you."

"I'd like that very much. I promise to write to you as well."

We made one more attempt to practice a piece, but it seemed clear neither of us could concentrate. After my third mistake, I dropped my bow and violin to my sides. "Maybe we should try later?"

"What's so important in that paper then?"

"I'm not sure," I said, storing my instrument in its case. "But it seemed to be for Colonel Williams." I related the man's actions during breakfast this morning.

When I concluded, she asked, "Do you think it has anythin' to do with that gypsy what got kilt in the stable?"

"How did you know—?"

Her eyes went upward again. "I heard my father and that Emily talkin' about it."

"I don't know if the man in the barn and the paper are related. I just thought the colonel's actions were…*odd.*"

"Why don't you take a gander now? I won't mind. Maybe I can help you look."

I spread the copy of the same newspaper Williams had been perusing at breakfast on the schoolroom desk. As I had noted in the pages at breakfast, it appeared to be simply listings of various advertisements. I flipped to the pages the colonel had carried away with him and studied each. My first impression was that the variety of items for sale was mind-boggling. Everything from furniture to animals (big and small) to farm implements. The first review indicated nothing out of the ordinary. Based on the number of announcements regarding secondhand wardrobes, I wondered if the colonel was in the market for that item. After all, he'd just returned to the country and might be in need of one.

I sighed and straightened up in the chair. "I can't find a thing that makes sense. Maybe I should show it to Mycroft? He's probably in the library."

"If he is, I bet he's not alone." Constance covered a smile threatening to appear. "I saw him on the way over walkin' with some lady."

"That would be Miss Meredith, the colonel's niece."

"They was comin' back from the stable. I could tell she

was a lady by the way she carried herself and all. Breedin'. It shows. That's how you get a gent."

"I do suppose it helps," I said, my mind working on what Miss Meredith had been doing in the stable—with *Mycroft*. As long as I could remember, he rarely moved beyond the library, his room, and the dining room, with an occasional visit to my uncle's workshop for special reasons. "What were they doing? Could you hear what they were talking about?"

"Just walkin'. Strollin' like." She shrugged. "They was talkin' too low for me to hear what they were sayin'."

The whole idea was a little more than I could fathom. Mycroft and Meredith? Another area requiring more investigation.

As if summoned by our discussion, Mycroft stepped into the entrance, a stack of newspapers under his arm.

"Oh, you're here," he said, drawing to a stop at the entrance. "I thought... Blast it. Are you practicing in here? I'd hoped to find some peace this high up."

"What's the matter with the library?"

"Colonel Williams is the matter. And Uncle Ernest. The two of them are using the room to play 'do you remember'?" He pulled back his chin and took on a broader accent. "'I say, Herbie, do you remember that lieutenant who found a cobra in his bed?' 'Screamed like a little girl, if I recall.' 'Ha, ha, ha. Jolly good times.'"

"And what's Miss Meredith doing?" Constance asked with a giggle.

She slapped her hand over her mouth when my brother glared at her but didn't drop her gaze under his scrutiny. My respect for her grew when she didn't kowtow to his intimidation.

"She's lying down, if you must know." He gave her another hard stare. "Not that it concerns you."

"Excuse me, your majesty," she said with a slight curtsy.

With a *harrumph,* he faced me, giving his back to her. His mouth pulled down. "God, I'd give my eyeteeth for the quiet of my Diogenes Society."

He and a few friends had formed a small group and taken over a space in the attic of one of Eton's dormitories. There, they would study or read in complete silence and had dubbed themselves "The Diogenes Society." Mycroft and the others who joined him at Oxford had continued the practice and the name. Those still at Eton had invited me, but I'd found their habits stifling rather than stimulating. My thought processes required more activity to remain engaged.

"You can have this room. We've finished practicing and were about to leave," I said, standing and gathering up the advertisements we'd been studying.

He stepped toward the table, and his eyebrows first dipped low, then arched upward. "What, in God's name, are you doing with that rag?"

My face burned from Mycroft's rebuke, but I recounted the events at breakfast, concluding with, "It's a rather odd publication. Mostly personal advertisements from what I can tell. People selling the odd item and the like. I'm afraid I haven't found anything that makes sense."

His palm outstretched, he motioned with his fingers. "Allow me to examine it."

With great reluctance, I handed over the ruffled pages, knowing full well he would lord it over me if he worked out the puzzle.

After he spread out the paper, I pointed out to him which were the ones Colonel William selected. He ran his finger down each column of announcements, flipped the pages over, and did the same thing again.

After flipping it back to the first side, he pointed to one. "There."

I read the brief announcement aloud. "'For sale: Steamer trunk. Empty. Contact Giles, c/o St. Barrens post.' Why this one?"

He drew himself up and took a deep breath, puffing out his chest. "There is no St. Barrens in England. In fact, there is no St. Barrens anywhere because there is no Saint Barrens."

I knew I could check his assertion by consulting the books in the library for Saint Barrens, town or person, but I had no doubt of Mycroft's knowledge of geography or religious history. "What does the message *mean*?"

"*That* is less clear. I would assume the key term here is 'empty.' It could mean 'all is clear,' or 'not ready,' or even 'danger.' Without more context, I'm not certain." He glanced about the room. "But for heaven's sake, whatever you do, don't ask the colonel. If he thinks you're spying on him—"

"I wasn't, but you have to admit, his behavior was—"

"Causing a guest to presume they are under scrutiny is the height of poor manners."

"Not to mention causin' problems with Miss Meredith," Constance said.

Both of us faced her. I sucked in my breath. For the second time, she'd called Mycroft out and I feared was finally about to experience his temper. While he prided himself on his ability to be above it all, at times, his emotions would get the better of him, and I now braced myself for the impending explosion. His cheeks sucked in and puffed out as he took several deep breaths in preparation for the verbal berating.

Checking on my friend, I could tell she had no idea of the eruption she'd set in motion. She remained calm, a smile playing at her lips.

He leveled his gaze at her and spoke with a steady but sharp tone. "You may think you have some special standing, given your acquaintance with my brother. But I remind you, your father is a *servant* in this house, and you, my dear, are overstepping your position."

His rebuke had more of an effect than a punch would have carried. Two bright scarlet spots formed on her cheeks, and she blinked rapidly as if to keep tears at bay. She glanced at me, and I dipped my chin to study my shoes. That peek struck me as a test of her early observation regarding her importance to me. I'd promised her only minutes earlier I would always be her friend. Mycroft, on the other hand, was my *brother*. In addition, one had to consider their temperaments. Constance could explode, but Mycroft had more opportunities to make my life miserable. In the end, as much as I wanted to defend her, I calculated my brother's reaction as the greater threat.

Following a moment of silence while I contemplated these various ramifications, she asked, "You're not goin' to stand up for me?"

My gaze shifted between her and Mycroft as I rocked on my feet seeking the words to rescue me. Ultimately, Constance concluded the encounter for me.

"So much for you bein' a *gentleman.* I'm goin' home. At least the children appreciate me."

She stamped out, leaving the door open.

A part of me wanted to run after her. I knew I should apologize. My brother's frozen posture, however, kept me rooted in place. Only after her footfall on the servant staircase echoed through the passageway did I take a breath. Mycroft merely sniffed and glanced about the room, as if to select the best place for him to read his papers, but after a moment, his gaze settled on me. "You have to be careful, Sherlock. You are getting too familiar with that girl, and it's affecting her attitude. Her remarks about Miss Meredith—"

"She was merely making a reference to having seen the two of you together earlier."

"We were seen?" He shook himself as if to resettle

himself and his thoughts. "Regardless, she shouldn't be speaking to her superiors in such a forward manner. It bodes poorly for her to forget her place. Her father is the assistant steward, and she needs to remember that. She certainly lacks the *breeding* of a lady, so clearly exemplified in Miss Meredith."

The remark jolted a puzzle piece into place. His reaction to Constance, although justified to a certain extent, was a misdirection from the true source of his irritation. I recalled his inability to eat at dinner, his furtive glances at the woman, his remaining with the women after the discovery of the body. "You…*fancy* her, Miss Meredith, don't you?"

"What? No. Well, she's certainly pleasing to the eye, but I-I-I've only met her."

"Then why did you walk with her to the stables?"

"I didn't walk with her. I met her in the yard. She was returning from the stables. Mrs. Simpson had said she had expressed an interest in riding, and I went to see if I could help her select a horse to do so."

"When do you help anyone select a horse?"

"I-I…." His face's crimson tinge told it all.

Rarely did I find a vulnerable spot in my brother, and this obvious liability proved quite tempting. At the same time, I could understand his interest also created a concern I hadn't considered until this moment. With my brother's feelings so exposed, the possibility of injury also increased.

Before thinking, I said, "Be careful, Mycroft. Don't share your feelings until—"

"You think I would be so dim as to actually *express* anything to her? Social convention alone would prevent me."

"Of course, I only meant—"

"I don't even know how we got onto this conversation." He pointed at the door. "Now leave me in peace."

He escorted me from the room and shut the door behind me. I sighed as the full import of my current situation hit me. At the moment, I had no room of my own to which I could retreat, and my best friend considered me a traitor. Currently at sixes and sevens, I decided to seek out my mother to help her in the greenhouse and perhaps even get an explanation of what I should have done and how I might repair the rift I'd caused with Constance.

The scent of damp earth and green growing things filled the warm, humid conservatory. The one item in the room Mother allowed the servants to touch was the stove in one corner. They were expected to maintain the temperature for her plants survive to the winter. Five rows of wooden benches ran from the wall the room shared with the house to the windows facing south and opening onto the backyard.

Mother continued to work along the middle row without even glancing toward me as I entered.

"Sherry, dear, can you please put on a pair of gloves and help me trim off the dead leaves on that row?"

"How did you know it was me?"

"Primarily by your footfall," she said. "Men's shoes sound different from women's. Heavier. And the heel on a woman's shoe is shaped differently. Also your steps are not as solid as that of a full-grown man, although yours is becoming stronger. I suppose before long, I won't be able to tell yours from Mycroft's."

Following her directions, I headed to the last row of pots.

She clucked her tongue. "With all the attention I've been giving to our guests, I'm afraid I've neglected my duties in here. But you didn't seek me out just to prune plants. What's troubling you?"

"And how did you know—?"

"Please, dear. I'm your mother. Some believe a psychic connection exists between mother and child, perhaps related to the umbilicus during pregnancy. I'm not certain of that strong a connection, but I have been aware of your moods since you were a babe, and your broodiness is not a mystery to me, only its origin."

I paused to snip off a leaf from the first plant, seeking to determine which of all the bits of news I should share with her and which should be first. As much as I was curious about Colonel Williams's behavior, I decided the mysteries of the female sex lay more at the root of my current disquiet. I faced her and summarized first Constance's report of Mycroft and Miss Meredith's conversation, then her exchange with Mycroft and my failure to defend her.

Mother's mouth drew further and further down as I did so. When I finished, she shook her head.

"I'm afraid I'm at fault in allowing your familiarity with

Constance." She sighed. "In France, despite your Uncle Horace's renown, an artist—even a Vernet—is considered part of the bourgeoisie. While the noble class still exists there, the English have much more marked distinctions than in France. *Liberté, égalité, fraternité* have never passed through British lips nor stirred hearts to revolution. You carry a more democratic spirit than your brother. Perhaps you inherited it along with your nose. We must recall, however, your father has a position within society here, and we must respect it."

"Are you saying?" I swallowed before speaking further. "Should I...should I avoid Constance in the future?"

"Not exactly, my dear." She turned her attention to the plant in front of her but continued to speak. "But I do believe you need to be mindful of your duties as the son of a country squire, albeit a second son. You will be expected to make your own way in life and, as such, have more freedom than your brother. All the same, your position will require you to keep appropriate company."

I paused to consider her observation. Until this moment, I hadn't thought of the future extending much beyond my returning to Eton and graduating in order to attend university, as Mycroft was now doing. In my mind, life here at Underbyrne would continue as it always had—with my mother and father in charge. I hadn't considered how I might be expected to find a path outside the borders of my family's modest estate.

Nor had I truly understood the expectations placed on Mycroft, of carrying on in my father's place someday as the inheritor of our family home and my father's position. Of course, there would be an expectation for him to marry and produce additional heirs. Was that partly behind his interest in…

"Miss Meredith," I whispered.

"What's that?"

"Miss Meredith," I said in a louder voice. "Mycroft fancies her."

Her mouth turned downward again. "I'm afraid your brother has had little experience with women. Living in the country as we do, few eligible prospects exist, and we have been negligent in affording him opportunities to meet young women. I must discuss that with Mr. Holmes. We will need to see he makes a good match. I fear he lacks context for evaluating her qualities."

"You have some reservations about her?"

She glanced away from me, down the row of plants, and blinked. I had the impression she was somewhere else, remembering another time. When she spoke, her voice was soft, and the remark was more to herself.

"First loves are so very special." She turned to me and added, "They can also be all-consuming, negating all except the two in love. Such an intense emotion devours everything, including the love itself, leaving nothing in its wake. *Engouement*."

Her choice of the French word wasn't simply a slip of the tongue. It came from the Latin for gorging oneself, and the term best described such an all-consuming passion. The word forced a shudder down my spine as I imagined my solitude-loving brother at the center of a blazing pyre fed by Miss Meredith. Surely that wasn't what I felt for Constance? I considered her my friend, but was that how Constance viewed it as well?

"Is that what Constance is afraid of? That our friendship will burn out?"

"Not so much be burned out as replaced."

"Which is why she's so mad at Emily." I shared with her the report about the cook's assistant helping out with Constance's younger siblings. "She's afraid she'll be replaced there, too."

"It seems to suggest that. Her resentment isn't truly anger but rather fear. She values your friendship and her father's love. Both appear in jeopardy at the moment." The grandfather clock chimed faintly in the background. "I had no idea it was so late. I need to change before luncheon. Why don't you finish this row for me, and I'll see you in the dining room?"

I had learned a long time ago that my mother had a knack not only for reading other people, but also for planting the seed needed for introspection and the time to do so. By the end of the row she'd asked me to tend, I had come to several decisions: I had most certainly failed to defend a friend, and regardless of English conventions when it came to class, I owed her more loyalty than I had displayed. Both an apology and the attention she deserved as a friend were due to her.

FOLLOWING THE MEAL, I headed to the assistant steward's cottage.

When Constance's father had accepted the position of Underbyrne's assistant steward, the Straton family moved from a dilapidated hut on the estate of Lord Devony to a cottage on our own land. In addition to being larger, the dwelling was in a much better state of repair and was divided into various rooms and had an actual floor, not simply swept dirt. It was also much closer to the stables, to provide Mr. Straton easy access to the animals and the manor house by a path through the bordering woods. Breaking through the trees and into the clearing surrounding the cottage, I paused to consider the neat brick building with its thatched roof, smoke curling from the chimney in the roof's center. A part of me envied the Stratons' simpler quarters. It held a fairy tale quality missing from Underbyrne's more massive structure.

As I admired her home, Constance stepped outside, carrying a bucket. She pulled a shawl wrapped over her head and shoulders tighter against a sudden gust of wind. When I saw she was heading to the well, I called to her.

"Here, let me help you."

She turned, her mouth and eyes rounded, but her lips quickly formed a straight line. "Don't sneak up on a body like that. I almost dropped dead from fright. What are you doin' here anyway?"

I dropped my gaze, my effort to make amends starting off badly. "I-I came here to apologize. I shouldn't have let Mycroft speak to you as he did."

She glanced down at the ground and kicked at the dirt there. "And I'm sorry for jumpin' on you just now. 'Specially since you were tryin' to help." She held out the bucket and pointed with her chin to the pump where she'd been heading. "You can bring in the water while I start the meal."

The moment I returned to the house with the full bucket, her younger brothers and sisters swarmed about me. The sight of the plump cheeks on the baby straddling Constance's hip delighted me. Four months ago, I feared it might not live. Following Constance's directions, I poured the water in the bucket into a barrel after filling a kettle. She hung the kettle on a hook over the fire and repositioned a fire screen in front of it. Her precautions brought additional respect for my friend. The papers carried stories all the time of children who were burned by the fire or scalded when trying to drink from a boiling kettle.

"I'll be makin' tea for the children. You want some?"

"That'd be nice."

Following her orders again, I put some of the water into a basin for the children to use to wash their hands and faces while she gathered the tea things. The three older children settled onto a bench and waited for their sister to cut some bread and cheese to go along with the tea. I took a seat on the bench on the table's other side and found myself staring at three pairs of wide eyes.

"My papa works for yours, don't he?" the oldest boy, Harold, asked.

I nodded, unsure of anything to add.

"And you've been teachin' my sister to read," said Mildred, his younger sister. "She's been teachin' us our letters too."

"A, B, C, D…" the youngest said, rapidly running through the alphabet.

"Very good, Victor," Constance said, stepping to the table. "Mildred, come take the baby. I gots to pour the water and don't want to burn anyone."

Once they all had their tea, Constance flopped onto the bench next to me and pulled her own plate toward her. "Papa's takin' me into town with him and Mrs. Simpson tomorrow. He promised me some ribbons for my hair."

With no interest in ribbon shopping, I made some noncommittal noise to let her know I'd heard. Her next remark, however, forced me to ask for her to repeat it.

With a roll of her eyes, she said, "Papa said the children can't come because of the gypsies. They steal children, you know."

While I would have liked to point out that their reputation was greater for helping themselves to more easily concealed and less troublesome items than children, I held my thoughts as her remark pulled up the image of the man in the stable.

Had the constable determined if anyone was missing from their number?

Another comment from her banished that thought from my head.

"I need to finish filling the water barrel. Let's leave the children to eat, and you grab the bucket."

After wrapping herself in the shawl, she led the way outside. Once away from the house, she turned to me. "What's troublin' you?"

Despite etiquette to the contrary, I stared at her. Both she and my mother somehow were able to read my mood even when I tried to mask it. Were women more attuned to others' emotions, or did I simply lack some training? I would have to work on this skill.

I sighed, glanced at the well, and then back at her. "I don't know. I just feel…like things are changing. Between you and me."

"I feels it too," she said and took the bucket from me to set it below the spout. She motioned to me to pump the handle. "I 'spect when you come back, it won't be the same between us at all. You'll be older. Met new people. Had new adventures. Me, I'll have been right here. Nothing new for me."

My heart squeezed in my chest. I didn't want to lose Constance. She said I'd have new adventures, but the ones I'd had with her had been the best. All strength drained from me, and when I lifted the bucket, it felt filled with lead rather than water.

I trudged back to the house, feeling as if each step was ticking away the time remaining. If only—

I stopped and turned to her, a smile breaking across my face. "Could I go with you to town tomorrow?"

"As long as your mother agrees, I suppose so. What for?"

"Just to get out of the house," I said with a shrug.

I couldn't share that I wanted to spend more time with her, to savor our friendship a little more before the inevitable arrived.

She cocked her head to one side, as if trying to gain a different perspective on me and my possible motives. "I suppose it best to go with me and Papa. You're a fine pick for the gypsies."

"I don't think they'd steal me," I said, barely able to hide my amusement about her concern for her younger brothers and sisters.

"It's not *you*. It's your *pockets* I'm worried about. They could fleece you before you even saw them."

I pushed down a retort about her having taught me the art well enough to know when someone was picking my pocket. My mentioning her own skill in that area hadn't been well received that day. Instead, I hurried back to the house with the bucket to finish filling the barrel inside, now feeling lighter despite my load. My friendship with Constance had been repaired, at least for the moment, and I could concentrate on other matters—such as seeking out the gypsies she predicted I'd attract.

CHAPTER FOUR

Market day in our town always brought vendors and buyers from all over the county, but with the holidays fast approaching, the variety and numbers of both increased greatly. Mother readily gave her consent for me to go with Mr. Straton and Constance and didn't even mention the possibility of Trevor being included in the trip, for which I was truly grateful. Vendors arrived before daybreak to set up their stalls in an open area just to one side of the town center. Their displays offered everything from eggs and butter straight from the farm to freshly prepared food to secondhand clothing and household items. Given the season, different stalls also offered toys, Christmas jellies, and other gifts.

Mr. Straton had arranged a cart for our trip. He and

Mrs. Simpson took the seat in front, leaving Constance and me to ride in the back. They had thought to include some blankets, and soon we were wrapped in separate tight bundles like two seated cocoons. Every time the wagon hit a rut or stone, it pitched to one side or the other. Unable to brace ourselves because our hands were bound inside the covers, we'd roll in the same direction, awaiting the next obstacle to send us to the opposite side.

By the time we reached the town, the sun had risen higher and warmed us enough that we could shed some of our layers. After securing the wagon and horse, Mr. Straton helped each of us descend from our perches.

Mrs. Simpson pulled out a list, studied it, and turned to Mr. Straton. "I'll need you to help carry my purchases. Follow me."

The man hesitated, his gaze shifting to Constance. I could tell he was torn between his promise to his daughter and the housekeeper's command.

"Mrs. Simpson," I asked, "would it be all right for Constance and me to explore on our own? Mother gave me some coins, and I do want a pasty."

"All right, but be back here on the hour."

With a nod to our elders, we were off. My nose led us straight to the row of food stalls, and we quickly purchased the meat pies, which we nibbled as we went in search of Constance's ribbons. Upon finding several vendors in a row, the variety of colors, patterns, and textures overwhelmed me. My mind spun at the diverse ways one could categorize the specimens. Constance, however, seemed to have some clear idea of what she wanted and scoured through the offerings at a number of stalls, considering some but finally rejecting them. I soon was able to identify her preferences and helped her select possible candidates. The process took us farther and farther down the row, and the volume of shoppers increased. I found myself being pushed and jostled about by those moving past.

We stopped at one booth deep in the heart of the market, and my friend applied herself to scrutinizing the man's wares as she had at the others. Almost at the same moment she brandished a satin indigo band with a squeal of delight, I yelped, aware of a hand digging into my pocket. I reached down to capture the culprit, and rough cloth grazed my fingers. Before I could close down upon the pickpocket, someone shoved me from behind, propelling me into Constance, and both of us landed on the stall's table. As we slipped on the churned-up mud in front of the stall, I caught a glimpse of a young Romani boy threading his way quickly through the crowd, leaving the row in the same direction as we had come.

I pulled Constance to her feet and dragged her behind me in pursuit of the gypsy.

"Sherlock, where are you going? My ribbon—" she said, twisting the arm still in my grasp.

I pushed on in an effort to overtake the boy, speaking to

her over my shoulder in quick pants. "That boy. Tried to steal my money."

"I told you to watch out for the gypsies."

"Did. Money wasn't in my pocket."

"Then why are you—?"

"Want to talk to him."

I could hear shouts behind me but ignored them, my attention fixed on the fleeing boy. He was having more trouble pushing through the crowd than we were and actually served us like a plow's chisel, clearing our way. He must have realized we were gaining because he slipped between two stalls. We did the same, and I managed to grab his arm just as he exited onto the next row's aisle.

He squirmed in my grasp, but I held fast.

"Let me go."

"Just want...to ask...a question," I said, forcing my words out between rapid breaths.

"I's don't have to—"

"Will you just listen?" I said as I caught my breath. I jerked his arm. "There was a man dressed as a gypsy killed two nights ago."

"I didn't kilt nobody."

"I know that, but did you know him? Is there anyone missing from your group?"

"Let me go."

"There they are," a man's voice boomed from farther up the new row of stalls.

The ribbon vendor, a rotund, red-faced man, was

waving his arms and shouting for the constable as he marched toward us. Behind him was an odd assembly of vendors, shoppers, and the simply curious, primed to enjoy what promised to be some free entertainment.

"Let him go," Constance whispered to me from the side of her mouth.

"But he hasn't answered my question."

"And he won't. He doesn't know. Let him go before they get here."

I wanted to argue with her, but she tugged on my arm, letting the boy slip from my grip and back through the stalls. Preparing to reprimand her for letting the boy get away, I turned to her, but the merchant's voice at my back signaled more immediate issues to be dealt with. Inhaling a deep breath, I spun back around and blocked Constance from the man. Squaring my shoulders, I braced myself for the oncoming storm.

"You've destroyed my business," the man said, shaking a fistful of muddied ribbons at me. He glanced over my shoulder at Constance. "And *she* ran off without payin' for that one."

Only then did I realize she still held the one that had caught her eye at the same moment as my pocket had attracted the gypsy boy. To my surprise, despite all the running, the ribbon remained pristine, albeit slightly wrinkled.

"What's goin' on here?" another voice boomed.

A chill traveled down my spine. I recognized the voice as

belonging to a police officer who'd almost arrested me several months ago. Thanks to Constance, our previous encounter had concluded with my escape. Given the throng about us this time, however, running off wasn't possible. He grabbed my coat collar and lifted me to study my face. He must have had a meat pie as well. A few bits of crust clung to his lips. I prayed he wouldn't recognize me as the same boy in apprentice clothes he'd caught spying into a hotel window.

I swallowed hard and glanced about at the crowd around me. "You see, sir, there was this boy, and he tried to steal my money, and someone pushed me—"

The officer turned to the still-vermillion-tinged merchant. "You want I should haul them in?"

I swallowed again, knowing my father would not look favorably upon his son being brought before the constable, regardless of the circumstances.

"That's not going to pay for my losses," the man said.

"How much?" I asked, thinking of my coins safely tucked away in a small pouch hanging about my neck.

The amount he named took my breath away. My little treasury didn't cover even a fifth of it. I glanced down at the muddy grass at my feet before responding. "I don't have that much."

"But I do," a man said beyond the circle of bystanders surrounding us.

The officer dropped me to the ground when Mr. Straton stepped up and stood beside us. I pulled my head down into my collar. For certain, this incident would be reported back to my parents. While the sum wasn't a great burden to them, my running through the market and other actions unworthy of my station would be pointed out to me in no uncertain terms—especially by my father.

Our assistant steward held out his hand, and I placed all that I had in it. After adding to it, he paid off the merchant, and the officer dispersed the crowd.

Once alone, Mr. Straton glared at each of us in turn, the two of us dropping our heads in response. After a moment, he turned on his heel and said, "Mrs. Simpson is waiting for us at the wagon. Come along."

The man's long legs soon put him several strides ahead of us. As his daughter and I trudged back through the stalls, all the vendors' and customers' gazes burned on my back. Once Mr. Straton was well ahead of us, a young man fell in step beside me.

After a glance at the man's back, he whispered to us, "How come you let Cappi go?"

"Cappi? You mean the Romani boy?" I asked and shrugged. "He didn't take anything."

"But you caught 'im with his hand in your pocket. How'd you do that?"

Another shrug. "I felt him."

"Cappi's the best dipper ever. He could even steal the halo from an angel."

I glanced at him and realized I recognized the coarse

coat he wore. "You're the one who pushed me into the stall."

He bobbed his head. "I had to do somethin' so's Cappi could get away." Another glance at Mr. Straton's back. "He said you asked him about a missin' gypsy."

"Do you know about it?"

"You seem a good cove. Come to our camp, and I'll tell you what we know."

"Can't you tell me now?"

Another glance. "Too dangerous here. Come to the camp."

Before I could respond or ask another question, the young man dashed off.

Constance stopped and pulled on my arm, turning me to face her. "You aren't thinkin' of goin'?"

"They might know something. I have to try."

"And you believe him?" she asked, shaking her head. "It has to be a trap. They wants to rob you of what they didn't get earlier."

"I have to know what happened to that man."

She opened her mouth, I'm sure to provide another reason for why I shouldn't go, but her father called to us before she could. We quickened our pace to catch up with him and loaded ourselves onto the wagon once again.

The way back was unbearably quiet, except for Mrs. Simpson's snoring. Every once in a while, she'd snort, raise her head, and grumble before nodding off again. Constance sat with her arms crossed, silent and scowling. I knew she would have scolded me like she did her younger brothers and sisters had we been alone. At the moment, all she could do was send her disapproval through wordless glares.

As much as I wanted to reassure her, I was as restrained as she was. I had gone, in part, to spend more time with her. To enjoy the day. The pickpocket had turned my plan on its head. In addition to putting her in a foul mood, I feared my father's reaction to news of the events in the market. I could only stare at the retreating landscape behind the sacks and baskets containing Mrs. Simpson's purchases and count the woman's snores, the knot in my stomach tightening with each turn of the wagon's wheels.

When we arrived home, Mr. Straton pulled as close as he could to the kitchen entrance, so the supplies could be unloaded. When we descended, Mr. Straton pulled the two of us aside and said, "I think it best not to mention to the others about the problem with the ribbon merchant."

I opened my mouth to confirm he didn't plan to share the incident with my parents, but Constance spoke first.

"Of course, Papa."

"It might be…" He pulled on his collar and glanced in the direction of the other servants before continuing. "Your parents, you see, Master Sherlock, charged me with your care. They might not be very understandin' to learn you almost gots yourself arrested. And you bein' under my supervision and all."

A great weight lifted from my shoulders as I understood the import of his words, and I quickly affirmed his assessment. With relief, I returned to the house after a cheery "goodbye" to them both, to which Constance only grunted in response.

No longer worried about the events at the market, I concentrated on the invitation to the Romani camp. Despite my arguments with Constance to the contrary, I did harbor some unease about the visit. After all, someone dressed as one of them was found dead in our stables. I spent most of the day preoccupied with different scenarios for making it to the camp and ensuring my safety when I did so.

My deliberations, I feared, affected my performance during my *baritsu* lesson with my mother and Mr. Moto late that afternoon. My reactions were markedly inferior to previous days, to the point that Mr. Moto cut the lesson short. The three of us bundled up and headed back to the house about half an hour early. I hung back a few paces from the adults, lost in my own thoughts until a remark my mother made penetrated my contemplations.

Taking a few quick steps, I joined them. "Did you say Mr. Moto was leaving next week?"

Despite having directed the question to my mother, he answered. "I received word of a sick friend who has asked me to come before the holidays. I will be leaving on Tuesday."

"But-but you were supposed to stay until I left for Eton."

"I regret that I cannot. My friend needs my help. You and your mother are now both quite skilled, and I must move on."

"I truly appreciate all your instruction," Mother said with a smile. "But let me point out that if the student achieves, it is because of the teacher." She sighed. "With so little time left, we will have to ensure we use each lesson to its fullest."

Her direct glance was enough reproach to bring heat to my face despite the chill wind.

He and Mother resumed their pace, and I followed behind, even more distracted than previously. Mr. Moto's imminent departure only served to remind me how close the holidays were and, more troublesome, my return to Eton. Events seemed to be swirling ahead out of my control and pulling me toward a destination I had no desire to reach.

MY DISQUIET CONTINUED THROUGH DINNER, during which Mycroft and Meredith kept glancing at each other. My brother once again failed to consume his usual share of the meal, and Mother raised an eyebrow when the maid took away his almost-full plate.

My efforts to sleep fared no better. In addition to my distress over Mr. Moto's parting and my return to Eton, I turned over and over in my head Constance's concern regarding our friendship, the identity of the man in the barn, and the Romani boy's invitation to his camp. To make matters worse, my cousin's steady breathing mocked my unrest and swirled my thoughts until I felt the urge to scream.

I had to get out of the nursery and find some means of distracting myself. Knowing that the schoolroom, at least, was empty at that hour, I slipped from my bed, donned my robe and slippers, and stepped from the room. Given my familiarity with that part of the house, I moved toward the room with confidence despite the darkness. To my surprise, the door was closed. Assuming Miss Bowen or one of the maids had shut it to keep the corridor warm, I reached toward the knob. A soft *thump* resounded from the other side and stayed my hand. A book had landed on the floor. My breath caught in my throat when I heard someone moving about in the room. Who would be in there at this hour? Not a thief. It contained nothing of any true value.

Before I could develop an explanation to these questions, footfalls from the other side of the door grew louder. A light appeared under the slit in the door, then went out. The person was coming toward me and had blown out a candle. I sped back to the nursery, leaving the door open a crack wide enough for me to spy whoever passed by. Unfortunately, the hallway was too dark for me to make out more than a slightly deeper shadow moving past. My heart thrummed in my chest as the man walked by without pausing, seemingly also having a sure foot despite the darkness.

And I knew it was a man—no rustle of skirts, only the

staccato *click* of a man's boots. When the sound faded down the servant stairs, I released a breath I hadn't even realized I had been holding and crept from my hiding place to glance first at the stairs and then back to the schoolroom. Torn between following the man and inspecting the schoolroom, I weighed which might present the greatest amount of information. Someone foreign to the household would have had no interest in the schoolroom. After all, what would some dusty books and even dustier furniture offer to anyone? My father's office, the library, or even the kitchen held more valuable and useful items. That someone known to us required stealth to move about represented the true threat. The identity of that person and his mission so near to where my cousin and I slept deserved priority. Whatever occurred in the schoolroom could wait.

My ears rang from my efforts to detect any hint of noise in the surrounding silence. I slipped to the stairs on stockinged feet, seeking even the slightest indication someone still moved about. After a moment of nothing, I descended as quickly as I could with minimum noise. At the second-floor landing, I paused, considering whether the person had stopped there or continued to the ground floor. When a frosty breeze blew up my nightshirt and sent goose bumps up my legs, I knew someone had opened the back door, allowing the winter air to make its way up the stairwell.

The man had left through the back of the house.

Fearing I would lose him in the dark, I rushed down the stairs as quietly as possible.

The kitchen was even chillier than the stairwell. Because the man had been unable to lock the door from the outside, it had blown back open, letting in the frigid air. I pulled on a coat and boots left for the servants to use for a quick trip into the yard. The moment the extra layers shut off some of the elements about me, I quit the shivering that had possessed me since the stairwell.

Stepping outside, I cursed under my breath. My luck in pursuing the man dissipated in the frosty breeze. Heavy clouds blocked the moonlight. I could barely see beyond my outstretched hand.

How was I to determine where my quarry had gone in the inky darkness?

Before returning to bed, I decided to make one attempt at finding him. As a first step, I considered the most logical options. If he wanted to leave, he would either go to the barn for a horse or head straight to the woods. The horses would raise an alarm if someone entered the barn at this hour. The woods required some light to keep on a path. I detected no sounds from the barn or light in the woods beyond, eliminating those options.

The final choice was my uncle's workshop. I headed there.

Fortunately, a well-worn path through the winter-dried vegetation marked the way. Stealth and my limited vision slowed my progress. As I neared the building, I decreased my pace even more to listen for any sounds from within. Some slight shuffling and scratching sounds rewarded my discretion.

A thin line of light also illuminated the door's edges. The workshop door had remained slightly ajar.

Keeping away from the sliver of light stealing through the crack, I crept to the entrance and peered around the corner. A lantern shone a cone of light onto a spot on one of the worktables and silhouetted a figure bent in deep concentration. Despite the light, I was unable to make out who he was or what he was doing—until the man reached to his left. I slapped my hand to my mouth to stifle a gasp that rose unbidden in my throat.

Uncle Ernest's *hira shuriken* crossbow lay on the table in front of Mr. Moto. In his hand, a pencil. He was making a drawing of the modified crossbow my uncle had designed to shoot razor-sharp stars.

Our *baritsu* master was stealing the plans for my uncle's invention.

Indignation rose from my stomach to my throat, and I called upon every bit of my reserve to refrain from stepping into the building and denouncing the man. Instead, I paused to determine the most appropriate course of action. Confronting him would most likely end with me unconscious and Mr. Moto disappearing before anyone was aware. I opted for returning to the house and informing my parents of the man's subterfuge. With luck, I might be able to convince my father to return and catch the thief in the act.

With a plan in place, I stepped away to hug the building's wall as I moved away from the entrance. After less than half a dozen steps, a crash from the direction of the open kitchen door reverberated across the yard. A second later, the light inside the workshop went out.

With the darkness now complete, I kept my focus on the workshop door and inched backward, watching for any indication of Moto leaving.

When I was about halfway to the building's edge, the door's hinges creaked, and I dropped to my stomach. After a moment, a rustle in the ankle-high grass told me our Japanese guest had stepped off the path and was heading to the left.

The greenhouse.

Several months ago, I had learned that while the enclosure's back door had a lock, it was rarely secured. Mr. Moto seemed to know this as well. When the rustling had moved a far distance away, I raised my head to see if I could make out how close he was to the house. The night's gloom, however, prevented me from even identifying the structure's outline.

I jerked my head to the right. Another swishing sound emanated from the direction of the stables and woods.

Had Moto seen me and circled back to deal with me?

I stilled, afraid to even breathe as the whispering continued past me.

Despite the movement in the vegetation, the wind carried the distinct *click* of the greenhouse door across the yard. The other person's movement stopped, then resumed —also in the direction of the greenhouse.

Perhaps they also had heard the crash from the kitchen and knew of the lack of a lock on the greenhouse door?

I sucked in a breath as my mistake became clear.

My discovery of Moto's deceit was accidental.

I hadn't followed Moto out. The man in the schoolroom had gone toward the woods, despite the darkness, but whatever had drawn him there had been fleeting.

Now faced with a new dilemma, I lay on the cold ground considering my options. Because I had no idea of the person's identity, should I follow him to discover it or inform my parents of Moto's activities? While whatever the other person was doing might be nefarious, Moto was definitely up to no good, and my parents needed to know of the malicious activity occurring within the household.

When I decided it was safe to return, I pushed myself off the ground and, with a stiff-muscled gait, made my way back to the kitchen door. When I reached for the latch, I held my breath, fearing it had been bolted by whomever had created the earlier disturbance that had spooked Mr. Moto. To my relief, it opened.

Emily squealed when I stepped into the kitchen.

She'd been stoking the oven fire in preparation for the day. She now spun about, wielding a log as if it were a weapon.

"It is I, Emily," I said and stepped closer to the light cast by the oven's fire.

Dropping her arm, she slapped her other hand over her heart. "Lords, Master Sherlock, you gave me quite a start. I thought it was the thief returned for more bread. He broke a crock of flour tryin' to get it."

She pointed to the half-opened door where a dusting of white covered the area in front of the larder.

I stepped to the edge of the powder and, with one glance at the mess, knew who had caused the crash that ended Moto's effort in the workshop.

Joining me, she pointed to the door leading outside. "The thief was in such a hurry to leave, he didn't close the door. But how he got in, I don't know. I locked it myself."

"I heard the crash," I said quickly. "I had come down to the…library…for…something to read. When I came in here and saw the door, I went to see if I could catch the thief. But it was too dark."

The young woman shook her head. "That was a mighty foolish thing to do. A thief like that, he might just cut you to save himself."

"Probably best I didn't catch him," I said. She studied me for a moment, and I became all too aware of my strange attire. "I borrowed the clothes to go after the thief. I'll bring them back in a bit."

After another head-to-toe inspection, she nodded, her lips in a straight line. "All right. Off with you."

She didn't seem convinced that I wasn't the one who had spilled the flour. I could have pointed out how a trail of white-powdered footprints led back to the main part of the house but decided to let her blame an outsider. I shuffled my way from the kitchen, erasing Trevor's small, bare prints.

My cousin must have gone in search of a snack, but I owed a great deal to his midnight nibbling. When the broken crock alarmed Mr. Moto and sent him back to the house, it kept me hidden long enough to be aware of the second person coming from the woods.

At my parents' bedroom door, I paused. Even though what I had discovered was important, Father wasn't going to appreciate being woken at this hour. Nor, I suspected, would he take kindly to my concern that we wouldn't be able to leave everything to Constable Gibbons. Swallowing, I rapped on the door. After a moment, shuffling footsteps preceded the door opening a crack.

My mother peered through and then widened the opening. "Sherry, dear, what are you doing up at this hour, and why are you wearing that old coat?"

"May I come in? I have something I must share immediately."

She peered over her shoulder and then stepped outside, closing the door behind her. "Your father's still asleep. What is it? Are you ill?"

I glanced up and down the corridor and shook my head. "We can't speak here." I dropped my voice to a whisper. "There are spies about."

Her hand flew to her throat, but rather than argue with me, she ushered me into the bedroom. Stepping to the bed, she lit a candle. In the flickering light, I could make out

Father's form in the large four-poster. Beyond that, I could see little, with the exception of the silhouette of the two chairs created by their fireplace's red-glowing embers.

"Mr. Holmes," she said in hushed tones, "you must wake up. Sherlock has something to share with us."

He rubbed his face and yawned. "At this hour?"

"It must be important for him to wake us."

"Whose coat are you wearing? What exactly have you been up to?" Father asked after he sat up and squinted at me.

"I couldn't sleep and heard someone in the schoolroom."

Father ran his hand over his face several times, and Mother licked her lips as I summarized my discovery of Moto in the workshop copying Uncle Ernest's invention and then the shadowy figure who trailed after him to the greenhouse. When I concluded, Father's eyes were fully opened, sleep long ago pushed away. His face darkened in color as he practically ground out his response to my story.

"Of all the…unmitigated…insolent…devious… He was a guest."

"Mr. Holmes, I do fear for your health if you don't calm down," Mother said.

"We have a thief amongst us, my dear. And a spy. I can't calm down." He shoved his bedcover aside and stood. "I'm throwing him out right this minute. On his ear."

Mother stood in front of him and placed her hands on his

chest. "I would caution you to consider a little more prudence. Please recall that the man is an expert in *baritsu*. You might meet more than a little resistance if you attempt to throw him out."

"Are you saying, Mrs. Holmes, I should let him continue under our roof? Who knows what else he might have stolen?"

"Exactly. We need to have an opportunity to search his room and ensure he doesn't leave with the drawings he made tonight or any other night. A little restraint will give us the time to do so."

Father's breathing, which had become almost a pant, calmed to a much more normal rate. "A search of his room. Right. Gather the evidence to have him arrested."

"And that, my dear husband, does require a plan. I would suggest the family gather after church to discuss how to lay the trap."

Church?

I opened my mouth to suggest that just once we should consider skipping it, but Father shared my thought before I could.

"Perhaps we should send the others on and we remain here?"

She tilted her head for a moment before responding. "Any change in routine might warn Moto and whomever went into the woods. Besides, Constance is singing."

"Quite right," Father said with a nod.

"I would suggest we all get some sleep before it is time to

rise. You in particular, Sherry, dear. You appear quite done in."

With that dismissal, I left them to any further discussions, but knew as I dragged myself up the stairs to the third floor, I would not go directly to bed. Mother was quite right in describing me as "done in." The lack of sleep and exposure to the cold had sapped my strength. But I had one more thing to do before retiring.

CHAPTER FIVE

Back on the third floor, I returned to the schoolroom, closing the door before moving to the teacher's desk, where I lit the lamp. I shone it about the room, seeking some indication of what the man had been doing there before going outside. Recalling the thump, I focused on the books scattered about the desks, bookcase, and cabinets.

At first glance, an inspection of all the volumes housed there seemed an impossible task, but I found myself invigorated at the prospect, despite the hour and lack of sleep. My mind whirled with the anticipation of discovering what had caused the mysterious sound. But where to begin?

Once again, I drew on Mother's admonition to examine a problem logically. Recalling the sound, I listed its characteristics. It had been substantial enough to carry through the door, but not so great as that made by a large volume. The object also had to have fallen from a height great enough to hit with some force.

Starting at the teacher's desk at the front of the room, I moved toward the back, checking each site with a book. About halfway through the room, I caught sight of the edge of a book on the windowsill. A curtain drawn across the window half-concealed it. The placement called my attention because my parents had my brother and me well trained to treat books with a type of respect. Leaving it by the window might expose it to the elements and damage it in some way.

I picked up the volume, recognizing it as one of the primers I used with Constance. It must have fallen off a desk. I turned to resume my search when I noticed a spot of wax on its cover. I might not to recall details as minutely as Mycroft, but I knew the book hadn't had the spot the last time I used it.

Pulling back the curtain, I discovered a small puddle of wax on the sill. The scenario seemed clear. The man I'd followed had signaled someone from the window and then gone out to meet them in the woods.

I considered those in the house and eliminated most of the servants and my family. That left only…

Colonel Williams.

I remembered then he was the first to arrive at the barn the night the man died. Then there was his interest in the secret message in the newspaper and now his nocturnal wanderings. All facts at this point indicated the colonel was not all he presented. I vowed, then, to keep him under observation until all was explained.

I yawned and realized I needed at least a few hours' sleep before church. I couldn't very well fall asleep during Constance's public debut. With a final glance at the window, I blew out the lamp and went to bed.

TREVOR WOKE me following what seemed only a moment of sleep.

"Did you see it?" he asked when I cracked my eyes open. "The ghost?"

"There's no such thing as ghosts," I said and rolled over, shutting my eyes. A moment later, I sat up in bed. "What do you mean 'did I see the ghost'?"

"I heard you last night. First you got up, then the ghost went down the hallway. Then, I heard you go down the stairs. You were gone ever so long, and I was afraid the ghost got you. I-I followed you to the kitchen, but it was cold, and I was afraid the ghost might come back, so I tried to hide in the pantry. But I knocked over something and it made a big crash. I thought for sure someone heard me, so I ran back upstairs. I tried to stay awake until you came back, but I fell asleep. I was ever so happy to see you this morning."

I wanted to ask him more about what he'd seen and

heard last night, not to mention admonish him for following me and possibly putting himself in danger, but Miss Bowen interrupted the conversation.

"Trevor, your mother wants you to be fed and dressed within the hour. And, Master Sherlock, I'm sure your mother expects you to be ready for services as well."

I would have leaped from my bed had Miss Bowen not been standing there. After all, it was unseemly for a woman to see me in nightclothes.

As soon as Trevor's governess left the room, I threw back the covers and rushed about to join my family for our weekly duties.

Of all the celebrations in the liturgical calendar, my favorite was Advent. The whole period was more festive, less somber, and filled with a sense of joy and anticipation. On this particular day, however, I found myself shifting in my seat, unable to repress my impatience with one of Reverend Adams's more elaborate homilies. I only stopped when I saw movement in the choir loft, and Constance stepped to the corner of the stalls to face the congregation. The organ groaned to life and wheezed out the first few chords of "Adeste Fideles."

Her voice rose clear and sweet. My stomach quivered as I watched those around me raise their heads as well, smiles creeping across their faces. The organ swelled as Constance began the final stanza, and her voice grew with it. The last chord held its note for an extra beat and then silence. The whole church remained quiet while the click of Constance's heels and the rustle of her skirts echoed throughout the chapel as she took her seat. The vicar broke the spell, raising his arms to call all to kneel for prayer.

In the churchyard following the service, well-wishers crowded about Constance and her father. Excusing myself from my family, I pushed through the crowd to reach her side. Along the way, I caught snippets of compliments about her and her voice. Not long ago, I had overheard some much-less-favorable assessments of the whole Straton family. After the death of his wife, Mr. Straton had taken to drink and neglected his children. Constance had held the family together, but only through some less-than-legal activities. While it thrilled me to hear this shift in public opinion toward her, I felt something slipping from me at the same time. Her talent had been a secret. True, she'd sung on street corners for pennies, but this appearance in church highlighted her talent before the whole village. The performance cut a secret bond with her I hadn't even known existed until I lost it.

I pushed down my regret to give her a smile when I reached her. She wrapped her arms about my neck and squeezed tightly.

"Isn't this grand?" she asked in my ear.

Overwhelmed with elation, and at the same time a sense of loss, I could only nod.

Behind her, a man cleared his throat, and I glanced up to see her father's scowling face. I gently pushed myself free of her embrace and held her at arm's length.

"It was perfect," I said.

Her father placed his hands on her shoulders. "That it was. We are most grateful for all the help you and your mother have given her."

His focus shifted to someone over my shoulder, and I saw Mother and Father making their way to my side.

Mother must have caught his remark because when she stepped nearer, she said, "Hers is the talent. We only assisted in refining it."

"Mrs. Holmes has assured me she will continue to work with her after Sherlock returns to school," Father said.

"Yes," Mother said, placing a hand on my shoulder. "I hope to increase her repertoire. Perhaps some Verdi. She has a lovely soprano."

"Oh, thank you, ma'am," Constance said. She shifted on her feet and turned to her father. "We need to be goin.' The little ones will be wantin' their Sunday supper."

"Yes, love. I'll take you home." He turned to my father. "With your permission. I'll take the cart and horse back to the stables in a bit."

We watched while they moved to the waiting cart, accepting a few more comments along the way.

When the crowd dissipated, Father turned to me. "Your efforts with the girl produced excellent results. Good job."

He slapped my shoulder, and warmth spread throughout my body from where he'd touched me despite the winter breeze. My father's praise was sparse and not given lightly.

This recognition, however, didn't dispel my anxiety about the shift in my relationship with Constance.

The conversation among the family on the way home only reinforced my concerns.

"It's a pity," Aunt Iris said, "the girl doesn't have more breeding. She has the air of a peasant about her."

"Manners can be taught," Mother said. "She might not be able to make up for her humble beginnings, but they can be corrected. She is a quick learner and quite clever. I've considered making her my personal maid to provide her additional instruction on proper etiquette."

My aunt sniffed, signaling to all she wasn't convinced such instruction was possible. For myself, Mother's announcement left me speechless. I had no idea she had considered making such an offer to my friend. While it did afford Constance some opportunities currently not available to her, including a better wardrobe and more training on proper conduct, it also clearly distinguished her social level from mine—hers, servant; mine, gentry. I recalled my conversation with Mother in the greenhouse and wondered if the plan was to elevate Constance or to reinforce the differences between us.

MYCROFT and I had been instructed to discreetly join Mother in her sitting room after luncheon, which seemed to drag on forever. The effort to converse on items of little import but appropriate for polite company made the whole meal tedious for me. Mother frowned at me more than once when a sigh escaped before I caught myself. Of course, Mycroft displayed the same disinterest in everything except making discreet glances in Miss Meredith's direction whenever possible.

When everyone finally rose from the table, Trevor approached me about the game of chess we had yet to play.

"I can't," I said. "I have something to do."

"Can I help you?" He fairly bounced from one foot to the other with eagerness.

"Not this time. Ask Miss Bowen if she can play with you."

In the next moment, he turned serious, dropping his head. "I don't like playing with her. She always lets me win." He raised his gaze to mine. "I know you wouldn't do that."

He was certainly right about that. As far as I could remember, not once had anyone in the household ever given any quarter during a match, and I wasn't even sure I'd know how to do so.

Out of the corner of my eye, I caught my mother drifting up the stairs to her bedroom. Finally, after a discreet interval, I was expected to do the same. With Trevor following me, however, a prudent retreat wasn't going to be possible.

"I-I have to go to the workshop. To help Uncle Ernest with something. When I get through, we'll see about the chess game."

The boy's chest rose and fell with a deep sigh, and I rushed off toward the back of the house before he could ask if he could accompany me there as well. Once out of his sight, I took the servant stairs up to the second floor and knocked on Mother's door. She opened it enough to let me slip through and secured it behind me with the key.

Mother's sitting room was off the bedroom she shared with Father but, as I learned later, not fitted out as most women's sitting rooms. In addition to the obligatory fireplace and overstuffed chairs, her bookshelf housed scientific treatises and the table by the window held a microscope for her biological studies. No embroidery or other typical "feminine" pursuits on display.

Father and Mycroft were already seated around a small table near the fireplace. Weak afternoon light shone through the window. The group seemed incomplete without Uncle Ernest, but I understood Mother's decision to exclude him at the moment. Given Ernest's sometimes-volatile nature, his reaction to news that his plans had been stolen might cause a stir when discretion was warranted.

"I do miss the schoolroom," Mother said as she settled into the overstuffed chair she used primarily for reading. "I found writing our observations on the blackboard quite helpful when we considered the death of Mrs. Brown."

Mycroft raised his head. "I could fetch some paper. To take notes."

"Not a good idea," Father said with a shake of his head. "Who knows who might find them?"

"Unfortunately, we have to assume someone in this house is not as they present themselves. We cannot trust anyone beyond us four," Mother said with a sigh.

I couldn't agree more with Mother's observation and fairly bounced in my seat to share my own discoveries about the colonel. Before I could speak up, however, she continued.

"Where shall we begin?"

"With what started this all. The man in the barn," Father said.

Eager to redirect the conversation again, I spoke up. "Didn't it start earlier? With Colonel Williams and Miss Meredith?"

Mycroft bristled. "I don't see how we can include the colonel. He's Uncle Ernest's friend. And a military man. Certainly beyond reproach. As his niece, Miss Meredith is also above suspicion."

"Mycroft dear," Mother said, "I'm afraid you may not be wholly unbiased with respect to our guests. Your uncle hasn't seen the man for years, and we have only the colonel's word as to Miss Meredith's identity."

Two crimson spots formed on my brother's cheeks, and I thought at first he was embarrassed that Mother chastised him. But he clenched his jaw before his spoke, barely keeping an even tone when he rebutted her observation.

"Now see here. We've no reason to question either one's identity or integrity at the moment. And you haven't even mentioned one other person who isn't known to us. That maid, Chanda."

"Quite right," Father said. "At the moment, we truly can't eliminate any one of the three, despite Ernest's assurances. Easy enough to confirm Colonel Williams's claims of recent retirement. The niece and the maid, of course, will be more difficult, but if we are able to establish the colonel's veracity, the two women can be given more credence."

"There is one other," I said, and shifted in my seat when the three adults turned to me. I coughed before saying, "Miss Bowen, Trevor's governess. He told me Aunt Iris just hired her."

Mother smiled and said in a tone that reminded me of her corrections of my schoolwork when she wanted to avoid hurting my feelings, "I don't believe the woman would be capable of—"

"If we can't put Meredith above suspicion, we can't do that for Miss Bowen," said Mycroft, straightening in his chair. "Both are as capable."

My parents stared at my brother for a long moment in response to his lack of etiquette. Mycroft had referenced the colonel's niece by her first name. Such familiarity was so far out of the bounds of social convention, they had been shocked into silence—not to mention his interrupting my mother.

Finally, Father pulled on his collar and said, "I think, Son, you have a point. I will contact your Uncle Thomas about Miss Bowen's references. It may well be she is not as she appears either."

"Having established that all the guests who are not family may possibly be involved in some type of subterfuge," Mother said, "we must go on to the next question. What exactly? And why?"

I shifted in my seat before directing the conversation back to my suspicions about the colonel. "I discovered something else that points to the colonel, and Mycroft knows about it."

Having garnered my parents' attention, I shared the information about Colonel Williams and the message discovered in *The London Gazette*. When I ended, both remained immobile to the point that I checked they were breathing. Mycroft, who'd been staring at the leafless branches moving in the breeze outside the room's window during my story, was the first to speak. "I grant that such actions appear dubious, but I contend other explanations, not all disreputable, are possible."

I stared at my brother, but he ignored my obvious reproof. While I didn't understand his attraction to Miss Meredith, I could comprehend his defense of her integrity. But the colonel? What influence did the man hold over him? My logical, taciturn brother was becoming someone unknown to me.

Father stood and pulled on his jacket to straighten it. "Corrupt or not, we certainly cannot withhold this information from Constable Gibbons. I'll send word for him to see me tomorrow."

My stomach sank. I had hoped to rekindle the cohesion within my family we had experienced when we solved the murder my mother had been accused of committing. Once the constable was brought in, we'd—*I'd*—be shut out. There remained, however, that invitation to the gypsy camp.

Before I could share that bit of news, Mother spoke up.

"Mr. Holmes, I recognize your concern about involving ourselves in what appears to be a matter for the police, but let us consider what we have to tell Gibbons at the moment. That our son observed someone making a drawing of a weapon developed by Ernest. In addition, someone appears to be passing messages through advertisements. We have no proof of the drawing, only Sherlock's word. While we all believe him, I'm afraid the constable doesn't have as high an opinion of our son. And as for the advertisements, they are neither illegal nor necessarily sinister. I'm afraid the man would only dismiss the information."

Father pulled on his beard. The three of us waited for his response in such silence I could detect the rasping of his hand over the whiskers.

With a sigh, he finally asked, "What do you propose?"

"That we gather additional information, something of substance that will cause the constable to act upon what we learn. And actually, I have a plan."

MOTHER and I stood outside Mr. Moto's room on the servants' side of the third floor. After rapping on the door to ensure he was out, she turned the knob and frowned. "It's locked."

Mycroft waited on the stairs between the first and second floor to run and warn us if our *baritsu* master returned early from his afternoon constitutional. Father was stationed on the first floor, prepared to distract him if needed.

With a shrug, she pulled a key out of her pocket and opened the door.

Given the man's limited time at Underbyrne and his rather simple lifestyle, the room held few personal possessions. One of the larger servants' rooms, it still contained minimal furnishings: a single bed, dresser, desk, and wardrobe. They seemed meager—almost monk-like.

The servants were enjoying their normal Sunday free half-day, going into town or visiting family, but I felt compelled to tiptoe. Every noise seemed amplified. Even Mother's footfalls in her knitted slippers resembled heavy boot strikes to me. As we moved about the room, my body remained tense, primed to flee at the slightest sound.

In addition to the furnishings, a trunk and a small chest sat open on the floor, a few items already resting in it. He was wasting no time in preparing to leave. Mother stepped first to the chest and examined its contents.

"I see nothing in here except for some of the equipment

used in the *baritsu* instruction," she said and closed it. "I'll take the trunk. You check what he hasn't packed yet."

While she busied herself carefully lifting out each item, I opened the top drawer of the bureau in the corner. A few white shirts were folded and stacked neatly on one side and several pairs of men's drawers on the other. I relaxed a bit as I completed the same cautious but thorough examination of the contents, mimicking Mother's process. My first reaction was relief that I'd been included in this task. It would have been inappropriate for my mother to handle another man's undergarments.

When I opened the bureau's middle drawer, I glanced over my shoulder. She'd turned her attention to the desk and the books lined there. She was flipping the pages of each before returning it to its place.

"This one must be a *baritsu* instruction manual. I wish I could read Japanese," she said and placed the book back on the desk.

Turning back to the drawer I'd just opened, I saw it contained socks and…

"Hello," she said.

My heart skipped a beat as I spun about. Had someone come in?

Mother was staring at a piece of paper lying on the floor. She still held a book in her hand.

We stared at each other for a moment before she reached down and picked up the tissue-thin paper. I knew immediately she had found what we had been seeking even before she unfolded it. I joined her to study its contents.

Several detailed drawings of Uncle Ernest's crossbow from different angles were arranged in neat rows across it.

"These are too detailed to have been done all at the same time," she said, glancing up at me. "He's made more than one visit to the workshop."

"Do you suppose he has more?"

She shook the book. No others fell out.

Footsteps sounded on the stairs a moment later. Both of us froze, our gazes locked on the threshold. Mycroft appeared and said in a harsh whisper, "Father has him in the library. You need to leave. Now."

Mother replaced the drawing and the book while I did the same to the items in the drawer. After a quick glance about the room to determine if all was as we'd found it, we rushed into the corridor. Mother locked the door and followed me and my brother down the stairs. About halfway to the second floor, we heard voices coming toward us. I glanced at the others, cold sweat breaking out on my forehead. I might have remained frozen on the stairs had Mother not passed me and Mycroft to continue down. Her calm bolstered me, and I followed her sedately to the second-floor landing where she turned into the hallway leading to the bedrooms. We had just stepped away from the stairs when my father's voice floated up the stairwell.

"Thank you so much, Moto, for that information."

"My pleasure."

We continued to move away from the stairwell and only stopped once we were inside Mother's sitting room once again. After shutting the door, she leaned against it, laying a hand on her chest. "We were fortunate."

Someone pushed on the door and she stepped away. Father joined us.

"Did you find anything?"

She nodded. "As Sherlock reported, he has made quite an elaborate study of Ernest's device. It had to have required several visits to the workshop."

"The man appeared almost as soon as I reached the first floor. I didn't even have time to warn Mycroft or think up a good excuse for calling him into the library. I pulled out my beetle collection and asked if he was familiar with any of the species in Japan." He shook his head. "He wasn't and was very annoyed at my questions. Thank goodness Mycroft got to you in time."

Mycroft said, "We were able to make it to this floor by the slenderest of margins."

"While we now have proof of his subterfuge, we're no closer to learning of Moto's motives or plans for the drawings," Mother said with a sigh. "I fear he might pass them off before we know to whom or for what purpose."

"And we have very little time," I said. "He's leaving in two days."

"I can promise you this," Father said, his voice taking on a harsh tone. "He'll be leaving with them over my dead body."

"Mr. Holmes," Mother said with a gasp, "you must be careful with such prophetic pronunciations. For the moment, I'm afraid I must see about dinner. To avoid any suspicion, I will leave first and each of you exit one at a time, with some period between."

After Mother left, Mycroft spoke up. "I'll go next. I have…something to do."

***

At dinnertime, Mycroft's errand became apparent.

When we assembled in the drawing room prior to dinner, neither he nor Miss Meredith had appeared when the clock struck the hour. Because we were expected to wait for all guests before entering the dining room, Colonel Williams, Uncle Ernest, Mr. Moto, and I were all dispatched to search for them. Never considering the two would be together (despite Constance's gossip, Mycroft with a woman —any woman—seemed absurd to me), I went to the library because it wouldn't be the first time he became so absorbed in some book he failed to hear the dinner chime.

To my stomach's disappointment, the room was empty.

At that point, I reexamined the situation. Perhaps they were alone together? While social conventions dictated against it, they had been spending time together.

I hurried to the kitchen to ask the servants if any had seen either of the two.

"I don't know where Miss Meredith is," Mrs. Simpson said in response to my queries, "but your brother asked about the lady as well. I told Mr. Mycroft fifteen minutes ago, and Colonel Williams five minutes after that, Miss Meredith had inquired about going riding tomorrow."

"And neither has returned?"

She shook her head.

"Would you please tell my father I'm seeking them out and perhaps they should start dinner without us?"

She wrinkled her nose but said, "I'll keep the plates for the three of you warm."

I thanked her and headed outside, choosing to ignore her warning that I needed my coat.

Within two steps from the back door, however, I doubted my decision. Despite my wool jacket and pants, a strong wind cut through the cloth, chasing away any vestiges of the kitchen's warmth. Ducking my head against the gust, I pushed on to the stables, in part to avoid giving Mrs. Simpson the satisfaction of knowing she had been right about the coat.

I'd almost reached the door when the wind carried a woman's scream in my direction. At first, I thought it just the wind whistling in my ears, but a second, longer shriek had me turn in the direction of my uncle's workshop. I took off toward the structure and was knocked forward, face-first into the frozen ground when someone hit my right shoulder. A boot landed inches from my nose. I might not have recognized its owner if Mycroft hadn't shouted over my head at the same moment.

"Meredith? I'm coming," he said over the wind and continued at a clip toward the building.

I pushed myself off the ground and followed after him, shouting his name. In all my thirteen—almost fourteen—years, I had only seen my brother run once. When he was fifteen, a large dog had chased him across the village square in pursuit of the meat pie he had just purchased. His agility at this moment bested even that youthful exertion. He didn't slow down until he reached the workshop's door.

I managed to catch up with him just as he placed his hand on the knob to open it. "Stop," I said with a gasp. "Don't open it. They might still be inside."

He stared at me as if considering my instructions before asking, "'They'? What 'they'?"

"Whoever or whatever made Miss Meredith scream. Crack the door open and see if you can see who's inside."

Mycroft gave me a raised eyebrow for one second before pulling back the door slightly and peering inside. A moment later, he threw the door back and would have hit me square in the face if I hadn't jumped out of the way. The door-frame provided a border to the tableau before us. Meredith was clearly visible several yards from the door, lying face-down next to one of my uncle's work benches. Chanda was leaning over her mistress's prone body. My brother rushed forward, pushing the *rajkumari* aside. She pinwheeled back-ward but managed to maintain her balance. I followed at a more measured pace after checking over my shoulder for anyone behind the door. I hadn't forgotten Mr. Moto's lesson of never giving my back to my opponent.

Mycroft now knelt over Miss Meredith, his hand

suspended over her mouth. His shoulders relaxed slightly. He must have felt her breath.

I took in a deep breath of my own and turned to Chanda.

She remained in the same place where Mycroft had shoved her, her eyes wide and a hand over her mouth.

"What happened?" I asked her.

She shook her head, unable to take her gaze from her mistress. "I do not know. She left me a note, requesting I join her in your uncle's workshop. I found her like this when I entered."

"Then it was *you* we heard scream?"

"Did I scream? I'm not certain…"

Mycroft rose from Meredith's side and spun about to face the woman. "What did you do to her?"

"I?" she asked, moving backward. "Nothing. As I said, I-I found her like this."

When he took another step forward, my jaw tightened. Never had I seen his nostrils flare as they did now. I truly feared for Chanda's safety. Without thinking on it, I inserted myself between them. "Maybe you should go and fetch Mother? I'm sure Miss Meredith is in need of attention." At my words, he shifted his gaze to me, and I cocked my head toward the door. "Go on. I'll see to her until you get back."

His arm shot out, and he pointed to Miss Meredith's maid. "Do not let that woman near her." With that command, he rushed out into the night.

As soon as the door slammed shut, I knelt at the unconscious woman's side to examine her. I saw no blood or other obvious injuries. I asked Chanda to help me turn her over, and with great care, we got her on her back. The cause for her fainting was immediately apparent. Her forehead displayed a lump at her hairline, and blood seeped from a scrape at its center.

Chanda sat on her heels on the other side of the woman and studied the abrasion I pointed out to her. "I don't know how she got that," she said, as if I'd accused her of making it. "When I came in, I found her just as she was. I hadn't had a chance to even turn her over before you and Mr. Holmes entered."

"Perhaps she somehow hit the worktable?" I said. "She is right below it."

At that moment, the woman moaned, and her eyelids flickered as if she were awakening. When she opened them completely a minute later, she stared at me as if trying to identify me. Her gaze then shifted from me to Chanda, and her mouth dropped open in a silent scream. She raised herself onto her elbows and crab-crawled backward away from the *rajkumari*.

"Meredith," Chanda said, her voice laced with distress, "what is it? What is the matter?"

She raised her arm and pointed at her companion. "Get her away from me. She was the one who did it."

"But I—" Chanda shifted her gaze to me. "I swear I haven't touched her."

"Liar!"

Meredith's voice bordered on hysterical, making Chanda's calm report seem more credible to me. All the same, I found little to indicate who was speaking the truth. Before I could voice any opinion, however, Mycroft returned with Mother and Father.

I joined my father and Chanda to watch Mother kneel next to the woman and examine her. Mycroft knelt on Meredith's other side, scrutinizing every movement our mother made.

Meredith's earlier emotional display must have sapped her strength, for now she swooned on the floor, unable to speak above a whisper.

"You took a rather nasty blow on the head here," Mother said, peering at the woman's wound. "Any dizziness? An upset stomach?" When Meredith reported the room did seem to spin a bit, Mother's brow wrinkled. "Let's see if you can stand. Mycroft, please take her elbow to help her up."

My brother reached out as if to take her arm, only to pull it back before touching her. He took a deep breath and extended his hand again. With a tenderness I'd never seen him show before, he cupped her elbow, and together, he and Mother helped her to her feet. Once upright, the girl wobbled a little and leaned a shoulder against Mycroft. Even in the workshop's rather dim light, I could see his cheeks deepen to a dark crimson.

"Oh dear," Mother said. "You do appear more than a bit unsteady. I think it best you not try to walk all the way to the house. If you would permit it, Mycroft should be able to carry you in his arms."

Only then did I realize both Colonel Williams and Uncle Ernest had not come out with my parents. Meredith's uncle would have been the logical choice for helping the woman back to the house, and Mother's suggestion that Mycroft substitute for him caused my brother to do an imitation of a beached trout. His mouth opened and shut in quick succession. Had the situation not been so grave, I would have laughed out loud at the man's discomfort. Never had I known him to project any image other than one of complete confidence in all things. Only a few moments before, he'd summoned all his courage to even touch our guest. Now, Mother wanted him to carry her?

When Miss Meredith assented to Mother's proposition, he pulled himself together and scooped the girl into his arms and set off to the house, Mother at his side. After she shut the door, Father glanced about the workshop and then at me and Chanda, a frown pulling down his mouth. "I'll send Stanton for the constable. We'll have to report the attack."

"You don't think it was an accident?" I asked. "The woman could have tripped. Fallen and hit her head."

He studied the area where Meredith had lain. "I see nothing to have caused her to lose her footing. If she hit her head, it was because she was propelled forward. Pushed, perhaps."

When he spoke the last observation, his gaze settled on

Chanda. In response, she rubbed her arms and glanced about her. "I do hope you are wrong. For it would mean Colonel Williams and Meredith's efforts to hide from our enemies were in vain."

"If we must look that far for the culprit."

The woman quieted and met my father's gaze straight on. Her tone was calm but carried an edge sharp as a dueling sword's. "If you are implying I had something to do with her injury, you are as addled as Meredith is."

I held my breath, fearing his reaction to someone questioning his good sense. Rarely had I observed anyone confront my father in such a direct manner. He held a position of respect and privilege in our village and was unaccustomed to impudence, particularly from a woman. While he would never raise a hand to a female, he would not be above a verbal lashing if he lost control, and the deepening scarlet beneath his beard hinted he just might.

"Now see here. You may be high caste in India, but I'll not have you speak to me—"

The workshop door slammed back against the wall, cutting off Father's thought, to my relief. All three of us turned to find Mrs. Simpson standing in the entrance, a hand on her side as if to hold back a pain. She wore no coat and was gasping for air, indicating she had come in great haste.

"Squire Holmes," she said between gulps of air. "You must....come at once."

"Is it Miss Meredith?" I asked as her agitation became apparent. "Mycroft was taking her—"

"No, no," the woman said, waving her arms as if to clear the air. "Miss Iris. Mrs. Fitzhugh. The greenhouse. Immediately."

Father spun on his heel and rushed from the building. Mrs. Simpson leaned heavily against the opened door and struggled to regain her breath.

Seeing the woman was spent, I decided not to wait for her to provide additional information and took off behind my father.

CHAPTER SIX

Despite my father having left before I did, I passed him less than a quarter of the way to the green-house. When I entered the glass-walled struc-ture, I could see Aunt Iris through the row of plants on the opposite side of the room. She sat on a bench in the passageway connecting the greenhouse to the rest of the manor. Her face was pale, and she leaned against the wall behind the bench. Two maids fanned the sobbing woman.

As I raced down the row toward her, I could see out of the corner of my eye, to my left, Uncle Ernest and Colonel Williams, but I was too concentrated on my aunt to deter-mine why they weren't attending my aunt.

A few steps from the woman, however, I stopped and shifted on my feet as I realized I had little to offer her. Given her emotional state, I could hardly question her, and without more information, little could be done.

My father entered the greenhouse, pushed past me, and rushed to her side. One of the maids stepped back to give him room, and he took her hand, rubbing it between his own, a tenderness and intimacy I had only seen him show to my mother, and then only once or twice.

"Iris, dear, what is it?"

Her response was only to wail louder and shake her head.

Two additional requests to share the reason for her terror produced similar results. I had thought Miss Meredith hysterical, but her outburst failed to rival my aunt's. Knowing one or more of the herbs growing in the room behind me would calm her down, I considered fetching something to have tea brewed when Trevor spoke up from the corridor's entrance.

"Mummy? Are you all right?"

At her son's voice, she pointed a trembling finger at him. With great effort, she croaked out a command: "Get. Him. Away."

Father spun about and glanced first at him and then me. "Sherlock, help Trevor bring a glass of water to his mother."

Despite his rather commanding tone, I recognized an undercurrent of concern. This sense of urgency spurred me to race to my cousin's side and grab his hand. The boy's eyes were the size of saucers, and I feared he was on the verge of an emotional display even more dramatic than his mother's.

As I reached Trevor, Iris found her voice and babbled to my father. "It's horrible, Siger. I'll never be able to sleep again. That man—how could someone—?"

Trevor turned to catch a glimpse of her, but I pulled him forward toward the kitchen. "Let's hurry and get her the water."

As we turned a corner, I checked behind me. The servants continued to fan her, but Father was not at her side. She had mentioned a man. And she had obviously seen something horrible. I then recalled seeing Ernest and Williams on the left side of the greenhouse. Was she referring to one of them? And where Father had gone?

I reprimanded myself for not going to investigate whatever called their attention. Being so focused on Aunt Iris, I'd rushed right past them. I recalled Mr. Moto's warning about being aware. No opponent was waiting for my inattention as he had during that lesson, but all the same, I knew now the true point of interest. My aunt was secondary.

By the time we got back, my aunt's face had shifted from pale to bright red and her cheeks glistened from perspiration and tears. Mrs. Simpson was now standing by the woman, having taken over the fanning from one of the maids. The greenhouse doors were closed, and my father had not reappeared. The moment Trevor stepped forward with the water, his mother grabbed for him with such force the glass tipped and doused her front.

"Oh, my son, my son," she murmured, running her hand over his head, oblivious to the bath she'd just given herself. "Such a comfort to me. Mummy's had a terrible fright. A terrible fright."

"What is it?" he asked, his voice muffled from being pressed against her bodice. "What did you see?"

"Just a mouse," Mrs. Simpson said before anyone else could speak. "I'm afraid it ran over her foot. That's all."

Trevor managed to pull himself free from his mother's grasp enough to raise his head. "Is that why Uncle Siger left? Is he helping them catch it?"

Mrs. Simpson forced a smile and smoothed her hand over the boy's head. "Exactly. We're going to take your mother upstairs to her room. Why don't you come with us?"

Aunt Iris took a deep breath. "Yes. Come with Mummy."

Mrs. Simpson and the servants helped my aunt to her feet and led her away. Trevor, his hand still in her clenched fist, tripped along beside her. "They need to get some of Uncle Ernest's traps. He could catch that mouse, I wager. Ask Cousin Sherlock. He knows."

"An excellent idea," Mrs. Simpson said over her shoulder to him. "I'll mention it directly."

Having stepped to the side to allow the group to pass, I stared at my cousin's back wondering if he truly did believe that a mouse had frightened his mother. If so, he was terribly gullible.

Once they rounded the corner, I moved through the

greenhouse door and toward where my father, Colonel Williams, and Uncle Ernest stood in a tight circle. Their conversation was low, but due to the acoustics in the room, quite clear. They were focused on something at their feet, but at this angle, I couldn't discern it.

"I'm surprised Mrs. Holmes isn't here yet," Father said. "Probably getting something together for Iris. Although I don't see how she'll be needed here. It's the constable that's required."

"You say Miss Meredith was attacked too?" Ernest asked.

Father nodded. "In the workshop."

The door opened, and Mother rushed past me, her medical bag once again in hand. I then knew the "something horrible" that had caused Aunt Iris's distress involved an injury or illness. I did a quick inventory of whom I'd seen lately, and my throat closed in on itself, making it almost impossible for air to fill my lungs.

I plunged down the center aisle toward the back door, then turned down a row running perpendicular to the one I was on. I pulled to a stop when the three men turned toward me. The colonel stepped sideways, as if to continue to obstruct my view of the dark form faceup on the floor where my mother now knelt.

"Sherlock."

Father's voice had a sharp tone to it, but I ignored the warning and dropped to my knees next to my mother at Mr. Moto's side. The man's mouth gaped open, and his eyes stared emptily ahead. No blood. Just like the gypsy in the stables. Bile rose in my throat, but the sensation was immediately replaced with a rush of anger so intense I dropped to my hands and knees and pounded my fists onto the boards.

"No," I said. "No. No."

Mother's skirts rustled next to me, and I felt the weight of her hands on my shoulders. "Sherry, dear—"

I spun about and buried my head in her lap. My litany shifted from "No" to "Why?"

She took my chin in her hand and pushed it upward until our gazes met. "Despite his deception and thievery, I know you had viewed him as your teacher. I, too, think he didn't deserve this death. You need to gather your emotions. The constable will be here again soon."

When she stood, I saw damp stains on her skirt. To my surprise, my cheeks were wet when I touched them. My focus shifted to the legs of the men behind her and trailed up to their faces. All were detached, stone-like, except for my father's. His disapproval of my emotional display was evident even from the distance.

I pushed myself up from the floor and turned my back on the scene, swiping at my face to clean any traces of my less-than-stoic response. Taking great gulps of air, I forced down the anger and sadness threatening a repeat of the panic I'd exhibited.

Placing a light hand on my shoulder, Mother said in a voice just barely above a whisper, "Let's go to the kitchen, and I'll make you a special tea. We don't want Trevor to see you in such a state."

The next hour passed in a sort of blur. Mother guided me to the kitchen, where I cleaned my face, and she prepared a strong infusion of chamomile and lemon balm for my nerves, ordering me to drink a cup and sending more upstairs for Aunt Iris and Miss Meredith. When I remained calm through these efforts, she suggested I wait in the parlor with the others for the constable and his men's arrival, Sunday dinner now all but forgotten.

Between the methodical clicking of the grandfather clock in the foyer and the mild sedative effect of Mother's brew, I found myself drifting between sleep and consciousness. Mrs. Simpson did enter at some point with tea and plates of sandwiches, but few touched the food. At another point, Gibbons arrived, and a low-voiced discussion followed concerning an examination of the greenhouse and Uncle Ernest's workshop.

My brain jerked back to reality and full consciousness when Gibbons strode into the parlor once again to interview the family and guests. Only Aunt Iris and Miss Meredith were absent, due to prostration, and as an officer of the court, Father shared what each had told him.

The constable pulled the pencil from his notepad. "I think I will start with your sons, Squire Holmes, as they found the two women. Shall we use your office again?"

Once Father, Mycroft, and I were seated, Gibbons turned his attention to my brother. He repeated his report of hearing the screams, running to the workshop, and finding Chanda leaning over Miss Meredith's prone body. When my brother finished, the constable eyed Mycroft and asked, "And just where were you when you heard the shouts?"

"The stables. I'd gone looking for Mer—Miss Meredith."

The statement rolled off his tongue without hesitation. All the same, I noticed, despite his usual ability to remain inscrutable in most situations, color darkened his cheeks. Had Gibbons noticed the flush indicating he knew more than just shared?

"Yes." Gibbons drawled out the word and scribbled on a pad before returning his gaze to my brother. "I understand both you and the lady were late for dinner. Disappeared."

"I wouldn't say we 'disappeared.' Late, perhaps. Miss Meredith and I had an…appointment. To play chess. When she didn't arrive, I went in search of her."

I dared not glance at my brother and focused on the fire in an effort to avoid revealing my skepticism around his story. Mycroft was very particular about his chess opponents and routinely berated females as poor competition. Either the "appointment" did not involve a game of chess or else he was willing to lower his standards to spend time with the young lady. Either way, Miss Meredith's effect on my brother was transforming.

"So, you went and brought the others," he said and turned to me. "What happened then?"

"She woke up, and she…" I paused, knowing what I was about to share would profoundly impact Chanda's life. Recollections of visiting my mother in gaol and of the other prisoners shuffling along the corridors in complete silence sent a shiver down my spine.

A glance at Gibbons told me he wouldn't wait long for an answer.

Before I could continue, Father spoke up.

"Go on, Son. I've already shared what Miss Meredith told me."

The accusation was already out. My report would at least not be the one to send the woman to gaol. Taking a deep breath, I finished my thought on the exhale. "She said not to let Chanda near her. That she had done it."

The man turned to Father. "I think I should see the Indian woman now."

Deep creases pushed Father's eyebrows low over his eyes. With a sigh, he waved toward the office door. "She's waiting in the parlor."

"Then we are excused?" Mycroft asked, popping up from his seat.

He hurried off as soon as Father nodded. He was already halfway up the stairs by the time I exited Father's office behind the two men. Were either of them aware of his concern, or more accurately, his obsession, with Miss Meredith?

Chanda perched in an overstuffed chair near the fire with Uncle Ernest and Colonel Williams on either side of her, whether to comfort or guard was unclear. Tears shimmered in her eyes, and her gaze shifted constantly, as if unable to focus on one person or object. The constable strode in, hands clasped behind his back. My uncle and his friend stood, partially blocking the woman from Gibbons's approach and making it clear where they sided.

Gibbons stepped to the colonel's side to get a view of the woman. "I have some questions for you about what happened before Masters Mycroft and Sherlock found you and the victim in the workshop. I understand you claim you found her on the floor?"

She swallowed and nodded mutely.

I observed the corners of his mouth twitching and knew he was savoring the thought of accusing the foreigner of the attack on Miss Meredith. "So you contend you didn't see anyone?"

"I didn't, sir," she said, a slight tremor in her voice. "But it was quite dark in there."

After another twitch of his lips, he set his mouth into a firm line and turned to focus on me. "Did you see or hear anything to give evidence of anyone other than the women in the workshop?"

"We were too fixed on caring for Miss Meredith," I said, then let my head drop. "I didn't think of searching the workshop."

"I'd expected as much. We have a building with only one entrance and no one seen leaving it. And a woman attacked from behind. *And* a man dead in the greenhouse. I believe the conclusion is obvious."

He stared down at Chanda. "Please stand, miss. I'm arresting you in the queen's name for the death of one Hiro Moto and the attack on Miss Meredith Williams. I'm certain that the evidence will also show you murdered the gypsy in the barn. That charge will be added later."

"B-but I-I—" The woman turned to each of the adults in the room, as if seeking someone to defend her.

The colonel dropped his gaze to the floor. My father shifted on his feet.

Only Uncle Ernest spoke up. "This is an outrage. She comes from a well-respected family. Is currently under the protection of—"

"I don't give a f—" Gibbons gave a sideways glance at my father and coughed before continuing in a more even tone. "—fig whose protection she's under. She's a murderess and must go to gaol."

My uncle stared at my father from around the constable's side. "Siger, please. You have to know she's innocent. She can't go to gaol. At least let her stay here. At Underbyrne. Under house arrest. As Straton did when they thought he'd killed his wife."

Gibbons shook his head. "A completely different situation. The man had been stabbed. Unconscious most of the time. And he was known here. If he'd left, someone would have recognized him and sent word that he was out and about. None of that applies here."

"I have to agree with Gibbons on this," Father said, his voice grim. He turned to Chanda. "I assure you, miss, if you are innocent, it will come out."

The constable took a firm grip on her arm and pulled her toward the door. She appeared dazed, allowing the man to lead her from the house without another word of protest.

When the front door clicked shut, the four of us remained where we had been in a sort of stunned paralysis. Uncle Ernest made the only movement, a sort of tightening and relaxing of his jaw as if he wanted to dispute the events once again but his body wouldn't cooperate. For myself, I too wanted to challenge what appeared to be Gibbons's illogical conclusion of Chanda's guilt but had nothing concrete with which to dispute it.

Colonel Williams finally broke the silence.

"I'd best get upstairs and check on my niece. Let her know what happened. She'll be—" He glanced at my uncle and shuffled his feet. "She'll want to know about Chanda."

The colonel's departure seemed to break the spell holding us all in place. Ernest slumped into the chair he'd occupied earlier. He appeared flattened, as if all the air had been sucked out of him and his legs could no longer hold his weight.

I understood the feeling. The distress of finding Miss Meredith attacked and Mr. Moto murdered had heightened both my senses and vigor. With the initial impact of the events now concluded, all vitality had drained from me. I feared I might not have the strength to make it up to the third floor.

Father must have recognized my sudden fatigue because he settled his gaze on me and said, "You should be getting to bed as well."

Despite my weariness and Father's command, I considered staying to comfort my uncle. I feared for his emotional condition if he remained in his current state for long. At the same time, I felt compelled to find Mother and let her know the outcome of the constable's visit. That she would most likely be aware of how to draw her brother out of his melancholy decided my course.

Taking my leave from my father and uncle, I ascended to the second floor. Mother must have heard my footfalls because she slipped from my—Miss Meredith's—bedroom. Placing a finger to her lips before I could ask how the woman was doing, she motioned to follow her toward her room.

Once we'd gone a good distance from Meredith's bedroom door, she said in a low voice, "I want you to have Mrs. Simpson send one of the maids up to sit with Miss Meredith...and Mycroft. His behavior breaches all etiquette, and I'm afraid I haven't been able to dissuade him from leaving. Her uncle came up a bit ago and is in there now, but I'm not sure how long he will stay."

"How is she?"

"Physically, she appears to have no lasting effects. But I'm a little surprised at her loss of consciousness. A blow to the head such as hers doesn't usually cause that result. Also, her emotional state is…unusual. A woman such as your Aunt Iris is prone to hysteria. Until now, Meredith hasn't seemed particularly high-strung. All the same, it took a good bit of the infusion I made to get her to sleep." She glanced over her shoulder toward Meredith's bedroom. "The colonel told me the constable took Chanda. How is Ernest?"

"He argued with Father before she left, but now…"

I wasn't sure of my words, but Mother read into them what I couldn't say. Her brows drew together, and she said, "I'd better check on him. Go find Mrs. Simpson and then go to bed yourself." She shook her head. "Such a sad yuletide for us."

After speaking to Mrs. Simpson about the maid, I rapped on Miss Meredith's bedroom door and entered after a barely audible "come in." If I hadn't been concerned for the woman's health, I might have found the scene before me quite amusing. Mycroft sat in an armchair by the bed. A candle cast an ocher glow across his face and that of the slumbering woman. Her hair spilled across her pillow, and her hands were crossed on top of the bed's quilt, almost as if posed by an artist. In the shadows on the other side, I made out Colonel Williams in a winged chair. His regular breathing indicated he had fallen asleep at his vigil.

Mycroft turned his face toward me. His appearance sent a tremor down my spine. Only a few hours had passed since we'd found our guest in Uncle Ernest's workshop, but the slight growth of beard, creases in his forehead, and downward pull of his mouth made him appear as if he'd been at her side for days.

I stepped to him and whispered, "Miss Simpson is sending Emily to watch her."

"I'm not leaving," he said, shaking his head.

"But it's not seemly for you to be here. When Father finds out—"

"To the devil with Father." His harsh whisper pushed my chin back against my throat. The colonel snorted and shifted in the chair from the other side of the bed. Mycroft evened out his tone. "I-I can't…I *have* to be here. With her."

"Think of her. Her reputation."

"It won't matter. Once we marry."

That pulled my gaze to his face. The skin about his bloodshot eyes softened, and he glanced in the girl's direction. "I plan to ask her as soon as she is recovered."

I stared at my brother, almost unable to recognize him in his present state. Mother's term *engouement* seemed to fit his current condition. What if Mother was correct in forecasting that such feelings were short-lived, burning themselves out? I recalled Uncle Ernest's appearance and how drained he'd become. Was this Mycroft's fate as well? If so, would he be able to recover? A desire to warn him, share my concerns with him, overwhelmed me. I had almost decided to say something when someone knocked on the door.

Emily entered, and the moment was lost. With her help, we woke Colonel Williams, and I accompanied him to his room after both the maid and Mycroft assured him he would be called the moment any change occurred.

As I ascended the stairs to the schoolroom and nursery, both my feet and mood were heavy. Each step seemed to bring a different concern to mind. Despite my discovery of Mr. Moto's deceit, a man, whose instruction and skill I'd admired only a day ago, had been brutally killed. On top of that was the attack on Miss Meredith, and the arrest of the woman under her and her uncle's protection. My own uncle's and brother's emotional states were in peril, their fates tied to that of the two women. Added to all this, the first murder had yet to be solved. Mother was correct in defining this yuletide: it wasn't the cheerful celebration usually anticipated.

When I entered the nursery room, I discovered one more concern to add to my list.

Despite the darkness, I could make out Trevor sitting up in his bed, the bedclothes pulled up to his chin.

"What are you doing up?" I asked from the doorway. "If your mother or Miss Bowen knew, they'd be very cross with you."

"I know," he said. The bedclothes bunched under his fists. "I-I tried to sleep, honest. Every time I closed my eyes… Mummy wouldn't tell me what she saw, but Miss Bowen said Mr. Moto had been hurt, and I know it scared her. Then I was afraid that maybe what happened to Mr. Moto would happen to her…or me. What if—?"

Unshed tears reflected the pale light from a crack in the

window's curtains. Right then, I saw him as something more than a nuisance. When my mother had been in gaol, accused of murder, I had been very afraid of losing her. Despite his rather clumsy explanation, I understood he feared the loss of his mother as well. Then again, we might all be at risk. I shivered in spite of the glowing embers in the fireplace. As much as I wanted to reassure him, I would have to first convince myself there was no danger.

After considering what assurance I might offer, an idea struck me.

"I think I know something that might help you. Wait here. I promise it will only be a few minutes."

After checking the corridor, I slipped to the servants' area and Mr. Moto's room. With some relief, I found the door unlocked and his things more or less as we had found them—had it only been a few hours earlier? I felt as if my world had tilted slightly on its axis during that time. I moved to a chest where Mother had found some of our instructor's equipment, retrieved an item, and rushed back to the nursery.

Reaching Trevor's bedside, I held out a polished wooden stick with a handle on one side. "This is called a *tonfa*. It's a weapon I've learned to use from Mr. Moto." Holding the stick's handle, I spun it about like a wheel in my hand. "This is only for an emergency. If you are being attacked. As long as you don't use it except for self-defense, you can keep it next to you in your bed. When you feel safe, you can give it back."

He ran his hand down the smooth, hard wood. "Oooh. This would give someone a good crack on the head."

"Remember, it's a weapon. Not a toy. You're not to play with it. If Aunt Iris or Miss Bowen find it, we may both find out what kind of crack it would make. So keep it hidden."

"I know I can sleep with this." He settled down in his bed, clutching the *tonfa* against his chest with one hand. He opened his eyes and turned to me. "Thank you, Sherlock."

"You're welcome."

After changing into my nightshirt, I crawled into bed. Trevor's steady breathing told me he had achieved what I feared I would not: peace of mind enough to sleep. Despite Mother's tea, I found myself staring at the patterns the three-quarter moon cast on the ceiling and walls through the clouds—all the while, in my mind, I could see my instructor's still form on the greenhouse floor.

THE NEXT MORNING, Mother left word with Mrs. Simpson for me to come to her sitting room after breakfast.

When I entered, her mouth pursed into a scowl. "Sherry, dear, there are circles under your eyes. Quite pronounced ones. Could you not sleep last night?" When I shook my head, she rose and put her hand first on my forehead and then on my cheek. "No fever—at least yet. I'll see about a stronger tonic for tonight."

"You don't sleep but a few hours. You've said as much many times."

"*I* am not a growing boy." She straightened her spine and studied me for a moment. "Perhaps what I had planned to ask you isn't prudent. If you aren't sleeping well now—"

"It will help if I stay busy. What is it that you wanted?"

"I had hoped you would accompany me to Mr. Moto's room." My breath caught in my throat. Did she know I had been there last night to get the *tonfa* for Trevor? "I would like to personally pack the man's things. I can see, however, this appears to have upset you. Perhaps it is better for the servants to do it, as your father suggested."

"No," I said almost before her last word was uttered. "I mean, I want to help you. We might find something we missed in our haste last time."

"Thank you, my dear, for agreeing with me. Given the man's brutal death, I consider it a last act of kindness. I know the man was a thief, but he was a good instructor. I can't bear a stranger handling his things."

With that pronouncement, we ascended to the third floor, and she turned the knob on Moto's door. "Oh dear, I'll have to go for my keys. It's locked."

"But it wasn't when I—" My lack of sleep had made me careless. My cheeks burned as Mother turned toward me. I paused before deciding to confess. "Last night, I took a *tonfa* for Trevor. He was scared, and I thought—"

She waved her hand. "I suppose it doesn't matter. After all, the man's…." Her voice trailed off. After studying the door, she tapped her finger against her lips. "If it was open last night and you went to bed after midnight, someone had to lock it during the night or this morning. I suppose a servant might have done it, but they wouldn't have had a key. Besides the one Mrs. Simpson has and mine, I can't think of another…"

"Mr. Moto?" I asked.

She smiled. "Of course. I suppose the events have taken a toll on everyone's faculties. If the man had a key in his pocket, there would have been opportunities for someone to take it while he lay in the greenhouse. I'll go get mine."

Once Mother unlocked the door, we both took stock before entering. The trunk with the neatly folded items she had so carefully examined was overturned on top of a mound formed by its contents, as if someone had dumped everything out to get to the bottom of the chest. The drawers in his bureau were pulled out and emptied in a similar manner, the smaller cases with the equipment also. The books seemed to have been given a comparable rough treatment.

"Oh my," she said after sucking in her breath. "The person appears to have done a quite thorough, albeit not orderly, search."

"The drawings? Do you suppose…?"

We both stepped into the room, picking up books as we went. We shook each one, hoping that the thin parchment we'd found earlier would appear. When she retrieved the last one and nothing floated out, my stomach dropped. We glanced at each other, both realizing whoever had rummaged through Mr. Moto's things most likely had done so for the now-missing plans.

Mother put the book on the stack she had in her arms and placed them in a short tower on top of the desk in the corner. I did the same with mine.

"What do we do now?"

She considered the disarray about us and shrugged. "Pack it away."

"What about the drawings? Shouldn't we tell Father?"

"We will, but at the moment, we have little to tell him. The room was ransacked, the drawings, gone. As we gather everything, there's a possibility we will be able to find something that points to the thief. Now help me upright this trunk."

With one of us on each side, we flipped it over, and Mother refilled it from the pile it had covered.

"What are we going to do with his things?" I asked. "Will you send it someplace?"

Mother frowned. "I'll write to the British consul in Japan. They may be able to work through their connections to arrange for someone here to collect his things or send word on where to send them. Until then, we'll store it in the attic."

I took charge of the chest with the equipment. Once that task was completed, I returned to the two stacks of books on the desk. When I turned to ask her about which trunk to put them in, I found her sitting on the edge of his slim bed, stroking the belt used to tie his *gi*. Tears shimmered in her eyes when she raised her head toward me.

"I'm rather silly, I imagine, to mourn the loss of the man. He was a deceiver. But—" She turned her head from me, and I knew she was trying to compose herself.

I stepped beside her and placed a hand on her shoulder. "I don't think it's silly."

How could I? After the emotional display I'd shown in the greenhouse.

She put her hand on top of mine and squeezed.

We remained in that pose, perhaps needing a concrete connection between us. Despite the man's treachery, I couldn't believe all of his attention was insincere. We had formed a sort of friendship, and I was certain Mother viewed him the same way. And only the two of us could understand each other's loss.

She sighed, and the bond was broken. "What's left, then?"

"The books. Should I put them on top of the things in the trunk?"

After her agreement, I carried first one stack and then the other. At that point, I paused as well, staring at the volumes in my arms. "Do you think it would be all right for me to keep this one? It's a *baritsu* manual. It's in Japanese, but the illustrations are still useful."

"I see no harm in you studying it—at least until we receive word from the authorities."

I flipped through it, Mother watching over my shoulder.

"Hold on. May I see it for a moment?" She turned back the pages until she came to a particular drawing. She held it toward me. "Have you seen that hold before?"

In the illustration, one man stood behind another, his arm wrapped around the neck of the one in front. In the next diagram, the man in front had slumped forward, limp in the other's arms.

I shuddered. "It looks…lethal."

"Without a doubt." Shutting the book with a snap, she held it out to me but didn't remove her grasp when I attempted to take it from her. "Promise me you won't practice that on anyone without supervision."

The severe tone of her admonishment caused me to shake my head almost involuntarily.

She glanced about the room, now bare of all of Mr. Moto's possessions except for the trunk and case. The exposed, scant furnishings gave the chamber an emptiness that sent another shudder through me.

Mother placed a hand on my shoulder, the warmth in her touch reassuring me.

"This wasn't an easy task, but I felt we owed it to the teacher we knew. I truly appreciate your assistance. I'll have the servants take these items to the attic." Tears reappeared in her eyes. "None of our guests appear to be what they seem. A maid is truly a princess. Moto turned out to be a thief. The colonel and Miss Meredith most likely have their own secrets as well."

I paused to consider sharing my suspicions regarding the

colonel to Mother. After all, I had no idea where he'd been when Meredith and Moto were attacked. And he certainly had time to ransack Moto's room after leaving his niece in Mycroft's care. I opened my mouth to say all this when Mother spoke up.

"I have a good idea who might know some of it. We must see your father immediately."

CHAPTER SEVEN

As soon as I stepped into the gaol the next day, my throat constricted, making it impossible to swallow. The same overpowering brew of sweat, dust, urine, and mold I had experienced on my first visit when Mother had been held there swept over me again. My head spun, and I worried I might be sick. What had possessed me to agree to accompany her and Uncle Ernest on their visit with Chanda?

Glancing at my mother, I confirmed the site had a similar effect on her. The color had drained from her face, and her mouth was pulled tight. She glanced at me, forced a quick smile, and pulled back her shoulders as if to steel herself. Mimicking her attitude, I followed her, my uncle, and one of the gaol's matrons down the passageway to the visiting room.

Mother had convinced Father to allow Uncle Ernest to serve as Chanda's solicitor, as he had done for Mother when she had been accused of murder, and he had arranged for a meeting with Chanda, bringing Mother as chaperone and me as his assistant. The room hadn't changed since I had been there to visit my mother. Benches lined the walls of the medium-sized room, and three wobbly tables, each with four spindly stools, occupied its center. We picked one of the tables while the matron went to arrange for Chanda to brought to us.

After we took our seats at one of the tables, Mother glanced about and lifted one side of her mouth slightly.

"It's rather odd to be on this side of the table. That poor woman. It's hard enough for someone from this country to be here. Imagine how difficult for someone from such a far part of the world."

"And recall, my dear," Ernest said, his face muscles drawn tight, "the poor woman is a princess. The rough conditions here were harsh enough on you. For her, intolerable."

"Which is why I had Cook prepare a curry and rice. I'm afraid it lacks something, although I'm not completely sure what. I do hope, however, it will bring her some comfort."

"The greatest comfort, of course, will be to get her out."

"*If* you can show I am innocent," a lilting voice said from a doorway.

Chanda stepped into the room, the matron escorting her a wall of blue uniform and brass buttons.

She continued toward us, raised her hands, her palms pressed together, and bowed. In the entrance, the prison guard stared at the four of us.

Mother rose and turned to the guard. "How are you doing, Mrs. Raymond?"

"Mrs. Holmes? My goodness, I almost didn't recognize you," the matron said. "But I do remember Mr. Parker."

"And I remember your preference for Cook's buns and tea," he said with a smile and lifted a basket. "Something to tide you over until supper?"

She took the basket and gave it an approving sniff. "I'll bring back the basket in a bit. You have a nice visit now."

The moment she shut the door, Uncle Ernest and Mother leaned forward over the table and spoke in low tones. "We've brought you something to eat. You'll have to excuse us if we hurry. We only have as long as they eat their own meal. Please enjoy yours as we talk."

Tears shimmered in Chanda's eyes as she glanced first at my mother and uncle and then at the plate they set before her. "You are most kind. I will try and answer your questions, but I do not fully understand how I came to be here."

"Let's start at the beginning. In India," Mother said. "How did you come to know Colonel Williams and his niece?"

"Through my mother," she said and took a bite of the meal we had brought. She spoke as she chewed. "As you know, I carried proof of my father's betrayal. Before her death, my mother had arranged an escort to get me to

Colonel Williams. When my father learned of my escape, he sent others to bring me back—or kill me. I do not know which. That was when the colonel decided to help me leave the country."

"Do you know of any reason why Miss Meredith would accuse you of attacking her?" Mother asked.

She set down her fork, as if the food had lost its appeal. "It is beyond comprehension to me."

"You said she left you a note? Do you know what happened to it?"

"I'm afraid not. It read 'Please come to the workshop. Hurry. M.' It had to be from Meredith."

"Mr. Moto," I said. "His name also starts with M. Could it have been from him?"

"I suppose…" She paused. "The note was printed. I'm familiar with her handwriting, but printing…"

I opened my mouth to ask about the colonel's writing, but Ernest spoke before I could.

"Regardless," my uncle said, leaning forward and placing his forearms on the table. "You received the note…"

"Not so much received it as *found* it. Outside my door. When I entered the building, I found her on the floor, just as Master Sherlock and Mr. Mycroft saw her."

"Did you see anyone?"

"No, sir," she said, a slight tremor in her voice. "But it was quite dark there."

"Mycroft and I were too fixed on getting help to Miss

Meredith," I said. "I didn't think of searching the workshop."

"An appropriate choice in priorities," Mother said, patting my hand. "But time may be short. Let's get to the man in the barn. We know he wasn't a gypsy, regardless of what Constable Gibbons says. He was…special. Your husband, perhaps?"

My mouth fell open, but the corners of Mother's lifted slightly. How long had she known?

"When the constable had all of you…view him, your eyes held great pain," Mother said. "It was fleeting but recognizable. Later, you clutched your chest. At first, I thought you were reaching for your heart, but I saw a chain around your neck and realized you wore a pendant of some kind. From him?"

"It is called a *mangala sutra* and is tied around the wife's neck by the husband during the wedding ceremony. He told me to wear it always. Never to take it off. But when I learned of his death, I removed it. I was no longer married, you see. It would be wrong to do so after becoming a widow."

"Who was he?"

"The person mother had arranged as my escort. Captain Vincent Rogers. A spy. I do not know how she knew him, but he had been observing the Russians. The escape was quite long and dangerous." She stared at what remained on her plate and turned her head as if the food were rancid. "He was…was kind, strong, and quite a gentleman, despite his trade. I was scared and grieving the loss of my brave mother. He comforted me. Please understand, my father didn't simply allow me to leave. We were pursued. More than once, he saved my life. We grew to love each other and married."

"Where is the pendant now?"

"Hidden."

Mother opened her mouth to ask for additional information, but before she could, the door swung back, and the matron entered the room. "The prisoners are lining up for their daily exercise. She must join them now."

Chanda's gaze met my mother's, her plea to remain with us awhile longer obvious. Mother, however, merely rose to speak to the gaoler.

"Thank you, Mrs. Raymond, for the warning. We won't detain her." The rest of us stood, and Mother took Chandra's hands in her own. "We will be back. Take heart."

The woman bowed slightly and raised my mother's hands to her forehead. "Thank you, madam. For everything. But most of all, for believing in me."

She straightened her back, joined the matron at the door, and faced to us once again. "I truly have appreciated your hospitality, Mrs. Holmes. I must warn you, however, that some of the boards in my room are loose. It would be unsafe for the next occupant."

With that, she turned back around and stepped from the room.

In the carriage ride back to Underbyrne, Mother tapped

a finger to her lips. "We haven't much time to prepare. Chanda's trial will be at the next quarter session in January. It will be here in no time."

"The evidence certainly is damning. Particularly with Miss Meredith accusing her," Uncle Ernest said with a shake of his head.

"I've considered that," Mother said. "When I examined Miss Meredith's injury, it is quite apparent she struck her head on the worktable. Given that position, I don't think she could have lost consciousness."

"Are you saying she was pretending?" I asked.

"Recall what Mr. Moto demonstrated. To render your opponent unconscious, you must hit the head with enough force for the brain to bounce violently within the skull and at certain points on the jaw or chin, but the forehead"—she shook her head—"highly unlikely."

Ernest gasped. "That's why no one was seen leaving the workshop."

"Precisely," Mother said. "Almost too perfect, wouldn't you say? Chanda did share one detail with us: we must search her room immediately."

MOTHER, Ernest, and I stood in the entrance to the small maid's room down the hall from Mr. Moto's room. Despite the few items Chanda had carried with her on her trip to Underbyrne, the disarray in the room rivaled that of Mr.

Moto's. Mother put her hands on her hips and studied the chaos of the dismantled bed, the mattress and coverings thrown to one corner; yards of brightly colored fabric, similar to the saffron one she'd worn the evening I met her, unfurled and strewn over furniture; papers scattered over the floor. But of greatest concern—what I stared open-mouthed at—were the floorboards that had been dislodged and thrown into another corner. I stepped into the room and stared into the shallow space now open in the floor.

"How did they know?" I asked.

"They didn't," Mother said, stepping to the corner and picking up a banner of bright blue fabric and slowly folding it. "At least initially. If they had, there would have been no need to cause such destruction. My guess is that they happened upon the boards after they had failed to find the pendant among her things."

"You believe the pendant is important?"

Uncle Ernest moved to my side and studied the area at my feet. "The *mangala sutra* denotes a married woman. It is usually made of gold and is, therefore, valuable. I suppose someone might take it for that."

"Possibly," Mother said with a frown. "She told us he said to never take it off. And he was a spy. Perhaps he hid something in it?"

"In either case, who did this?" I asked.

"Perhaps we may find other answers among her things," she said, reaching for a length of scarlet fabric. "Let's straighten up the items and see what we may find."

With an odd sense of familiarity, a repeat of our actions in Mr. Moto's room, Mother and I, and Ernest this time, collected and folded Chanda's clothing, remade the bed, and replaced the floorboards. Throughout the process, I kept vigilant for anything that might point to the culprit but found nothing. Mother's movements, too, seemed very deliberate. Only my uncle's actions, while slow almost to the point of glacial, appeared distracted.

I paused to watch him turn what appeared to be a gold hair ornament over and over in his hands. His thoughts, I imagined, were thousands of miles away. Did he recognize the piece? Had it belonged to Chanda's mother? He had told me a few months ago he had been in love once, in India. How hard it must be to see the young woman and contemplate what might have been. All the more reason to help her. To preserve what was left of his memories of that time.

Mother broke into both our thoughts. Smoothing out the blanket that now lay taut over the narrow bed, she said, "This exercise provided us with two bits of information. Whoever searched this room, while destructive, was meticulous and left nothing to indicate the perpetrator. All the same, it also points to Chanda's innocence. If she were guilty of attacking Meredith or Mr. Moto, why search her room, or why not leave something to point to her guilt?"

"We have nothing more to help her than when we arrived here," my uncle said and glanced at the object in his hand.

As if seeing it for the first time, he studied the ornament again before placing it on a small table serving as a night-stand next to the bed. A thought crossed my mind about how common it was for women to decorate their hair with items like that ornament and—

"Ribbons," I said, only realizing I had said it aloud when the other two turned to me. Swallowing, I explained. "The other day, when I went to market with Constance, we had a little mishap with some gypsies."

I quickly summarized our encounter with the pickpocket four days earlier. At the conclusion, I said, "The boy indicated he knew something about Chanda's husband. I think we should find out what he knows."

"We certainly have no other direction at the moment," Mother said, tapping her finger to her lips. "If anyone would be attuned to the less savory elements of the village, this group would be. If we all agree that Chanda is not behind the murders or the attack on Miss Meredith, that leaves either someone from outside…or in the household."

"Are you suggesting—?" I shuddered, recalling my discussion with Trevor. Suddenly, an outsider held much more appeal as the culprit than any of our guests or servants.

Ernest shook his head. "It's too dangerous to go to the gypsy camp. The boy may have been merely setting a trap."

"For what purpose? He could have robbed Sherlock there in the market. Like Sherlock, I think the offer was sincere—a repayment of a debt for not pointing out his companion."

"All the same, a woman of your stature can't very well go traipsing about in the woods with a bunch of gypsies."

"Romani. They prefer the term 'Romani.' And no, I wasn't considering going myself. After all, they haven't invited me." She turned her gaze to me. "They invited Sherlock…and Constance."

Another shudder raced down my spine. Four days ago, I'd been eager to visit the camp, to learn what the young man had promised to share there. That was before Mr. Moto's death. Now, I wasn't so confident. Uncle Ernest, however, was the one to express such concerns out loud.

"Two children? Alone? Too dangerous."

"They wouldn't be alone. We would go with them, just not into the camp. Close enough to hear if they call out."

"This is madness," my uncle said, throwing up his hands. He paced in a circle and stopped only with my mother's next statement.

"At the moment, I see no other way to save Chanda."

With that pronouncement, he stared at her for a moment and then at the stack of neatly folded fabric on the bed. With a sigh, he asked, "What sort of plan do you have in mind?"

Despite her warnings to me as well as her siblings, Constance agreed to Mother's request to accompany us to the Romani camp. After lunch, they met in her sitting room. Afterward, my friend sought me out where I was finally playing that promised game of chess with Trevor.

"So I'll see you tomorrow morning," she said after we exchanged greetings.

"Are you going somewhere?" Trevor asked, glancing first at me and then Constance. "Mightn't I come too?"

"We're not going anywhere," I said in a tone I hoped warned Constance to change the subject or at least make the appointment less appealing.

"That's right. We'll just be practicin' some more. Mrs. Holmes still wants us to perform after your Aunt Rose arrives." She glanced at us and the board. "I can tell you're concentratin' now, and I've got to get back to the children. See you later."

After she'd gone, my cousin stared down at the board and picked up a pawn he'd captured from me. He rolled it between his two palms. "I'm not sure we'll be here when Aunt Rose comes. Mummy wants to leave. Miss Bowen told me."

He set the piece down with a sigh. I gazed at the board but found my thoughts kept returning to this bit of news. Despite all that had happened, I saw no prospect of Meredith or the colonel leaving soon. While she was no longer confined to bed, she appeared less than hardy and required help from her uncle or, at times, Mycroft's arm when a bout of dizziness hit her. I now had to consider she might be *acting*. And maybe not just for pretense sake—perhaps to ensure Mycroft's attention as well.

If Aunt Iris left, however, it would mean new sleeping arrangements could open up. Iris's departure would mean Miss Meredith could abandon my room and move into my aunt's. A few days ago, the idea would have caused me great joy.

Now, however, Aunt Iris's parting would mean Trevor's as well, which struck me as…regrettable. I glanced at the boy. His head was down, and his lower lip protruded, not in concentration, but in melancholy. We both were upset about the prospect of him leaving. His presence had been a constant this past week and, although at times annoying, had provided some pleasant pastimes. Not to mention some valuable observations on the night of Chanda's husband's murder.

"I don't think your mother will be ready to travel for at least a few more days," I said, hoping to raise his spirits. The woman remained in bed, and Mother continued to send up pots of tea to keep her nerves calm. "By then, who knows? She might change her mind."

"I hope so," he said, picking up his knight and placing it on a space occupied by one of my own. "There's so much more to do here than in London."

ERNEST ARRANGED with Mr. Straton the use of one of the wagons the next morning on the pretext of bringing some supplies for his workshop from town. He, mother, and I all dressed as laborers, using some of the costumes we kept for playing charades during family visits. When she'd opened the trunk, a small tremor traveled down my spine. The last time I'd worn a disguise, the midwife's murderer had kidnapped and almost killed me.

Mother must have noticed my reaction because she put a hand on my shoulder and said, "Don't worry. We'll be within shouting distance. One call, and we'll come running."

While their presence nearby was comforting, I kept my concern that I might not be able to call out to myself.

Mother and Ernest took their places on the driver's bench, and my uncle slid a rifle onto the boards underneath his feet. He winked at me when he saw I'd observed him. "Can never be too cautious, I say."

Constance and I lay in the back of the wagon, cocooned in blankets once again. As we moved onto the road, she placed her hands under her head and focused her gaze on the brightening sky.

"This is my favorite part of the day," she said with a sigh. "When everything is peaceful, waitin' like. When you can ask, What's this day goin' to bring?"

I grunted in response and stared at the sky, trying to see it from her perspective. I considered whether I had a favorite part of the day and decided I'd not given it much thought. For most of my life, my days had been regulated in one way or another. My parents and social convention determined a regimented schedule of schoolwork, meals, and evening activities. My private time, time in which I determined what I did, I realized, were the moments I most cherished. They were not necessarily spent alone, but they were mine to choose to use as I saw fit. Even at Eton, although my time there had been short, I found the "free time" the most enjoyable.

The rocking of the wagon bed lulled me into a half-stupor, and I found myself drifting off in the semidarkness. After what seemed only a short time later, the pace slowed, and I could hear other traffic moving about us on the road to town. Constance and I raised ourselves on our elbows to see over the tailgate.

Carts and other wagons similar to the one we were in carried all manner of items. I also caught the scent of smoke and the aroma of meat grilling over an open flame. My stomach rumbled. Despite the breakfast I'd eaten before we left, I knew now I should have had more.

As if following the scent, Ernest pulled the wagon to a halt by the side of the road and let us jump out before moving on. Our plan was to appear as if we'd walked into town. After the wagon passed a slight bend in the road, we moved on foot toward the Romani's fires.

I glanced at Constance. Her mouth was a determined line. I didn't share her unease. While I knew I had to be vigilant, I was also quite eager—and more than a little curious—to actually see the camp. Before my brush with the pickpocket at the market, I'd never had more than a glimpse of the Romani secondhand stalls on market day and only from a distance. Father warned us the items had probably been stolen from another village. He'd actually had a case where a gentleman had tracked a band to our market and identified several objects taken from his home only three days earlier.

Because we didn't want to appear as if we were sneaking up on the camp, we tramped through the woods without any attempt at stealth. I wasn't surprised, therefore, when five men stepped forward to stop our progress on the edge of the camp. They wore the same type of colorful pants as the man in the stables had. Dark vests covered blousy-sleeved white shirts, and short-brimmed hats topped off their long hair. Behind them, about twenty colorful wagons circled five fires set about to cook their meals in a large clearing.

Constance moved closer and slightly behind me.

I swallowed at the sight of the heavy blades they carried at their sides. At that moment, I wasn't sure the decision to come here had been a prudent one, and my earlier curiosity dampened considerably. Forcing a bravado I didn't feel inside, I met their stares with one of my own.

The oldest, a gruff man with a rather greasy, unkempt beard, eyed us from beneath the brim of his hat. "You have no business here. Turn back."

"We were invited," I said a little more loudly than needed, "by a friend of Cappi's."

The men glanced at each other, and the one who'd spoken to us shouted over his shoulder. "Cappi? Get over here."

A door to one of the wagons opened and slammed shut. The boy who'd tried to pick my pocket hustled down a short set of stairs by the wagon's door and across the grass. Two of the men stepped aside to let the boy through. He glanced at me and turned to the apparent leader.

"You know these two?" the man asked.

He squinted at me and said, "The girl, I saw in the market the other day. The boy, I don't recognize."

"He tried to pick my pocket," I said, raising my voice. "I got him, but I let him go before the police officer arrived. Another boy invited us."

"That'd be Gallius," the boy said. "He was my crow."

Crow. The word brought back an incident only a few months before when I'd been Constance's crow, keeping watch for trouble, when she'd spied on the constable. Now I understood better what Gallius had been doing in the market that day.

Following another scrutinizing squint, the bearded man called out again. "Gallius?" Another brief wait as the young man exited the same wagon and trotted to our little group.

"Did you invite them two here?"

"They wanted their fortunes told, Fonso. They asked on market day," he said after he studied us for a moment.

Fortunes? I opened my mouth to protest but caught his steady gaze on me. Pushing down my first reaction, I held up a penny instead. "We have coins to pay."

The man's huge hand wrapped itself around my fingers with the money. "Of course you do."

He squeezed hard, and I released the coin into his grasp. He studied it as it lay in the palm of his hand and dropped it into his pocket. "You got more?"

I paused, knowing if I answered affirmatively, he would take what I had in my pocket. If I denied having more, he'd probably search me, and it might go worse when he found them.

Constance must have sensed my dilemma because she spoke up for the first time since we got off the wagon. "They're for our fortune."

The men chuckled, but Gallius pointed toward another trailer. "Then you need to see Drina. This way."

The men parted, and we followed him into the camp proper.

As we passed the man, Constance slipped her hand into mine. Her palm was damp in my grasp, the only indication she wasn't as confident as she appeared. Crossing the camp, I knew the men continued to stare at us the whole way, their suspicions weighing on my back.

We crossed almost the entire camp before Gallius ascended the steps of one wagon. He pulled open the dark-green door painted with a large eye and waved us inside.

The space was crowded and the air stale. In front of us

stood a table draped in a dark cloth with another flowered one spread over it. A woman sat behind the table, a similarly flowered scarf draped about her shoulders. A deck of cards lay on the table. Behind her, a heavy curtain appeared to mark off a part of the space, probably for sleeping.

"Drina, these are the two I told you about," Gallius said. "The ones from the market. They want to know about the man the constable questioned us about."

Drina now lit a tallow candle and peered at us from the other side of the flame. The candle's smoke seemed to push all the air from the room. While I normally didn't experience discomfort in tight spaces, the dank, oppressive surroundings raised a strong urge to turn and flee outside, if for nothing more than to breathe fresh air. I glanced at Constance and saw a slight sheen on her upper lip.

"You can pay?" When we nodded, the woman pointed to two stools in front of the table. "Sit."

Obediently sinking onto the seat, I placed the coins on the flowered cloth. Without a glance at Constance, I said, "Like Gallius said, we want to hear about the gyp—Romani found dead in the barn."

She squinted at me. "What's this to you?"

"Our papa works there. In the barn," Constance said.

"We already told the constable we didn't know him. Anyone can put on baggy pants, a vest. That doesn't make him Rom. I didn't see him. The constable took Fonso to identify him, but he told us the man wasn't Rom."

"How did Fonso know? That the man wasn't Rom?"

"The man's hair was too short."

"None of you had ever seen him before?"

"I never said that. I said he wasn't *Rom*, but Fonso said he'd seen him. Wandering in the woods."

"And he was not the only one." Gallius spoke up from the corner where he stood. "Fonso's seen another about as well."

"A lot of people take shortcuts—"

"But he was not dressed"—she paused and examined me from head to foot, as if she recognized my disguise for what it was—"*appropriately* for such a place. Any more information, you'll have to speak to Fonso."

The image of the man and his blade flashed through my mind, squelching any desire to pursue the question.

I shook my head. "I'm out of coins."

"And our papa's going to be wondering where we've gone," Constance said.

The woman's gaze rested on the table and the two pennies there. "I think you deserve more for your coins. Before you go, I'll tell one of you your fortune."

Before I could protest, Constance thrust her hand forward and Drina took it. Moving the candle closer, she leaned over Constance's upraised palm and ran a finger along a line curving around the thumb.

"This is your life line. See how it breaks here? There's a change in your future."

"I wants to be a singer. Is that it? I'm going to be a singer?"

She shook her head. "I cannot tell what the change is. Only that it will occur and while you are still young."

"What else?"

"This line," she said, drawing her finger from the base of her palm through the middle, "is the line of destiny. It is very deep for you. Your fate is being ruled by events outside your control. See how it breaks here? Changes directions? You will be pushed and shoved by these events. Your life will not be your own."

Constance frowned and pulled her hand away. "I don't believe you."

"I'm only telling you what your palm shows," she said with a shrug. "Believe it or not."

My friend popped to her feet and turned to me. "Let's go. Papa's waiting."

She'd moved toward the door before I could even rise from my seat. I barely made it to the back of the wagon before she rushed outside and stepped to the ground. Gallius was right on my heels. The two of us trotted to keep up with her. She focused straight ahead and continued a quick march out of the camp and toward the trail we'd taken in. Gallius broke off from us, heading toward a group of men at the camp's edge. He apparently convinced them our exit was no threat because they sank back to their places as he spoke to them.

Once clear of the camp but still in the woods, she finally paused and, turning her back to me, took a deep breath. She let it out in a quiet sob that shook her whole body.

"Constance," I said, putting my hands on her shoulders. I tried to turn her toward me, but she shook off my touch and refused to face me. "What is it? You said you didn't believe her."

She took a few more deep breaths and finally turned to me. After running the back of her hand across her eyes, she said, "You won't understand."

"If you don't tell me, I won't."

Another deep breath that ended in a sigh. "All my life, I've done what others needed or wanted. I took care of the babies when Mama died. Saw to my Papa when he was sick. When I sang at church, for the first time, it was something for *me*."

I waited through her pause, understanding her concern at least in part. Just as my days had been regimented, so she felt her life had been—and just as my free time had been the most precious for me, I realized: "You want to decide your fate, not have it decided by outside events—as Drina predicted."

She raised her gaze to mine, her eyes wide, shimmering behind unshed tears. "You understand?"

"A little. You want to be a singer, but—"

"But what if something else happens? Stops me from being one?"

With a shake of my head, I indicated I had no answer. At the same time, I imagined her traveling about, singing in music halls in London and beyond. I already had a taste of what it meant to share her with others after the performance at church. The thought filled me with dread. As much as she fretted about not achieving her dream, I realized the misfortune of her accomplishing it. That small amount of attention she'd received at church would be multiplied a hundred—a thousand—fold and most likely rupture our friendship.

I swallowed, seeking for some words of comfort that I didn't feel and grabbed on to the one logical argument which I also believed. "She's a *gypsy* for pity's sake. Most likely a thief and definitely a liar. She can no more tell your future than…than Trevor can."

With a sniff and a swipe at her cheeks, she turned to face me. Tears had turned her lashes into spikes, but her face was dry. "Do you truly believe she was making it up?"

"Without a doubt. Lines in the hand no more indicate the future than the position of the stars in the heavens. As I said, *we* make our future, and you can make yours."

"When you put it that way…" She sighed. "I just so much want to do more than live here in the country like my mum. And it scares me that I won't ever leave."

Gone was the optimism she'd expressed on the ride over. Perhaps that hope she noted she felt at dawn couldn't maintain itself in the light of day? A desire welled in me to reassure her, tell her what she wanted would come to pass, but I tamped it down. For the first time, I truly felt the chasm between her status and mine. I could help her develop her talent, but I wasn't in any position to do more. Before my impotence impacted my own mood, I decided to focus on the matter at hand—the information shared by Drina and Gallius.

I waved my hand toward the road. "Come on, we need to share with Mother and Uncle Ernest what we discovered."

She gave a little gasp. "Not about my fortune?"

"No. Of course not. I need to let them know we must search the woods. More than one person's been lurking about out there, and we need to find out who."

CHAPTER EIGHT

M other, Ernest, and I stood in the center of a small clearing. In the waning light, we studied the items scattered about. Mother's application of basic logic had led us almost directly to a small camp set up in woods surrounding Underbyrne. After leaving the Romani camp, we identified what we considered to be the attributes for someone wishing to stay in the woods. We determined the camp had to be accessible but not visible. This required it to be near the path that the villagers had blazed to reach Underbyrne and other large estates. Constance had shared their existence with us only a few months ago. Lastly, if the purpose was to spy on our home, it had to have a vantage point with enough vegetation to hide the individual's presence.

From these characteristics, we narrowed the area to begin our search. By late afternoon, we had discovered the place. Branches, their dried leaves still attached, hid a small tent, and a ring of stones set not far from the tent held the remains of a fire. Both were in a hollow that would have kept any flames from being seen below. At the same time, from the hollow's raised edge and placement between two trees, the side and front of our house, the barn, and part of my uncle's workshop were all clearly visible. I could even make out Mycroft strolling toward the barn and opened my mouth to comment on his sudden interest in the structure as well as my surprise that he wasn't with Miss Meredith when Mother spoke.

"A week ago, I would have said it was ridiculous to consider someone spying on us. What is here that would require such stealth?"

"My inventions," Uncle Ernest said. Hurt tinged his voice.

He was quite proud of the devices he'd developed and was constantly sending letters to the War Office with his latest plans. While he'd never received a single reply, he always attributed it to the secret nature of his ideas. I had considered them as never of much value to a government office until Mr. Moto showed us that not all of Uncle Ernest's designs were without merit.

Mother must have had similar thoughts because she patted her brother on the arm and said, "Quite right. Moto proved their value beyond the War Office."

"Do you think it's abandoned?" I asked. "I mean, if this belonged to the man in the barn…?"

Uncle Ernest knelt by the firepit and stirred the ashes. "These are less than three days old."

"If not the man in the barn, who's staying here?" I asked.

"We might find something in the tent," Ernest said.

While he crouched to crawl inside, I continued about the perimeter, kicking up rocks and leaves in case something had been covered in a hurry. About a quarter of the way around the clearing, my boot toe caught on a tree root, and I fell forward, barely missing a tree trunk. Mother rushed to my side, and I pushed myself up. When I did so, I disturbed the leaves covering the ground beneath.

Mother stooped next to me and pointed to the tree's roots. "Hello."

Following her finger, I noticed a piece of cloth protruding from a space at the base of the tree. I swiped at the layer of loose dirt covering the cloth and uncovered a shallowly buried knapsack.

"Open it," Mother said.

Her breath quickened, and I shared her anticipation. She called my uncle over, and they peered over my shoulder as I removed its contents one item at a time.

I withdrew first a pair of coarse wool workman pants. Below that, a heavy jacket and cap, also of wool and for a workman. No boots, but a blanket, one side dusty with several dried leaves attached to it.

Once the items were all out, I stood, and we studied them.

Mother lifted the three items of clothing one at a time and then placed them back on the ground.

"Another disguise?" Ernest asked.

"Perhaps, but I don't think for a man," Mother said and gestured to me to stand next to her. She held the pants in front of my legs. "How tall would you say that the man in the stable was?"

"Certainly taller than Sherlock," Ernest said. "Those pants wouldn't have fit him."

"The owner of these pants was short and thin. A boy, perhaps? But older than Sherlock."

His gaze lingering on the clothes, my uncle rubbed his chin and then raised his head to address his sister. "What do you propose we do? Line up all the young men and have them try on the pants?"

"Like Cinderella?" I asked, a giggle escaping my lips.

When Mother didn't join in on our chuckle, we faced her. She tapped a finger against her lips. "It would be easier if we could somehow have him come to us."

I glanced back at the house, and my gaze fell on the schoolroom windows on the third floor and drew in a sharp breath.

"I may know how to call him," I said.

I SHIFTED on the ground and tried to adjust the weight on my backside in the tight space. Despite my wool pants and coat and Uncle Ernest's close proximity, the air in the tent was frigid enough I would have been able to see my breath —if any light had existed for me to do so. The tent was close quarters for the two of us, and I wasn't even fully grown. Could two grown men ever share such a shelter and in the middle of winter? It certainly provided minimal protection against the elements. Having read the history of Napoleon's defeat at the hands of the Russians, I was all too familiar with the concept of *gelure*, frostbite, and its effects on a soldier's extremities. If they were forced to bed in such meager defenses against freezing temperatures, no wonder so many suffered as they had.

A cramp seized my leg, and I pushed it forward to ease the muscle.

"Will you keep still?" Ernest whispered.

His harsh tone cut worse than a slap. My uncle rarely lost his temper with me, but the waiting seemed to have taken a toll on him as well. He pushed open the front flap and peered out through the slit. In the slice of wan moonlight on his face, I perceived the sheen of sweat on his brow. How could the man be perspiring when I was thinking about frostbite?

He let the tent flap drop back into place.

"Anything?" I asked.

He shook his head. "They might not come tonight."

A sigh escaped me. I had hoped that the candle in the schoolroom window would signal the man I'd followed the other night to come to the camp. Of course, we had no way of knowing if Mother had been successful in communicating with the person. If no one came tonight…

"We might have to do this again?"

When I'd offered to assist my uncle in this vigil to capture whoever had been using the campsite in the woods, I'd imagined a less frustrating task than I'd endured up until now. Sitting in a tent awaiting the rogue had sounded… adventurous. Up to this point, it had only been uncomfortable and a little…boring.

"Did you do this often? In India?"

"More than once. Of course, we were waiting for an armed party of thieves or rebels." He drew in a shaky breath. "Hours of holding ready for minutes of battle."

I could feel as much as hear him grip the pistol in his hand even tighter. At that moment, I understood the origin of the sweat on his face—this was no escapade for him, but an all-too-real return to the combat he'd experienced during his time in the military.

"That's where you learned your patience," I said, hoping to calm him as much as I could. "What you've taught me about taking deep breaths, finding my center, and keeping my thoughts outside."

"Right," he said with a sigh, tension dropping from his voice. "Right."

Following his lead, I took in and let out a deep breath. My ears fairly rang as I sought to hear a sound that didn't belong. Unlike the woods in summer, the same area in winter lay quiet under the moonlight. No insects, the scurry of small creatures, or leaves rustling in the trees to mask the breaking of a twig or crunch of dried grass or leaves underfoot. As much as my muscles burned to be stretched or at least readjust, I remained immobile and found my eyelids threatening to droop. I forced my head up, willing myself to remain vigilant. My chin drifted toward my chest, only to jerk to attention when my uncle tapped my shoulder. The rhythmic tramp of feet through the brush signaled someone approaching.

The slight *click* of my uncle's pistol let me know he was preparing for some sort of confrontation. The footsteps drew closer. A shift next to me also signaled he was moving toward the tent's front flap.

The plan was for me to remain inside with a rifle to cover my uncle once he was outside. I put my hand on the weapon, ready to take my position.

My uncle's speed in exiting our canvas enclosure startled me as much as I'm sure it did the person outside. Despite the tight quarters, hours of confinement, and advanced age, the man's agility astounded me. He was out of the tent and on his feet before I had a chance to grab the rifle and throw myself onto the ground to point it out of the flap.

The pitch blackness of the tent's interior made the

moonlight shining through the leafless limbs almost as bright as day. Beyond my uncle and his raised arm, I could clearly make out a young man in dark trousers and a hat pulled low over his brow. The man was unarmed, his hands held high in the air. Something familiar struck me about the hands…

"Don't shoot," I said, scrambling from the tent and leaving the rifle inside.

Without dropping the pistol, my uncle glanced toward me. "Sherlock, what are you doing?"

"That's Miss Bowen. Trevor's governess."

Before he could respond, another crack of twigs pulled our attention behind us. My heart rose in my throat. Would I never learn Mr. Moto's most important lesson? With my attention focused on Trevor's governess, I'd dropped my guard and allowed someone to sneak in behind us. My inattention had placed me in a vulnerable position. Again.

Thankfully, Ernest had been alerted as well and spun about, pistol in hand. He aimed it at a man's dark form at the edge of the clearing.

"Come forward slowly. Hands over your head," he said, an authority in his voice I'd heard only on rare occasions.

The crunch of dry leaves marked the man's movement into the clearing's moonlight. He appeared older than Mycroft and was wearing country hiker's tweed, complete with cap. He said nothing, only stared past us to the governess now sniffling behind us.

"Oh, Richard," Miss Bowen said, "we've been found out."

Both Ernest and I checked both the governess and her...

My mouth dropped opened as the whole scenario fell into place. Given her use of his first name, she and the gentleman—and I used the term based solely on the cut of his tweed—were obviously well acquainted. Just as obvious, they had been meeting in the clearing. Had she been the one Trevor and I had heard in the hallway at night?

I checked my uncle to see if he had come to the same conclusion. He still held the pistol pointed at Miss Bowen's...*Richard*.

"Uncle Ernest," I said. The man didn't move, so I spoke up a little more. "Uncle, I believe you can put away the pistol. These are not dangerous criminals. Miss Bowen is a guest in our house, and Mister...*Richard* is her acquaintance."

After a glance at the two, he dropped the pistol to his side. "What are they doing skulking about in our woods? I-I might have shot them."

"Perhaps we should all return to Underbyrne? I believe Mother and Father will want to hear their explanation as well."

Following a deep breath, he nodded. "Most definitely. Come along then. And don't forget I'm armed."

I retrieved the rifle from the tent, and my uncle and I followed the couple through the woods.

Miss Bowen and Richard, whose last name we learned was Dunn, sat on the edges of two straight-backed chairs placed by the fire in Father's office. Uncle Ernest, Mother, and I sat across from them in leather armchairs. Father, in his dressing gown, paced between the two groups toward and away from the fire, hands gripped behind his back. From the whiteness of his knuckles, I knew he was restraining his fury. For my part, I was grateful it wasn't aimed at me. Although I was almost certain some amount of it would be once his decision with respect to the couple was completed. He'd muttered something about recklessness and weapons after I'd awakened him upon our return to the house.

After several minutes of pacing, he stopped and faced the two. Both shrank under his glare, dropping their gazes to the floor.

"Look at me." All five of us raised our heads. "I want to be quite certain I understand the details. Miss Bowen here has been secretly meeting with this Richard Dunn for…how long?"

"A-a-almost two months, s-sir," she said. "We met at your sister's—Mrs. Fitzhugh's. Richard—I mean Mr. Dunn is an employee of her husband, and they had a party—"

He waved his arms as if to clear the air of her words.

"I don't give a d—er, drat about any party. What I want to know is how you considered it appropriate for a woman of your status to be traipsing about in the woods to meet some *man*. Given the mixed company we have at the moment, I won't even ask what you were doing in the tent."

Scarlet crept up the woman's neck into her cheeks, but Dunn spoke up for the first time. "See here. We have conducted ourselves quite *appropriately*. Nothing untoward was going on. Yes, we used the tent, but only to keep from being found out by accident."

"It's cold," she said. "All we did was…cuddle."

My father's *hurrumph* suggested he didn't believe them, but Mother spoke up for the first time before he could say so.

"I suppose it is up to your sister to determine Miss Bowen's fate, and Mr. Fitzhugh, Mr. Dunn's," she said. "But not tonight. Poor Iris is just now showing signs of improvement following her shock, and I don't think it makes sense to share this mess with her now. I suggest we confine Miss Bowen to the house, and Simpson can escort Mr. Dunn to the train station in the morning."

The two opened their mouths, most likely to protest. I almost considered adding my own to theirs. Miss Bowen's departure would mean no one would be in charge of Trevor. Even if he did follow me around quite a bit of the time, his governess kept him occupied with lessons and other activities so that his tagging along wasn't all that constant. I wasn't sure how I'd survive his visit without her. Father raised his hand, however, and all three of us remained silent.

"Someone will see you out, Mr. Dunn," he said and rang

for a servant. "And there'll be someone at the train station to see that you board it in the morning. Do not attempt to set foot on Underbyrne again. I will warn my staff. We would be in the right to shoot trespassers."

The two exchanged glances and rose to leave. Before they moved, however, Mother spoke again.

"Just a few quick questions. Did either of you see anyone else in the woods?"

"Do you mean the man from the barn?" Miss Bowen asked.

"You were afraid he was Mr. Dunn when they first found him?" Mother asked, and she nodded in reply. "That's why you watched them bring him around for the others to see before he was taken away."

"How did you—?"

"I saw you. In the upstairs window."

I'd almost forgotten the person in the window that night, but Mother hadn't. And somehow, she'd determined it was Miss Bowen. In hindsight, I could see the process she had used. Who else would have been on that floor at that hour?

"I hadn't seen the man before. Nor anyone since."

"I have," Mr. Dunn said. When we all turned to him, he cleared his throat and shifted in his seat. Dropping his gaze, he continued. "I mean, of course I've seen village people using a path through there. Used it myself once I found it, and that's when I had the idea of the tent. But there was one gent I saw once or twice that—he caught my eye, you see. He didn't seem to *belong* there. Not like a villager at all."

"You said 'a gent.' Do you mean he was older? Or just how he was dressed?" Mother asked, her voice shifting slightly from troubled and annoyed at the governess's behavior to excitement at this bit of news. While most might not have caught it, having heard her in all her moods, I detected a slight shift in the speed of her speech. I glanced at Father. He frowned and his jaw muscles tightened. He'd sensed the change as well and was none too pleased with it.

"Both, actually," he said. "Older. Dressed in good clothes. I was on the way to the clearing when I saw him get on the path and head toward this house."

"What was he like? Tall? Short?" she asked.

"I couldn't rightly say too much. It was dark, you know. But he was about average."

I weighed what he had said and eliminated most of the servants. Besides, if they had found such an encampment, surely they would have reported it? And besides—

"Then how do you know he was old?" I asked. "You said it was dark, but you knew he was old."

He touched the top of his head. "A branch knocked his hat off. I could tell his hair was white."

Uncle Ernest drew in a sharp breath. When he exhaled, he muttered a name with it: "Herbie."

My father must have come to the same conclusion as I that the colonel was behind it. His face darkened as his neck muscles formed thick cords. He managed to force out a few words between his clenched teeth. "I should have known."

Before any of us could comment, Mrs. Simpson stepped

into the room. She still wore her nightcap and robe. "You rang, sir?"

"Wake your husband and have him take this…this *man* into town. Then tell Constable Gibbons to have one of his men escort him to the train station and make sure he's on the first train to London in the morning."

Our housekeeper's mouth formed a thin line as she waited for the man to exit and followed him out of the room.

After the door closed, Father spun about to face Miss Bowen. "As for you."

The woman paled, her lips and chin quivering. She appeared to be on the verge of falling off the chair in a dead faint.

"You are confined to this house until Mrs. Fitzhugh determines your fate." She bobbed her trembling chin in response. "You are dismissed as well."

After the door closed for a second time, Father strode to the fireplace and stared into the flames. He took several deep breaths, but even from my view of his back, I could tell his neck muscles had never relaxed.

"I was going to discuss this in the morning, but I suppose we might as well consider it now. A telegram arrived this evening. A response to my inquiries at the War Office regarding our Colonel Williams," he said to the logs glowing bright red at his feet. He turned to face my uncle. "They say Colonel Williams retired from the army in 1860. Seven years ago."

Uncle Ernest leaped to his feet. Crimson rose in his face, almost matching Father's color earlier. "What of it? They aren't denying his service, are they?"

"No, but you tell me what the man has been doing for the past seven years. And why did he show up the same night that a man was murdered in our stables?"

Ernest clenched his fists at his side, and I drew in a breath and held it. I truly feared they might come to blows. Never had I seen the two so at odds. They'd disagreed and shouted in the past, but the tension in the room was almost visible. Mother stepped between them, and I released the air now burning to escape my lungs.

"Mr. Holmes. Ernest. It has been a long night, and obviously everyone is tired. I agree this is most distressing news, but we do not have to deal with it tonight. I believe we can all agree we need to speak with Colonel Williams, and I would suggest it best to do so in the morning. When all is fresh. At times, situations appear less…grim in the light of day."

Miss Bowen and Mr. Dunn's secret meetings did not appear quite as resolved in the morning as they'd appeared the previous night.

Before I descended for breakfast, the governess joined Trevor for his. Her red-rimmed eyes and distracted manner were apparent even to my young cousin. When he asked if she was all right, I excused myself and hurried downstairs. I feared I wouldn't be able to maintain my feigned ignorance of her clandestine activities. I had recently determined Trevor had uncanny observational skills at times and didn't want to be caught off guard.

When I arrived at the breakfast room, I could tell from Father's frown his mood had only improved slightly from the previous night. I chose to finish off my toast and tea—my own unease had curtailed my appetite—and retreat upstairs, only to pause before I reached the second floor. I had no interest in returning to the third floor, nor tiptoeing around Father. I had almost decided to pass the time on the stairs when Constance appeared.

"What are you doin' just standin' there?" Before I could answer, her mouth thinned to a straight line. "You forgot again, didn't you?"

I swallowed several times but found my mouth dry despite my efforts. I'd forgotten about our scheduled rehearsal and lesson. She crossed her arms when I hesitated in my response.

"I'm sorry. I truly am. But you see, a lot happened last night." I quickly summarized finding the camp, encountering Miss Bowen and Mr. Dunn, and learning about Colonel Williams's fabrications. I concluded with, "I know what Father extracts from Colonel Williams will be important, and I just wish I could hear it for myself."

She tilted her head and studied me for a moment. "Where do you think he'll speak to him?"

"His office, most likely. That's where we took Miss Bowen last night."

"It's next to the library?"

"Yes, but how do you—?"

"'Cause the servants talk. That's why. Emily and Father, they talk sometimes in front of me." She snorted as if the thought was distasteful to her. "Like I wasn't there."

"Talk? About what?"

"About what goes on here."

"You mean they *spy* on us?"

"Not necessarily *spy*, but they do know a lot of what goes on here. Just like they don't always see me, your family doesn't always see them. Of course, sometimes, they know how to hear what goes on in one room by bein' at a certain place in another. Like there's a spot in the library where if you stand there, you can hear what's goin' on in the office."

In response to my wide-eyed stare, she shrugged her shoulders. I wasn't sure whether I was more surprised at her revelation of our servants' eavesdropping or that she was aware of it.

CONSTANCE and I squeezed next to each other in a space at the end of a bookcase next to the outside window. The velvet forest-green curtains, pulled back to allow the weak winter sunlight, hid us from anyone's view. Because the library and the office shared a window (at some point, a former Holmes had created the two rooms by adding a wall), conversations in one could be heard in the other. The curtains usually muffled such sounds, but someone had stumbled onto this fact and now the staff seemed to know.

We'd sneaked back down using the servants' staircase and slipped into the library after observing Father, Ernest, and the colonel cross the foyer from the breakfast room. Just as I had been excluded, my father had chosen not to include Mother either. I knew she would consider the action a direct slight, but at the same time, without her audience, the men might speak more freely. At least, I'm sure that was the argument he would have used with her.

Now, in such close contact with my friend, I found it somewhat difficult to concentrate on what was happening in the other room. In addition to the dust from the curtains and the aroma of lemon oil the servants used to treat the wood paneling, the tang of the soap used to wash Constance's clothes and the scent of winter's sharp wind in her hair called my attention to her instead of the disembodied voices drifting in from my father's office.

With a concerted effort, I forced myself to ignore her presence and concentrate on imagining the scene in the adjacent room. I started with the furniture arrangement. Similar to the placement of Miss Bowen's and Mr. Dunn's chairs the previous night, Colonel Williams would occupy a straight-backed chair next to the fireplace. Next, I focused on the voices of the other two men to determine their positions in relation to Williams. Given the ebb and flow of his voice, Father appeared to be pacing. I imagined him moving about in front of the colonel. My uncle appeared to be stationary, most likely flanking his seated friend.

"I received some very disturbing news yesterday," Father said. I could imagine him pausing, arms crossed, to give the man a steady stare as he would a defendant brought before his court. "In response to my inquiry, the War Office has informed me they do not have a Herbert Williams currently serving in India or anywhere else for that matter. Do you care to explain your audacity in presenting yourself as such?"

"Do you truly think," the colonel said, "that the army would acknowledge a spy, regardless of where he is found?"

Constance gave a little gasp, and I poked her to remind her not to reveal our hiding place. She put her hand over her mouth, as if prepared for the next revelation.

She didn't have long to wait. Having shared that first bit of news, the colonel appeared to be primed for sharing even more. He discharged his words in a belligerent staccato.

"I have been since the rebellion. Even before. Information is vital to maintaining peace. Keeping an eye on those who would usurp us."

Now Ernest drew in his breath and released it with two words. "The surveyors."

"Yes, and you almost destroyed that as well."

"I don't understand," Father said.

"Some of the local men were recruited and trained to take measurements of various areas of the country to map it," Ernest said. "But there was more to it than just noting mountain heights. They traveled with caravans, recording the terrain and the peoples. Where settlements were and the sentiments of those who lived there."

"But we weren't the only ones collecting such information. The local princes had their own network of observers who reported information back to them. We were able to get some in the household to then share that information with us," said Williams. A chair creaked. He must have shifted to get a better view of my uncle. "When you courted Susheela, you put that whole operation in jeopardy."

"You mean, she was a… No, I don't believe it."

"Why do you think she was able to make it out to see you? We'd developed a secret exit for her. Of course, she used it to see you as well. When her father discovered her treachery, he almost killed her—not to mention uncovering what she had been doing for us. It was only by some manipulation on our part that neither occurred."

"Instead, you sent her away. From me."

My heart went out to my uncle. His voice cracked on the last word, his heart breaking all over again.

"You would have preferred her dead?"

"No." He sneered the word into a snarl. "But of course, you put her where you could continue to use her."

The blood pounded in my ears. The venom in both

men's voices made it clear they were on the edge of a physical confrontation. Father must have seen how volatile the situation had become.

"We can discuss the past later. Sit down, Williams. Parker, step away."

Another creak of the chair. In the silence that followed, the men's heavy breathing drifted across the divide.

"You contend, then, you're running some sort of ring of spies," Father said. "And you expect us to accept your word. When even the War Office denies your existence."

"I explained why they report they have no record. I've been posing as a merchant the past few years, overseeing a group of men working as traders who passed information— maps, the presence of foreigners, any talk of dissent—back to me."

"The man in the barn, Captain Vincent Rogers," my uncle said, his words crisp and emotionless, "helped Chanda escape from her father. Was he one of your men?"

"How did you—?" his old friend asked and then sighed. "Chanda, of course. She had no reason not to share with you. The man was one of the best. Great at disguises. He'd taken another ship to England. Advance guard, if you will. They were going to start a new life here. When we received word we'd been followed, I was the one who thought of hiding out here. We sent word through the newspapers of the change in plans. His last order was to set up a post in the woods to protect us from a distance."

I willed my uncle to watch his words. He'd already shared too much from our discussion with Chanda. The only proof of Colonel Williams's true reason for being here was his own explanation. My opinion of the man's true nature had slipped quite a bit since his arrival. His deceptions went beyond the misrepresentation of his military position or the secret messages in the newspaper.

"I want you out. Now," Father said, his voice dropping so low I almost couldn't hear him. The tone told me he was trying to contain his anger.

A shuffle signaled Williams had stood. "We can't leave. Not with Chanda in gaol."

"We had no issues until you three arrived."

"Have you forgotten about the man in the greenhouse? He wasn't one of ours, but he was murdered. Don't you understand?" Williams's voice rose even louder. "Two murders in less than a week mean your whole family is in danger. *We* can provide the security needed for your family. Meredith and I are trained—"

"Are you saying Miss Meredith is one of your spies as well?"

Another creak of the chair. The fight in the colonel must have drained him, and he'd collapsed into the chair.

"In a way. She's not truly my niece, but we had to pass her off as part of the ruse to get Chanda out of the country."

"But she resembles your sister," Ernest said.

"We have found that providing certain suggestions to

people often will mold their perceptions. I told you she was my niece, and you took that at face value and used it to assemble the features you felt were appropriate. The woman was actually recruited from an orphanage. A survivor of the rebellion, her Indian nurse disguised her and managed to help her escape. She's quite adept at the local dialects. And disguises. Also, quite the skilled combatant. A real street fighter. She's been on more than one mission with Rogers. Worked well together as a team. Often posed as a married couple. That's why Sherlock noted her finger had previously worn a ring. She continued to wear it until just recently."

Now I gasped and clapped my own hand over my mouth. At thirteen—almost fourteen—even I knew the reputation of a young woman traveling with an unrelated male would be in tatters if the situation became known. Above that, an orphan with no social standing? But most importantly, the man was sharing the girl was a spy as well. Clearly Miss Meredith wasn't an appropriate match for my brother. But would Mycroft see or understand that fact?

And how could I tell him? After all, I wasn't supposed to be privy to this conversation.

Ernest cleared his throat, but his words remained clipped. "Spies are sprouting everywhere, it seems. You. Moto—"

The colonel stuttered out a response. "Moto? A-a spy? Are you certain?"

A man's muffled footsteps indicated my uncle crossed

the rug where the chair holding the colonel rested. I was certain he was directly in front of the man.

"Don't act as if you didn't know. I'd shown you the crossbow myself. Asked you to share the design with your superiors. Moto certainly saw its merits. *He* copied the design."

"I had no knowledge of Moto before we were introduced at the house. If he was spying on you, it's news to me."

"Then what happened to the drawings he'd made of my invention? They went missing after his murder."

"I don't know. I came here for one purpose and one purpose only: to hide out until we could safely get to London. Chanda has information valuable to maintaining British dominance in the region."

"So you say," Father said.

Even without seeing him, I could tell from his tone Father's mouth would be twisted into a sneer.

"Good God, man, what must I do to convince you?"

In the silence that followed, I could hear Father's and Williams's breaths, fast and deep. Each were most likely staring at the other, fuming, in some sort of standoff.

My uncle broke the tension by speaking in a calm tone. "Siger, please, we can't force them out. Not now. Not with Chanda in gaol and Meredith recovering. Perhaps in the meantime, you could send another inquiry?"

"The foreign secretary knows of our predicament," the colonel said with a sigh. "Pity the former Viscount Palmerston isn't here anymore. I doubt even you would dismiss assurance from the prime minister."

"Quite convenient to suggest as a character reference a man who's been dead for four years."

Father might not be seething anymore, but he'd hardly lost his suspicions regarding the man.

"Surely we can wait a day or two?" Ernest said. "To confirm the man's claims. We can't very well turn these people out if we're putting the empire at stake."

Ernest struck a nerve with that statement. Father was, if nothing else, loyal to the Crown, and little would be on the same scale as the whole British Empire.

After a moment, he sighed. "All right. I'll send the request off immediately and let us hope they have not all gone on holiday. Two days. I'll give you two days. But if you have put my family in jeopardy, you'll have hell to pay."

"You may all wait for us to be murdered in our beds" came a woman's voice from the other side of the room. "But I'm not."

My widened stare met Constance's. Aunt Iris was out of bed?

My surprise at her recovery turned to concern. What had she heard about Williams? I had never known my aunt to be discreet. If Williams and Miss Meredith truly were working for the foreign secretary, their secret would not be safe in Aunt Iris's hands.

While I'm sure Father would have liked to question her on the matter of her eavesdropping, she didn't give him an opportunity. She continued in the same heated tone as her first remark.

"I'm leaving in the morning with Trevor. I've already sent word to Mr. Fitzhugh that I'm returning and not to come and join us. Don't try to stop me."

Following her pronouncement, the office door banged shut.

CHAPTER NINE

A moment later, the library door opened and shut again, and I could hear Father call after her.

"Iris, you can't be serious. Please reconsider."

Their footsteps passed the office door—hers, a stomping march, followed by his, a quick staccato as he ran to catch up to her. They both stopped at the stairs. He must have reached her at that point. I moved to leave our hiding place, but Constance held me back. A fortuitous precaution because the next snippet of conversation we heard was my father cajoling his sister.

"Iris, let's talk about this. Come into the library."

Constance and I flattened ourselves even closer to the paneling. Now, not only did I notice the scent of her clothes and hair, but also became very aware of the warmth of her body, the touch of her breath against my neck. Sensations stirred within me once again. My heart seemed to pick up its pace and my breath came quicker. A part of me wanted to touch her hair, but I knew any movement behind the curtain could be detected. Instead, I straightened my back and willed my attention to the other side of our velvet screen, painfully aware that if I didn't control my breathing, I could give us away.

The door opened and closed, and two set of footsteps signaled Father had convinced his sister to discuss her departure in private. The sound stopped about halfway into the room. Some shuffling indicated they had taken seats on the couch in the center near the fireplace.

"Iris, dear, we hardly see each other anymore. And Trevor…the last time I saw him he was still wearing shifts."

"If we don't see each other more, it's because you refuse to come to London. But that's not the issue at the moment. My safety and that of my son's is. My nerves can't take any more stress. People attacked. Dead bodies. *Someone* in this house is a murderer, and I, for one, am not going to wait around and be the next victim."

She rose from her seat and marched to the door. "I have already told the servants and Miss Bowen to pack my things and Trevor's."

"You've missed the morning train. There won't be another until afternoon. By the time you get to London, it will be late. At least wait until tomorrow. In the morn—"

"I can't shut my eyes, let alone sleep here one more night. I keep seeing that…that…*scene* in the greenhouse."

"I can talk to Violette. See if she can't make you a sleeping draught. Stronger than what you've had, if needed."

"The only sedative I need is a few hundred miles between me and this house." She sniffed and her voice quivered as she continued to speak. "I had such high expectations for the holidays. Such happy memories growing up here. I'd hoped for Trevor to have the same. It's all been ruined. Thanks to those dreadful people you let into our home."

The sentence ended in a sob, and I had an overpowering urge to run and comfort her. I certainly could see her point of view. I couldn't think of the greenhouse without bile rising in my throat. The image of Mr. Moto would forever be etched into my brain. At the same time, the thought of her leaving and taking Trevor created the same hollow feeling within me I had felt when he told me of his mother's plans to return to London during the chess game a few days ago.

I realized I had grown accustomed to my young cousin. True, his constant questions were annoying, but I had enjoyed sharing some of my knowledge with him. At Eton, when I had tried to point out some fact with the other boys or sometimes even the instructors, it was not always well received. Trevor, however, hung on my every word and was quite disposed to hearing what I had to share.

"I had no idea... I won't stop you. I'll arrange for

Simpson to take you to the station in time for the afternoon train."

Another rustling. The two rose to their feet.

"I've already written to Rose and told her not to come. That it is not safe here."

When they reached the door, Iris gave a startled cry, and my mother's voice floated into the room.

"So sorry, Iris. I didn't mean to startle you. I'd heard you were out of bed, and I wanted to—"

"You'll have to find someone else to push your vile concoctions on. I'm leaving. Today. Now, if you'll excuse me, I need to oversee the packing."

The door closed again. This time I was the one to restrain the other from making a too hasty exit from our hideaway. A swishing of skirts informed us that my parents continued to occupy the room. I'd imagined they would stay for a private—well, not as private as they thought—conversation. After all, social convention would not have allowed them to discuss my aunt's pronouncements beyond closed doors.

"I can't blame her, you know," Father said.

"I suppose not. I'm sorry, my dear. I know you were looking forward to having everyone here."

"This Christmas hasn't exactly been what I had planned by any means. And I still haven't found the opportunity to inform her of Miss Bowen's actions. I'd hoped to tell Thomas when he joined her in a few more days. Now, I suppose I'll have to write instead. If it weren't for all that has happened, I might suggest we follow Iris back to London. At least then, we'd all be together."

"Perhaps we could—?"

Mother's thought was cut off by screams echoing down the stairwell. By now, Aunt Iris's wails were familiar to the whole household. I held Constance back until I heard my parents exit the room.

Once I knew we were alone, I checked at the door before I flew up the stairs, Constance at my side, to join a number of servants on the upper floors.

My first thought was that she had found another person injured—or worse. When it became clear her cries were coming from the third floor, my throat tightened. Only one person's mishap would have caused my aunt's anguished shrieks. That thought spurred me into taking the steps two at a time, shoving my way past others, all the way praying I was wrong, and she'd found a mouse or something else as innocuous.

By the time I reached the children's room, Aunt Iris was seated in a chair, my parents on either side of her. Father fanned her with his hands while Mother held one limp wrist. Miss Bowen sat on the edge of Trevor's bed. An open trunk stood at the end. Several piles of clothes were stacked about it. The governess's face was drawn and white, a reflection of her employer's. Even their lips were white. Iris had stopped shouting and lapsed into a sort of catatonia.

Blood pounded in my ears from the exertion and the conclusion that Trevor was the cause of both women's distress. I froze in the threshold, unable to enter and hear her pronounce what I already knew. I glanced about. Aside from my parents, none of the household was present. That the colonel wasn't there didn't surprise me. But neither was Ernest nor Mycroft.

Constance stopped at my side and whispered, "What happened? Where's Trevor?"

I shook my head, my voice failing me. She would have to wait for someone else to share the particulars.

As if in response to Constance's whisper, Miss Bowen drew in a deep, shaky breath and recovered herself enough to mutter repeatedly, "It's my fault. It's all my fault."

That pronouncement broke my paralysis, and I asked the question that everyone else carried on the tips of their tongues.

"What happened to Trevor?" All turned to me, even Iris. Constance's open mouth made me aware that panic had made my question come out too loud for the room. I cleared my throat and asked in lower tones, "Where is he?"

Miss Bowen found the strength to reply.

"Mrs. Fitzhugh told me to pack Trevor's things. He was upset. Said he didn't want to go back to London. He was having a temper tantrum and grabbed some of his clothes and threw them to the ground. I told him to go to the schoolroom until he could behave. He stomped out. I thought he was in there. But when Mrs. Fitzhugh came here—"

Her choked sobs prevented her from continuing, but my

aunt was able to finish the thought. "My son. My son," Iris murmured, "is m-m-missing."

Father exchanged a glance with my mother in a silent discussion. From the creases about their eyes, I knew they were both concerned, but also knew they would diminish it for Iris's sake.

"Now, now, my dear," Father said, "we don't know that he's missing. He's a boy. They tend to take off by themselves. Sounds very much like he went off in a huff. Maybe to hide so you can't go today. More than once we've searched the house for Sherlock or Mycroft only to find them engrossed in some pursuit and totally unaware that the whole house was searching for them."

"We'll send the servants to join with all of us to seek him out. I'm certain he will be found in no time," Mother said. She raised her gaze to the governess. "When did you last see him?"

"When I sent him to the classroom. About an hour ago."

Another glance between my parents, and again, I could read the silent discussion passing between them. In an hour, the boy could go far. And if unfamiliar with the area, get quite easily lost in that amount of time. Aunt Iris didn't allow him to stray far from the house, and if he had decided to go into the woods…

A shudder passed through me, and I forced my thoughts away from that scenario to focus on what my mother was saying to her sister-in-law.

"I think it best if you were to lie down completely. Mr. Holmes and I will take personal charge of the search and keep you informed of anything. Mr. Holmes, why don't you and Miss Bowen take her to her bedroom? Prop up her feet and make sure her corset isn't too tight to allow circulation. Then, if you will meet me in the kitchen, Mr. Holmes, we'll ask the servants if any of them have seen Trevor."

With a nod, my father helped his sister to her feet, and he and the governess led her toward the door. Constance and I stepped back to let them pass.

I couldn't stop thoughts I was certain were identical to those racing through my aunt's head. Trevor, cold and shivering, scared and possibly injured, unable to return to the house. My legs shook, barely supporting my weight, and I leaned against the wall, its firmness bracing me.

Mother paused upon entering the corridor to speak to me. She laid a hand on my cheek. "You're almost as pale as Iris."

"Trevor—" I paused and licked my lips. "Do you think he's all right?"

Her smile failed to reassure me. "Under normal circumstances, I'd say he's fine. You probably don't remember, but when you were about five, you disappeared one afternoon. The whole household went on the search. First the house and then the grounds. You'd gone out to your uncle's workshop. He'd been busy and thought you'd left. Ernest insisted you weren't there until we searched the place and found you asleep on the cot in the back."

I blinked, trying to keep my darkest fears from overcoming me. As always, Mother seemed to have read my mind. She cocked her head to one side and studied me before speaking again.

"You know, Sherry, dear, you and Constance are most familiar with your cousin at the moment. What interests him? What might have lured him away? And where? Put that information to work while we organize the rest."

I nodded, grateful for something to do. After she moved past us and down the stairs, I turned to Constance. "Let's go to the schoolroom."

"I don't think—"

"That he's there? I agree, but he may have left something to show where he did go. It was the last place we know he was."

She followed me into the room, and I studied the now-deserted space. After a cursory review, my gaze fell on the teacher's desk. Black smudges marked its surface. These were new.

While I moved in that direction, Constance moved to a cupboard and opened it.

Rubbing my fingers across the desktop, I asked her, "Do you truly think he's hiding there?"

"No," she said, shutting the cupboard doors, "but everyone assumes he's no longer in here. You said this was the last place anyone knows he was. Maybe he's just hiding."

I stared at charcoal smudges on my fingers and around a clean area on the top. Someone had been drawing on paper and taken the sheet with them. "Why wouldn't he just come out? Surely he knows we're all searching for him."

"Precisely," she said and moved to another cupboard. "He could be too frightened now to tell everyone he'd been hiding on purpose." She sighed when that cupboard revealed only stacks of old papers.

After a final glance at my fingertips, I lifted the lid on the desk.

She spun around and glared at me, hands on her hips. "You aren't going to tell me you think he's hidin' in that desk?"

I held up a finger to silence her and examined the detritus hidden there. Mixed in with two more charcoal drawing pencils were various broken nibs, lead pencils stubs, and chalk for slate work. To one side lay several pieces of paper, and…

"Hold on," I said, more to myself than Constance. I closed my eyes and considered the series of events.

Trevor had drawn a picture with the charcoal and had gone to…?

I met Constance's gaze. "I think Trevor drew a picture. For someone. He was angry with his mother, Miss Bowen…"

"But not with you," she said. "Maybe he went to give it to you."

My eyes widened. "Come on," I said and grabbed Constance's hand. "I think I know where he went."

Trevor would have known I wasn't on the third floor, so

he would have gone downstairs. Of course, I was hidden in the library listening to Father question Colonel Williams. Trevor wouldn't have found me inside and…

Would have gone to the workshop.

With a goal in mind, I rushed down the stairs and into the kitchen, dragging Constance behind me. Along the way, I noted how deserted that part of the house was. The servants had obviously been sent out already to seek my cousin. Only after I rushed out the door did I realize I'd forgotten a coat. The wind sliced through my jacket and pants, causing me to gasp. Cold air filled my lungs, and I coughed in response.

Constance had a similar reaction, and I turned to her.

"Go get your coat. I'm going to the workshop. If you find either of my parents, send them there as well."

She rushed back inside, and I ran the distance between the two buildings, stopping only when I reached the door. Just outside I paused, deciding whether I should knock or simply enter. I listened for moment in case I could hear him or someone else already in there. All quiet.

I pushed the door open and stepped into semidarkness.

Another pause, listening for any indication of movement or someone else's presence. The structure appeared to be deserted, but the rush of blood in my ears made it difficult to hear. Between the cold, the brisk run to the workshop and my own growing concern over my cousin, my breath took up the beat set by my heart. I drew in a lungful of air and considered my next step.

Deciding that the search would go faster with some light, I took a lantern my uncle always kept by the door and lit it. The flame's yellow circle cast elongated shadows in all directions. The posts and various tables scattered about the room loomed as dark shapes at the edges of the lamplight.

"Trevor?" I said.

The only answer was the scurry of some of the caged mice from my uncle's experiments.

Recalling my mother's story of me asleep in the cot in the back, I made my way through the building, checking under tables and around posts as I went.

As I stepped behind the screen Ernest used to mark off his sitting area, I cast the lantern light around, expecting to find my cousin asleep on the narrow bed.

My stomach dropped as I found the top blanket pulled taut in my uncle's neat military fashion. The rest of the furniture was equally empty.

With a sigh, I turned to leave. Out of the corner of my eye, a flash of white caught my attention. I turned back to the sitting area and raised the light again. The white was a bit of cloth peeking out from the lid of a wooden trunk shoved against the back wall. While I was not certain what the trunk held, I was confident it had been shut tight before now. Setting the lantern on the ground, I stepped over and opened it.

My first reaction was relief. Trevor lay curled up inside, atop what appeared to be some of my uncle's old military items. At first, he appeared asleep on his side, his legs pulled up to his chest. Bile rose in my throat, however, when I saw the blood staining the dun-colored blanket underneath his head.

I rushed out of the workshop, yelling at the top of my lungs for the others to come, and met Constance halfway, my parents trailing right behind her.

MY TONGUE ADHERED to the roof of my mouth as I tried to swallow. Mother leaned over Trevor's still-curled body, checking his breathing and pulse. When she rocked back on her heels, I bit my tongue to avoid shouting out *What?* to her. If the news was as bad as my panic suggested, I knew I'd have to find a place to sit.

Mother's gaze met mine for a brief second before she announced her observations. "He's breathing, but barely."

"He's—he's alive?" I asked, unable to keep the tremor of relief out of my voice.

"If you hadn't found him, Sherlock, I'm certain he would have suffocated in that trunk. You most likely saved his life." She rose to her feet. "We need to get him to his room. The wound to his head is not deep and the loss of blood not too great. Given the trauma to his head, however, I do fear a brain commotion."

My father shook his head slowly. "How am I going to tell Iris? Her nerves are already strung tight. Now that something has happened to Trevor, she might very well become catatonic."

"She need not know all the truth for the moment. Simply tell her Trevor hurt his head and will not be able to travel for a few days. I doubt he will even remember being in the trunk. He was unconscious when he was put there."

"How do you know that?" Father asked.

"If you were put in a trunk awake, wouldn't you push on the lid? Fight to open it? The items underneath him were neatly folded. No signs of struggle in the trunk." She glanced at me and Constance. "Remember, share as little as possible with your aunt. Mr. Holmes is right. She will be quite distraught when she learns of her son's injuries. No need to exacerbate the problem."

The three of us nodded in silence. Having all witnessed her reaction to learning her son was missing, we could all imagine her response upon hearing of his current condition.

Following Mother's instructions, my father gathered the boy in his arms to carry him back to the house. As he lifted him from the trunk, I caught sight of Trevor's hands. They had been folded underneath his head, and I studied them to see if he held the paper I suspected he'd taken before searching for me. My shoulders drooped when I ascertained them empty.

In the hopes it might have fallen from his grip, I remained to search the trunk after my parents left.

Nothing.

"No paper?" Constance asked when I straightened up.

I shook my head. "Perhaps it fell inside? Let's take everything out."

Stepping to my side, she reached for the blanket that had lain underneath my cousin, then stopped.

"Th-that's blood, isn't it?" she asked, pointing to the dark stain on the blanket.

She swallowed hard enough I could hear her effort, and I feared she might be ill.

Retrieving the blanket, I saw the blood had already begun to dry, making it stiff and heavy. "I should show it to Mother, then take it to Mrs. Simpson for cleaning. We should make sure my uncle's military uniform and equipment haven't been…stained."

Setting the blanket aside, I checked the articles below. As I did so, I caught a strong whiff of naphthalene, used to repel moths. The blood hadn't passed beyond the blanket. The pair of pants below remained creased. With great care, Constance and I removed each item. With every piece, my jaw tightened, only to relax again when nothing out of the ordinary appeared. By the time we reached the bottom, we'd found nothing of interest, and the heavy odor of naphthalene gave me a headache.

I glanced at Constance. Her face had paled, whether from inhaling the moth repellant or thoughts about Trevor, I wasn't sure.

"Let's find your mother," she said when she caught my gaze. She glanced at the blanket resting to the side. "And show her that."

With leaden limbs, I replaced all but the blanket, taking care to return everything just as I had found it. What could poor Trevor have seen or done that would cause anyone to harm him? All because I'd been hiding in the library. On some level, I felt that what happened to him was my fault.

When we stepped from behind the screen to the main workshop area, we found my uncle shutting the door behind him. He joined us and studied the item in my hands.

"Was that in my trunk?" he asked.

I nodded. "I'd hoped to find something that Trevor might have been carrying with him before he was attacked. I found this and thought I'd take it to Mrs. Simpson to be cleaned."

His gaze fell immediately upon the blanket.

"Odd. It isn't mine." He pointed to the cot. "That's the only one I brought back from India."

I stared at the woolen cloth in my hand. I had assumed it belonged to my uncle in good part because of its color. The tan resembled that of his uniform. Now away from the trunk, I noticed the blanket didn't carry the strong odor of the moth-repellant that permeated the rest of my uncle's things.

I turned to Constance. "We must share this with Mother immediately."

In response to our knock on the nursery door, Mother stepped from the room.

She glanced at the blanket but didn't ask any questions. Instead, she shared about my cousin and his condition.

"He's resting, which is what he needs at the moment. Both to replace the blood loss and to recover from the blow on his head. You don't recall when you had your brain commotion after tumbling down the stairs. You slept a long time then as well."

I swallowed again, remembering with a shudder the pain and dizziness I'd experienced in my effort to keep Constance from arrest. She'd tried to help us by stealing a book taken from my mother. I pushed down the memory and the concern for my cousin. I had to focus on the moment.

"There may be an additional reason," I said. "The trunk reeks of naphthalene."

"I smelled it too," she said with a nod. "I was too focused on him at the time, but I wouldn't doubt…" She paused, as if considering the implications. "I don't recall reading anything specific on exposure to the repellant, but given it was inhaled, I assume exposure to fresh air will help relieve him. I do believe I have read of children *eating* tar camphor. I'll research it if I have a chance."

"And Aunt Iris?"

"Resting. I did get her to take a sedative. Your father is sitting with her for the moment." She placed a hand on my cheek and gave me a slight smile, I knew for sympathy. "They are both mending. We must focus on finding who did this."

Before I could share my information about the blanket, Constance spoke up.

"Did you find any paper on him? No chance something appeared in his pocket? As you undressed him?" When Mother shook her head, Constance continued, her voice gaining speed as she did so. "Sherlock thinks Trevor drew a picture for him and that's why he left the schoolroom. We didn't find it in the trunk so maybe he had it with him."

When she paused for a breath, I added, "But we also found this blanket, and I think it might reveal something as well."

Mother had pulled her head back as Constance spoke, and then quieted as if taking in her information. When she finally moved, it was to tap her finger against her lips. "Given we don't have the picture, let's start with the blanket and see what it might reveal."

She waved her arm toward the schoolroom, and the three of us stepped inside. After quietly shutting the door and locking it, she turned to us. "Constance, please be so kind as to open the curtains. The sunlight will allow us to examine the blanket properly. And, Sherry, dear, do you think you might be able to find some magnifying glasses? We should still have some from your science studies."

While Constance and I completed our assigned tasks, Mother repositioned the teacher's desk to catch the largest square of sunlight. I managed to find two magnifying glasses and carried them to the table.

I dropped my gaze before meeting Constance's. "I'm sorry. I could only find two."

"That's all right," she said, crimson creeping into her cheeks. "I'm not sure what I'm supposed to see anyway."

"It's not a matter of seeing," Mother said, taking one of the glasses from me and putting the blanket on the desk. "It's a matter of observing. Follow over Sherlock's shoulder and see if you catch something he misses."

With the blanket sitting in the sunlight, the side next to Trevor's head now appeared more worn than I had noticed in the workshop's dim light. Definitely not something my uncle would have kept. A round circle of blood toward the top fold indicated where Trevor's head had lain.

"Odd," I whispered when I considered it.

Mother turned her gaze to me. "What is, Sherry, dear?"

"The stain, it's almost circular. I don't recall seeing any blood on the floor of the workshop, but he must have bled. And you said head wounds bleed profusely. If he was hit and then placed in the trunk, there should have been blood."

"What if someone wrapped his head?" Constance asked.

"That would explain the lack of blood," Mother said and tapped her finger to her lips. "But the attacker didn't use this blanket."

"Exactly. The spot wouldn't be so...so..." I searched for a word to describe the spot that didn't make me sound insensitive to Trevor's plight.

Mother seemed to have understood my discomfort. "It's almost perfectly round, isn't it? I would say it was formed from a bleeding wound at its center. Let's focus on this blanket now." She flipped the blanket open, following the bloodstain through the various layers, each one growing smaller in circumference until only a spot appeared on the last layer and nothing on the far side. "Shall we see what we can observe beyond the stain?"

After opening the blanket and spreading it out on the table, she gestured to me to move to the other side. Using both the magnifying glass and my unaided eyesight, I examined the surface, starting at one end of the cover and working toward the center while Mother used a similar method from the other end.

As I proceeded across the item, I found I had to force myself to concentrate on the task at hand. Once again, Constance's presence at my side drew my attention to the warmth radiating from her body, the scent of her hair, and the slight prickle on my neck when her breath passed over it. My thoughts flitted briefly to my brother. Did he notice similar aspects in Miss Meredith? Is that what attracted him to her?

For a moment, I found myself understanding some of his infatuation.

I gave myself a mental shake and refocused my thoughts, reminding myself that allowing my thoughts to wander would do no good for my cousin. Perhaps because of such random notions, Mother was the first to discover our first indication of the blanket's origin.

"Hello," Mother said, peering through the glass. "What do you make of this?"

She passed her glass to Constance, and she and I trained our gaze on the area Mother indicated with her finger.

"That's hay," I said, straightening my back.

"Do you think the blanket is from the barn?" Constance asked.

"You can ask your father," Mother said. "He might be aware of whether any blankets are missing."

"If it did come from the barn, why are there not more bits of hay or straw?" I asked. "I'm afraid I haven't found any on this side."

"Perhaps it came from Trevor," Constance said.

"A possible explanation." She paused and closed her eyes. She had to be remembering her original examination of my cousin. "Miss Bowen helped me undress him, bind his head. I'm afraid I was too focused on the boy to notice anything else, but she or one of the servants will know where his clothes are."

Knowing now to keep an eye out for straw, we returned to the item. Once again, I observed the unemotional detachment required for such work. Mother's concentration had been elsewhere and had kept her from noticing the state of Trevor's clothes when he had been undressed. By now, the items could have been washed and any hints as to where he was before the trunk could be lost. When lives were perhaps at stake, one couldn't allow emotions to block one's attention.

With our second review of the item, we found a few more bits of straw. Similarly, when the blanket was turned over, additional traces appeared, along with a long, dark strand of hair.

"This couldn't be his," I said, holding the strand by one end. It swayed gently in the breeze as the sunlight bounced off it. "Only a woman would have hair that long."

"Or an animal, like a horse or cow," Constance said. "And horses are around hay."

At that suggestion, my gaze met Mother's as if each of us knew what the other was thinking. A thrill ran down my spine, as I knew where to go next.

The barn.

I opened my mouth to suggest we search the place at once when someone rapped on the door.

Mother motioned to me and Constance to stand in front of the table holding the blanket before opening the door to Miss Bowen.

"Mr. Holmes is asking for you. Apparently, Mrs. Fitzhugh has awakened and is quite distraught."

"Please tell Mr. Holmes I'll be there directly."

After the governess left, Mother turned to me and shrugged. "As much as I would like to continue with our efforts, I'm afraid I must leave you two to explore the barn yourselves."

Once Mother had shut the door behind her, Constance turned to me.

"How did she know we are to go to the barn? Because of the hair on the blanket?"

"That's right. There may be something there to tell us who attacked Trevor."

Her entire body then straightened, and she stared at me as if an idea occurred to her. "Do you think they are out for children? Like the gypsies?"

"At the moment, we can assume he found something that someone else didn't want him to have," I said with a shake of my head. "I don't think the attacker is interested in children in general."

"Still, it ain't right. Hurtin' a little one like him. Let's go to the barn."

WHEN I ENTERED THE BARN, my gaze strayed immediately to the spot where I'd found the man, and a shiver passed through me. Had it only been a week and a half? So much had happened during that time. The attack on Miss Meredith. Mr. Moto's death. Now Trevor. I shook my head. As Mother had observed, this was hardly the peaceful country Christmas we'd intended.

A strong wind blew the straw and dirt about the stable floor as Constance used her weight to close it.

With the door to our backs, I scanned the brushed-dirt floor, seeking any signs to indicate where Trevor might have been. Or of any struggle taking place there. The horses, aroused by our presence, pawed and stomped the ground with their hooves.

"How should we do this?" she asked. "I've never been searchin' for anything like this."

"But you've played that game. The one you taught Trevor."

"Hot and cold?" She paused and a smile flitted across her lips. A memory of Trevor? Or her own brothers and sisters? "You know, I suppose I have done somethin' like searchin'. When I used to play the game with my mum, I learned to check for somethin' out of place. And to learn where they hide things. Like with Trevor. Bein' short and all, he always hid everything on the ground, under something."

I stiffened as her comment brought an idea to mind. "What if he came here not to look for someone but to hide from them? We need to check the stalls. Maybe he tried to cover himself with hay? I think we can eliminate the ones with the horses. He wouldn't go in an occupied one."

"All right," Constance said and waved her hand to the left. "I'll take this side. You take the other."

The first few I examined contained a bit of straw strewn about but nothing to indicate either man or beast had occupied them recently. About halfway down, a large pile of hay filled the back corner. I called to my friend, and she watched from the stall door as I brushed the hay aside with great care, examining it for any sign of blood or other indications that Trevor had been there. As I reached the bottom, my hand connected with something metallic. Ignoring caution,

I dug it out, then sat back on my heels to stare first at the box in my hands and then at the rafters above me.

"That doesn't look like something Trevor would have."

"It's one of my uncle's rat traps." I lifted the box in my hand to measure its weight. No rats. When I moved it about in my hands, however, I felt something shift inside. "There's something in there, though."

Constance stepped behind me as I pried open the trap's top. She drew in her breath as I retrieved the item. The necklace was a most unusual design. A double strand of black beads linked by a circle of gold.

"Is that your mother's?" she asked.

I shook my head. "I believe we've found Chanda's *mangala sutra*. She took it off and hid it in her room before she was arrested. Then someone stole it."

"Trevor wouldn't have done that."

"No. But he might have found it and hidden it here. Maybe that's why someone hit him on the head."

"That means someone might come back for it. What if they were to come——?"

As if her very thought were a prediction, the barn door creaked open, letting in a gust of cold air. I pulled her down next to me, and we crouched at one side of the stall as someone stepped into the barn.

At first, I thought a stable boy had come in to check on the horses. The step was light and quick as the person moved to shut the door. With the wind now cut off, I could hear the rustle of skirts. Had I not known my mother was attending to Trevor, I might have thought she'd followed us to the barn, but with all other possible women being eliminated, I knew Miss Meredith had joined us. Once the door closed, her footsteps were slow but steady, and she moved back and forth from the stall on one side to the one across from it.

My mouth dried as she came nearer and nearer. Having not made our presence known from the beginning, we would surely be accused of improper conduct. Not only might we be accused of some sort of eavesdropping, but our conduct might also be questioned because of our different genders. It was one thing for us to be together in the open and quite another to be found hiding together. I didn't relish the reprimand my father, brother, or the colonel might bestow upon us if found out.

I dared a glance at Constance. Her eyes, bright, blinked rapidly at me, and I knew she would bear the brunt of any blame. As the daughter of a servant, she would be the one who would be considered trespassing.

The muscles in my legs cramped from the crouch I held, but I feared moving them would create enough noise to attract the woman's attention. My breathing came shallow and fast as the woman continued in our direction, and my thoughts whirled about as I debated making ourselves known, weighing it against the commotion it would create should I do so. Then, my thoughts paused and focused on Miss Meredith.

My concern was resolved when the door opened and

closed again and a set of heavy footsteps echoed through the room.

"Meredith?" Mycroft said. "What a delightful surprise."

My mouth fell open. Did she truly believe he hadn't followed her? I knew of no other reason for him to come to the barn.

A swish of skirts suggested a quick spin on Meredith's part.

His footsteps grew louder as he approached her. "I was hoping we might have a moment alone."

She giggled, and he chuckled along with her.

My mouth snapped shut to keep from drawing in a breath loud enough to be heard over the horses' restless movements. In all my life, I'd never heard my brother sound so amused. Laugh, yes, often with derision tainting the outburst, but the giddiness he displayed represented a side of him I wasn't aware existed.

Constance and I exchanged glances. Unfortunately, whatever she wished to convey was not clear to me. My concern was no longer for us, but for the other couple. Should Mycroft and Miss Meredith be caught, I wasn't certain that the colonel might not demand my parents restore her reputation by announcing their engagement. After what I had learned of the woman's history during the interrogation in my father's study, I knew they would hardly be considered a good match.

Had the colonel encouraged Meredith to beguile Mycroft for just this reason? To attach her to our family?

Meredith sighed, and a rustle of skirts signaled her movement toward my brother. Another sigh followed and then what sounded like a kiss.

"Meredith, you have made me…your presence at Underbyrne is…" He paused. "I can't bear the thought of this place without you. It would be so…empty."

"I've grown quite…fond of you, too, these past few days." Another swishing, and from the sound of her voice, she'd moved away from him. "I will miss you very much when we leave."

"Surely you don't mean—"

"My plans are my uncle's. Whenever he decides the time is right, we will move on." More shuffling about. "I can't bear the thought of being without you."

"Or I, you. If you go to London—"

"I have no idea if we will do that anymore. The whole purpose of our trip was to carry Chanda to safety. And she repays us by attacking me…" The last word was choked off in a sniffle.

To that point, I had considered the declaration of her affections legitimate—and my brother's own besotted tone rather amusing. Her disparagement of Chanda, however, raised my doubts about the sincerity of all her pronouncements. For her to imply she was the *rajkumari*'s protector when they arrived and now raise doubts about the woman laid all her assertions open to suspicion.

The muscles in the back of my neck tightened, and I knew I had to remain hidden. Under no circumstances should Mycroft marry this…this deceiver. While I'd developed a slow burn, Mycroft had continued in his response to Meredith.

"My…dear, don't think of that night. You are safe. I would stay by your side forever to keep you that way."

"I do feel safer…in your arms. I want to stay in them always. And we could, you know. That is, if we were…"

"Are you suggesting…?"

"How far is Gretna Green from here?"

"I-I'm not certain…from London. I'd have to consult Bradshaw's."

My eyebrows flew up at this point. The one thing my brother would *not* have to do is to consult the train tables. He *knew* them. By heart. Thanks to a memory even greater than mine.

Why was he lying to her?

After a pause, he said, "Good heavens. You are truly serious about—"

"Aren't you?" she asked.

Although I couldn't see him, I had a clear image of my brother. He was hardly ever at a loss for words, but when it happened, his chin would quiver as his mouth worked itself as if to force his lips and tongue to pronounce the words.

Surely he was tongue-tied because he realized he'd been duped? He had gone from expressing a vague fondness for the first woman, as far as I knew, who had shown any interest in him to running off to Gretna Green in the span of a few seconds.

I glanced at Constance. Her eyes were round, and she clamped her hand over her mouth so tightly the flesh around her fingers was white. The import of this conversation seemed as clear to her as it was to me.

Meredith seemed to take his hesitation as a refusal. In the next instant, she moved toward the door, pausing at the entrance. "I allowed you certain…liberties because of what I considered sincere feelings. Now I see, however, you were just…you were just—" The last bit ended with a slight whimper and another sniffle.

A series of quick steps sent him toward her. "I would never dishonor you in such a fashion. My feelings for you are genuine."

"Then what's keeping you from acting upon them? Why not simply agree to this plan?"

"What about Christmas? Don't you want—?"

"You don't think they have Christmas in Gretna Green? If you are truly sincere, I don't see why you are objecting."

I could think of any number of objections, not least of which was that, other than Colonel Williams's vouchsafe, no information on the woman existed. And who vouchsafed for the colonel? Could someone make such a life-changing decision in just a few days?

The answer came in Mycroft's next statement.

"My intentions, my dear Meredith, have and always will be honorable toward you. It is my deepest desire to keep you at my side. Always. And Gretna Green would appear to be the most expedient means of doing so. Will you do me the honor of becoming my bride?"

"Oh." The word escaped Meredith's lips as a little squeal. This expression was followed by a louder but breathless, "Yes. Yes, my dear Mycroft." Before my brother could respond with his own enthusiasm, she added, "Let's not dally. Tonight. Tomorrow night at the latest."

"Tomorrow would allow me time to arrange our route."

"We need to make our departure when we will not be missed. Let's discuss this on the way back to the house, before our absence is questioned."

Their footsteps led them out of the stables.

When the door shut off their voices, I leaned back against the stall's side, and with a deep exhalation, I rested my head against the rough boards. Only then did I realize how stiffly I had held myself, and I twisted a bit to stretch my muscles.

Turning back to face Constance, I was surprised when she peeled her hand from her face and let out a howl of laughter. "If she put a ring in his nose, she would no better be able to lead him."

For the first time ever, my anger truly flared at her. I'd been frustrated, annoyed, and peeved, but never had I been as furious with her as I was at this moment.

"What do you find so amusing? My brother is about to —" I paused, unable to even mouth the words or come up with a reasonable explanation. "She's…she's…*bewitched* him."

"Ain't no witchin' goin' on here. She's just usin' what God gave her to get what she wants."

"You don't think she's in love with him?"

She shrugged and giggled. "I don't know that. But I's can tell you, she wants somethin' else as well. And it must be in that Gretna Green place."

"I fail to see any humor in this. My brother is about to ruin his life."

"Won't be the first man to do so. 'Sides, I sort of thinks it's justice-like. Him, all high and mighty, bein' taken down a peg or two by a woman."

Her lack of concern at what I considered a quite disturbing turn of events only pushed my anger to the boiling point. So what if he'd been less than respectful to her? I failed to see this as appropriate punishment for his behavior. At that moment, I wanted to hurt her, and I knew exactly where to plant the sword.

"I suppose your father is another." She sobered immediately and fixed her stare on me. I drove the edge to the hilt. "You said so yourself. Emily has her hooks in him. Maybe she'll take him down a peg or two as well."

Her fists convulsed at her sides, but her voice was calm and slow. "Maybe. But at least the children will have a mother. All you'll have is a *liar* for a sister-in-law. And you'll never be able to trust her. And you can't tell anyone why 'cause then you'll have to tell them how you were a spy and a liar yourself."

Before I could respond, she pushed past me, shoving the

stall's gate open so hard it swung around and slammed against the wall.

The anger drained from me, and I stared at her retreating back. She held her head high as she stomped from the stables, leaving me frozen in place by both anger and regret. I'd hurt my friend. Part of me wanted to run after her and apologize. The other part wanted to preserve my wounded pride. After all, she'd hurt me first. The second part won. I waited until she had left the barn to go in search of my mother.

The elopement had to be stopped.

CHAPTER TEN

No sooner had I entered the house than a hand clamped onto my forearm and another onto my mouth, and I was pulled tight against a man's chest.

I knew it was a man because of the breadth of the hand covering my lips and the tweed cloth on the hand's arm. My breath whistled through my nostrils. What if this was the person who accosted my cousin?

My breath slowed only slightly when my brother hissed into my ear. "You and I are going to have a private conversation, Little Brother. One sound out of you, and I'll break your arm, do you understand me?"

I nodded, and the pressure on my face disappeared. The force on my arm, however, increased as I was pulled down the corridor. While my respiration had slowed, my dread had intensified. Mycroft was not one to make physical threats, and his doing so only made clear both the fervor that currently possessed him as well as how it pulled him out of character. For this reason, I allowed him to drag me toward our father's office. I might have been able to release myself from his grip thanks to my *baritsu* training, but I feared Mycroft's reaction given his odd state of mind. I had heard that those not in control of their faculties often possessed superhuman strength. As such, he might prove a more formidable opponent than I would anticipate.

In addition, I wanted to share what I'd learned about Miss Meredith's history, hoping, in part, to dissuade him from a hasty marriage. Of course, divulging this information presented a dilemma. I'd no way of sharing it without also revealing how I'd obtained it.

At the end of the foyer, my brother yanked me into Father's office and shut and locked the door.

Releasing me, he said, "Now we can talk without being overheard."

I rubbed the spot where his fingers had gripped my arm, knowing I would most certainly carry a mark for several days. My glare followed him as he moved to stand with his back to the fireplace. With no other illumination in the room except for the embers glowing in the grate, he appeared almost demon-like. A tall silhouette flanked by a deep crimson glow.

"What were you doing in the barn?"

"How did you—?"

"Please," he said, a sneer coloring the word. "I heard that Straton girl's cackle. Even through a closed barn door."

I opened my mouth to remind him she had a name and that it was quite rude to refer to her laugh as he did, but a greater concern rose as my brain sorted out the import of his explanation. Instead, I asked, "Did Miss Meredith hear her too?"

He shook his head. "She'd gone on ahead so we wouldn't be seen together. You didn't answer my question about being in the barn. Please tell me it was nothing untoward. An involvement with that sort of girl won't end well. For either of you."

My throat contracted at his reference once again to Constance's class rank and my association with her, burning with a thousand retorts to his warning—chief of which were my knowledge of Miss Meredith's questionable heritage and reputation. If both or either were made public, Father's disapproval of Mycroft's "involvement" with the woman would not be dissimilar to his issues with Constance—most likely with an even greater vehemence given Mycroft's position as successor to the Holmes estate.

Mycroft must have taken my silence as a sort of affirmation because he raised the derision in his voice. "That *was* what you were doing in there. I'd hoped you had better sense than that."

This second insult jarred my tongue free.

"If you must know, Mother sent us there. We were trying to find out what happened to Trevor. And Constance is ten times—a hundred times—better than Meredith. And you're the fool if you take her to Gretna Green."

The reference to his secret plans spurred him to take the few paces between the fireplace and my position until he was standing over me. "You little sh—" He clamped his mouth shut, his lips forming a thin line, and his jaw muscles tightening.

I couldn't tell if his anger or the fire had deepened the flush in his cheeks, but I knew my remark had wounded him. Only when truly furious was he at a loss for words.

After several breaths, he said in a slightly calmer voice, "You stay out of my affairs. I swear by all that is holy, if you breathe one word of what you overheard, I will make your remaining days on this earth a living hell."

He gripped my forearms and leaned into me. His face inches from mine, I could tell he'd eaten kippers with his eggs that morning. "Swear to me," he said. "Give me your word you will not tell a soul what you overheard."

His grasp tightened, making me squirm. The pressure increased until I fairly shouted out. "All right. I swear."

"And the girl too. Tell her she's to keep that loud mouth of hers shut as well. I can make even more trouble for her."

The threat paralyzed me. Despite his anger, I knew his warnings to me carried little actual danger. What, after all, could he possibly do that would truly make my life "a living hell"? Constance, and in fact her whole family, were, however, at the mercy of my father's benevolence. He could dismiss Mr. Straton from his position and send him and the children packing. How much influence my brother might hold to achieve such a turn of events was not clear, but I didn't want to risk it.

I quickly bobbed my head, eager to end this whole exchange with my brother.

Never had I feared Mycroft's mood as much as at the present moment. In the same measure, I feared *for* him. He seemed oblivious to Miss Meredith's manipulations. For someone I considered quite astute, he was plunging head-on into a situation that would only end in disaster for him.

I recalled Mother's description of *engouement*. Had he truly lost his senses? Did that explain such reckless fury?

He released me and stepped back two paces. Waving his hand toward the door, he said, "Now get out. I need to check the train tables."

Needing no additional instruction, I was moving toward the door before he'd even completed the thought. After checking through a crack to ensure no one would see me leave my father's sanctum, I opened it wide enough to slip through. As I did so, I turned to check on Mycroft. He had turned to the fire again, and the light from the hallway fell on his back. That perspective gave me a different view of the display of emotion I'd just witnessed. Certainly, he was angry, but now I considered the rage as symptomatic of another emotion.

Fear.

What had my brother so alarmed?

As much as I wanted to report my observations to my

parents, I couldn't jeopardize Constance and her family's precarious situation. Only a few months ago, the children had been on the brink of starvation. I wouldn't be the cause of sending them there again. The ache in both my arms buttressed my resolve to protect my friend.

Mycroft had made it perfectly clear I wasn't to interfere with his relationship with Meredith Cummings. If he wanted to destroy his future by eloping with a woman who would ruin his social standing, I decided not to try and stop him. A part of me hoped he would follow through with his plan. It would serve him right if it led to his downfall. He'd put me down one too many times.

I shoved my hands in my pockets to emphasize my resolve. As I did so, my hand hit the necklace Constance and I had found in the barn. The events following its discovery had pushed the missing piece out of mind. I turned to head upstairs and show it to Mother.

Mother stood from her chair by Trevor's bedside and smiled at me when I entered the nursery. I opened my mouth, ready to share all I had learned in the stable, not to mention the necklace.

As if she sensed my desire to report all, she put her finger to her lips to silence me before announcing, "Good news. Your cousin is awake."

She stepped aside to give me clear view. The boy lay on a mound of pillows. His complexion, while still pale to me, did have a tinge of pink I hadn't seen earlier. He turned his head toward me, his lips curved upward.

"Hello."

I swallowed in an effort to remove the lump in my throat, but it refused to disappear. I forced my words through a constricted windpipe. "H-how are you feeling?"

He closed his eyes for a moment, perhaps conducting a short inventory of his ills. When he opened them, he said, "Dizzy."

For the first time since he'd come to visit, the boy limited himself to a one-word reply. The lack of a rambling response created a wave of guilt through me. An over-whelming urge to fill the uncomfortable silence pushed me to speak.

"I was, too. Dizzy, that is. I had a brain commotion after I fell down some st—fell out of a tree. Don't worry. It'll get better. Mine did."

A slight smile pushed up one side of his mouth, providing me with the first bit of hope. My anxiety returned a moment later, however, when he said, "You found me. In a trunk."

While it was a statement, a question lay underneath. A request for confirmation of what had happened. Did he recall the event? Or had someone else shared that bit with him? I considered my answer, uncertain whether I would add to his trauma if I substantiated the story. I glanced at Mother for guidance. She nodded, which I took as a sign to share the circumstances of his recovery.

After shifting on my feet for a moment, seeking the most appropriate words, I said, "Yes. We found you in my uncle's workshop." When he remained silent, I decided to press a little and see what he did recall. "Do you…do you remember how you got there? Or what you were doing before?"

Another shutting of the eyes and a long hush. I feared he'd gone back to sleep, but he finally opened them again. "I-I can't remember."

His chin quivered, and I feared he might cry. Before tears could flow, however, Mother spoke up.

"It's not uncommon after a blow to the head. Your memories will come back. Maybe just in flashes, but the pieces will come together. Like a puzzle."

"Maybe you can begin with what you remember doing last?" I said, hoping to jog his memory. "Miss Bowen said she sent you to the schoolroom."

"I was angry. I didn't want to go." His mouth turned down, and his forehead puckered. He pushed himself up on his elbows. "Are we still leaving? I-I want to stay."

Mother stepped to the far side of his bed and placed a hand on his chest. "Don't worry. You won't be going anywhere for now. Your mother plans to spend the holidays here."

"Truly?" he asked, relaxing back onto the pillows. "I wouldn't mind living here forever."

"And we wouldn't mind having you," Mother said, cradling his cheek in her hand.

I wasn't personally in favor of *that* prospect, and Aunt Iris had probably agreed to remain at Underbyrne because

Mother and Father had somehow convinced her returning to London was not in her son's best interests. All the same, I recognized the need to keep such opinions to myself and changed the subject by returning to my original questioning.

"Did you draw a picture while you were in the schoolroom?"

He screwed up his face, making evident his effort to remember what he had been doing after leaving Miss Bowen. "I drew...drew...." He shook his head. "I don't remember."

"That's all right. As Mother said, it will come." I glanced at my mother and took a breath, weighing my thoughts and words. I decided to plunge ahead. "I found this in the stables. Do you know anything about it?"

I retrieved the *mangala sutra* we'd found in the mousetrap from my pocket. My hope was that it might trigger more memories, but my expectations collapsed when he squinted at the necklace in my hand for a moment and then shook his head.

"I-I... No. I don't think so. It looks very pretty."

With a glance at my mother, whose rounded eyes told me she understood its significance, I placed it back in my pocket. She then gave me a slight shake of her head, and I knew she wanted me to avoid pressing him more.

I reached out and patted his shoulder. "You rest. You'll remember."

"I am rather tired," he said with a sigh and closed his eyes again.

"I'm going to see about some broth for you," Mother said. "I'll ask Miss Bowen to stay with you while I do. Sherlock will visit you again later."

She accompanied me to the schoolroom. While I knew she wanted to know about the *mangala sutra,* another concern pressed more heavily on my thoughts and conscience.

"How is he, really?" I asked when I turned to face her after shutting the door.

"He'll be fine," she said, placing a hand on my cheek. "He did lose blood, and he is weak, but he will recover."

"And his memory?"

She shook her head. "I didn't want to worry the boy, but his recollection of the full event may never be retrieved."

"I wish he could remember how he came across this," I said, withdrawing the necklace from my pocket again. "From her description, I would guess it is Chanda's *mangala sutra.*"

"Based on drawings I've seen, I would agree. Where did you find it?"

"The stables. In one of Uncle Ernest's mouse traps. We think Trevor hid it there and then tried to hide from someone. Probably the same person who put him in the trunk."

"We?" Mother said, lifting one eyebrow. "Why didn't Constance come with you to share this development?"

I dropped my gaze to my shoes, resisting the urge to share what we overheard while in the barn. Mycroft had warned me not to tell anyone and to stay out of his affairs. At the moment, I had no desire to disregard his demand.

"We had an argument," I said with a sigh and raised my head to meet her gaze.

"About…?"

Pausing, I considered how to explain our difference of opinions about Mycroft and Meredith's discussion without giving away their plans. Finally, I chose a half-truth.

"Miss Meredith. She thinks the woman is amusing. I find her…dangerous."

"I'm not sure I would go so far as to say that." She paused, her forehead creasing. "But I do believe Mycroft's relationship with her is not…healthy."

"*Engouement.*" Her lips thinned to a flat line, and I knew we shared the same opinion of our guest. "That's what I mean by 'dangerous.' Constance thinks Meredith's control over him a sort of joke."

"I have to agree that I find no humor in that. But one must consider your perspective. He's your brother, and you know him quite intimately. From what you told me the other day, his encounters with Constance are few and haven't always been courteous."

I pondered her observation—particularly with respect to his treatment of Constance—and my own encounter with him just now in the library. That meeting called into question any understanding I had of my brother. He'd always been rather cerebral and dismissive of me (and just about everyone else). But he'd never threatened me with bodily harm. Had I truly never had any comprehension of my brother?

She studied me as I considered these thoughts. "You're worried about Mycroft."

Again, I weighed my words, finding it difficult not to share all with her. Finally, I said, "He's…changed."

"Under different circumstances, I would have your father speak to him about his behavior…" Her voice trailed off.

I knew she was reviewing all the events that had taken place in the past twenty-four hours and the stress it had taken on both her and my father. I assumed she didn't feel it possible to add to my father's concerns at the moment.

As if my mind could carry no more unpleasantness, the one positive consequence of the attack on Trevor occurred to me. "Will Constable Gibbons be releasing Chanda now? After all, she couldn't have attacked Trevor. If the same person attacked the others, she could not be the one to have done so."

"Quite right, but I have yet to discuss this with your father—or Ernest. Earlier your father suggested the colonel had encouraged her confinement for her own safety—the gaol being more secure than our house."

As much as I detested the idea of an innocent person being imprisoned or even agreeing with the colonel given all his deceits, I had to allow that, at present, being a guest in our house carried some risk.

"I will discuss these matters with your father when it seems appropriate. Including the *mangala sutra*. For the time being, why don't I keep it?" She held out her hand, and I dropped the necklace into it. "I have a special place I keep my jewelry, and I'll put it there. It will be safe until then."

"Should we let her know? That we found it?" I asked. "I could tell Uncle Ernest, and he could pass on—"

"I think it best for the three of us alone to know it has been found. If whoever had it was the one who attacked Trevor, the fewer who know it's been found, the less risk we run of anyone else being hurt." She dropped it into a pocket of her dress. "Speaking of Trevor, I must see to the broth I promised him."

She left me in the schoolroom, where I continued to ponder the strange turn this holiday had taken. So many problems and so few solutions. The urge to review all the events pushed all other thoughts out of my mind as I stepped to the teacher's desk at the front of the schoolroom and pulled out some paper and a pencil to examine the events to date and consider them all logically.

At the top of each paper, I put the names of the victims: Captain Vincent Rogers, Mr. Moto, Miss Meredith, and Trevor. Underneath each, I placed the names of those I knew to be associated with each, what Mother had once referred to as "common denominators." For Captain Rogers, there was Chanda, Colonel Williams, and Miss Meredith. For Mr. Moto, Mother and me. After a moment's reflection, I added Aunt Iris because she had found him. For Miss Meredith, Colonel Williams, Chanda, and Mycroft. For Trevor, I again placed my own name, Miss Bowen, and Aunt Iris.

Staring at the lists, I sighed. No more than two shared a common denominator. With more force than necessary, I tossed the pencil onto the desktop in frustration. I felt certain all the attacks were related, and I simply wasn't seeing the connections. The pencil rolled across the desk and came to rest against the spine of a book.

My attention shifted to the volume, recognizing it as the one from Mr. Moto's collection I'd borrowed when Mother and I had packed his things. Finding myself unable to make any sense of the lists, I picked up the book and flipped through the pages.

I stopped to study the page I'd found the last time I looked through it, the one mother and I considered lethal. I glanced up from the text when Mother rapped on the door. A servant stood behind her with a tray.

"I happened to speak to Cook when I went for the broth and learned you haven't eaten since breakfast. I've brought you a sandwich."

Mother directed the girl to place the tray on one of the student desks and shut the door after her.

"It is unwise not to eat, Sherry, dear," she said, stepping up behind me and glancing over my shoulder. "What have you been working on?"

"I tried to sort out what I know about the attacks, but I'm afraid I haven't gotten very far. Then I came across this book. Do you remember this hold?"

The next moment, she pulled my chair back and tapped my shoulder, indicating I should rise. "Let's try it."

I stepped away from the desk, and Mother moved behind me. In one swift action, my chin was nestled in the crook of her arm. The pressure on my neck seemed to build pressure in my head. When I tried to tell her to stop, my mouth moved, but no words escaped. In a few heartbeats, black spots drifted across my field of vision. Instinctively, I grabbed her arm to pull it from my neck. An instant later, the pressure was gone, and my vision cleared.

"Oh dear," Mother said, turning me around again and studying first my face and then my throat. "I had no idea… Did I hurt you?"

"I could feel myself losing consciousness."

Mother pulled open my collar and studied the neck intensely. "No markings here…" She gasped and stared at me. "The man in the barn. This *has* to be how he died—no marks on the throat."

"And Mr. Moto the same way?" Returning to the desk, I pulled the book toward me. "Maybe a countermove is provided as well."

After turning to the diagram we found earlier, I flipped to the next page but found nothing indicating a defense against the hold. Mother watched over my shoulder and turned back to the original hold and one additional page.

"The Japanese read right to left. So, the front of a book would be the back to us. I believe this may be what we were seeking."

The following pages included more diagrams of a person caught in the same hold. In one, the victim knelt in the choker's grasp and pushed against the attacker's fore-arm. In another, the victim was turned, and one leg was behind his attacker. The third drawing showed the victim pushing his aggressor over his leg.

"Shall we try these two moves? I promise not to squeeze this time."

After a few practices, first with me as the victim and then Mother as the victim, we found both countermoves effective.

When we'd finished, she closed the book and caressed the cover. "I know he turned out to be deceitful, but he was a good teacher. Even in death, we learned from him." She raised her chin and frowned at me. "I hope I haven't hurt your throat and that the sandwich isn't a mistake. Let me see you swallow a few bites before I check on Trevor."

After she had confirmed no permanent harm had been done, she left to check on my cousin. At the schoolroom door, she paused. "You should destroy those papers before someone else sees them. I will give them some thought as well. There is a connection. We simply haven't seen it yet. In the meantime, I would suggest you consider making your peace with Constance. This is, after all, Christmastime, and a good time to put any…disagreements aside."

Closing the door behind her, she left me to consider how best to apologize to Constance for my hurtful behavior.

AN HOUR LATER, I made my way through the waning afternoon light toward the Straton cottage. Passing the stables on
the way to the path in the woods, I shook my head to clear
away the memories of all that had occurred inside earlier.
Was I making a mistake not telling my parents about
Mycroft and Meredith's plans? Somehow, I just couldn't see
my brother following through with such a life-altering decision. The man I knew calculated every move, including the
order in which he ate his food—hardly the type who would
up and run off with a woman, especially one he'd known for
less than two weeks.

Even if my brother hadn't threatened me, I probably
wouldn't have reported what I'd overheard to my parents.
They had too much on their shoulders already. Regardless,
my resolve to stop the possible elopement hadn't wavered. I
simply needed a plan that thwarted their leaving without
causing a scandal.

The avoidance of scandal was the tricky part. Should
they be caught while still at home and no one outside the
family alerted, marriage might be avoided. Discovering
them after leaving home, either on the way or in Gretna
Green, would most certainly end in a wedding anyway.

As I pushed through the sparse woods to Constance's
home, I considered various scenarios, from the ridiculous to
the feasible—locking one or both in their rooms, disabling
the carriage, putting something in their food to sicken them.

I paused at that idea. Any number of plants in Mother's
greenhouse would do the trick. Enough to make them too ill

to consider travel without truly injuring them. The delicate part would be assuring only they consumed the item. Quickening my pace, I knew how that might be achieved.

Constance opened the door in response to my knock and frowned when she saw who it was. "What do you want?"

"To apologize. And to bring you something."

I pulled several ribbons from my pocket. Mother had allowed me to take them from her own collection. Recalling the ones she had considered at the market, I'd selected some similar in texture or color.

She opened the door wider to allow me to pass. Her younger brothers and sisters ran up to me when I entered.

Her sister Mildred eyed the ribbons I held. "Oooh, them's pretty."

"They're for Constance," I said, feeling rather foolish I hadn't considered something for the others. "What color do you like? Maybe I can bring one for you later."

"Pink," the girl said without hesitating.

I nodded. "Pink it is."

Before I could say more, Emily stepped through the front door, several logs in her arms. She must have been to one side of the cottage. I hadn't seen her in the yard.

"Oh, Master Sherlock, I wasn't expecting you. I thought it was Joseph. That is…Mr. Straton. Did you need him for something?"

Despite the heavy burden in her arms, she remained in the open doorway, as if unsure what to do. Without knowing why, I shoved my hand into my pocket to hide the ribbons I'd been displaying and stepped up to her.

"I came to see Constance for a moment. We weren't able to rehearse today, and I hoped to set up a time tomorrow," I said, holding out my arms as an offer to take her load.

She hesitated, then dumped the three split logs into my arms. I carried them to the fireplace, and she shut the door behind her. "I was making dinner for the children before I had to get back to help Cook."

She studied me and Constance for a moment, and then turned her attention to a pot hanging over the fire. After learning about the gossip servants shared among themselves, I hesitated to speak to Constance in front of Emily. I had no way of knowing what might be shared.

Seeing Emily fill the kettle from the water barrel gave me a means of speaking to my friend privately.

"Let me fetch some water before I go," I said, picking up a bucket next to the barrel. "Constance, can you help me with the pump?"

"I'll go," Mildred said.

Constance had glared at me slightly when I'd asked her to come outside with me, but she spoke up quite fast when her younger sister offered to help. "No. You're not strong enough yet to pump the handle." She spun on her heel and headed toward the door.

"Take your shawl," Emily said, her back to us. "It's quite windy out there."

My friend rolled her eyes but grabbed a shawl from a hook by the door. Together we stepped into the darkening afternoon.

As soon as we were away from the house, I brought out the ribbons again. "I hope they didn't wrinkle."

She took them and hung each over her fingers. "I can press them, if they are. They're grand," she said and raised her gaze to mine. "What are they for?"

"To say I'm sorry." I stared at the hard ground below my boots. "I shouldn't have said what I did about Emily."

When I glanced up at her, she stared at me, her head tilted to one side. "You came all the way out here. Just for that?"

"How else was I going to apologize?" I glanced back at the house. "I didn't know Emily was going to be here."

"I told you. She's workin' her way in." She took several steps toward the pump. "Come on. We need to get the water like you promised."

When we were returning to the house with the water, I tripped on a root and the bucket swung forward, splashing water on her. She stopped and faced me. My hand flew to my mouth.

"I'm so sorry," I said as she blinked at me. "I-I tripped on a root. Check and see if it passed through the shawl. It's not ruined, is it?"

Watching her pull the shawl around and squeeze out the water, I chewed my lip, waiting for the conclusion.

"It should be all right. I'll put it on the chair in front of the fire. It'll dry out. Thing is, it isn't mine. I grabbed the first shawl on the peg. It belongs to Emily. I suppose she can borrow mine to wear back to the big house tonight."

"'The big house'?" I asked. "Is that what you call where I live?"

"Well, ain't it?" she said with a shrug. "What else should I call it?"

Staring at her for a moment, I considered our home compared to where she lived. Ours was certainly much larger. In comparison to Hanover, the Devonys' manor house, Underbyrne shrank considerably. Once again, the difference between my family's fortune and those of the Stratons and others like them became evident to me.

She pulled off the wet shawl and bundled it so the dry end covered the wet. "Hurry up. I need to get inside before I freeze to death."

"Let me tell Emily about her shawl," I said when I stepped to get next to her. The water sloshed in the bucket, and I slowed to keep from spilling it.

She stopped and faced me. "If you don't mind…"

I shook my head.

"She might think I did it on purpose."

True to Constance's prediction, the woman's features hardened when she learned about the shawl but seemed to temper her emotions when I explained what happened and apologized for splashing the wrap. I even offered to accompany her back to Underbyrne, so Cook wouldn't scold her for being late because we took so long fetching the water.

Emily seemed quite appeased by our solutions, and shortly after, we returned together through the woods. The afternoon had grown quite dark, and I regretted not having a lantern to light the way in the woods. Emily, however, seemed to have little problem with the path and warned me more than once of a root or large stone that might have tripped me up in the dark.

Once we passed the stables, the woman turned to me. "I can walk from here alone. You don't have to follow me into the kitchen."

"But I promised to speak to Cook."

She glanced first at the door leading directly into the kitchen and then at me. After shifting her weight about, her gaze strayed to the barn, and she shrugged. I realized she'd wanted a moment to see Mr. Straton but then decided against it.

"Let's get inside," she said with a sigh. "It's getting cold."

Together we made our way across the lawn. At one point, I thought I heard one of the outbuilding doors creak —whether opened on purpose or by the wind, I wasn't certain. Checking behind me, however, all seemed secure, and I decided I'd been mistaken. With so much wind, almost anything could have creaked.

AFTER ASSURING Cook wouldn't discipline Emily for any tardiness, I returned to the third floor to check on Trevor. Miss Bowen reported that he had fallen back into a deep sleep—due at least in part to a draught Mother had prepared after he'd drunk his broth. She left word, through the governess, that I was to dress for dinner. Despite more than a few in the household preferring to sup in their rooms, Father must have sent word we should dress properly for dinner this evening.

As expected, those at the table were few: Father, Mother, Mycroft, Uncle Ernest, and myself. With only the immediate family present, we soon lapsed into our regular habits. French was chosen for the *langue de jour*. Even though Mycroft usually chose this time as an opportunity to correct something about my ability to speak my grandmother's native tongue, he paid no attention to my pronunciation, word choice, or grammar. His distraction was so complete, I even baited him once or twice by using a totally incorrect word. He didn't lift an eyebrow.

Of course, I knew what lay behind my brother's preoccupation, and I wondered what his decision would be about Miss Meredith's proposition. Were they eloping?

His expression was inscrutable. I had no clue as to his plans regarding Gretna Green.

If the others had similarly noticed his inattentiveness, no one questioned it. All seemed lost in their own thoughts. The usual table conversation boiled down to "please pass the salt" and the like. Had I had a room of my own to which to retire, I would have requested that I be excused.

After the meat course, I set my fork down and prepared to ask to be excused anyway. Before I could speak, the sound of someone running drew everyone's attention to the dining room entrance. Mr. Straton rushed in.

Father rose. "See here, Straton——"

The man panted out his words between gulps of air. "Come. Quick. The. Barn."

CHAPTER ELEVEN

When we arrived at the stables, we found Mr. Simpson and Emily sitting on a hay bale. The girl shivered despite the shawl and Mr. Simpson's arm around her shoulders. Mr. Straton knelt in front of her but addressed my mother.

"I found her just outside the stables. I'm not sure how long she'd been lying there. There was a dish not far away. She was bringing me my dinner."

Mother knelt next to Mr. Straton and dipped her head until she could see Emily's face. She took the woman's hands in her own, rubbing them for a few seconds, and then stood.

"She needs to lie down. Find a blanket and wrap it around her so we can take her back to the house. I will need a glass of your brandy, Mr. Holmes."

"What is it, ma'am? What's happened to my Emily?" Straton asked.

"H-h-hit me," Emily muttered through chattering teeth. "S-s-somebody hit me. P-pushed me down."

"We need to get her warm. Calm her down," Mother said. "Let's get her back to the house."

I rushed to the tack room and pulled a blanket from a stack on one shelf and hurried back. Straton and Mr. Simpson helped her to stand, and we wrapped the blanket around Emily's shoulders. With her leaning on the widower, we all made it back to the house. Mr. Straton seated her near the fire, and Mother gave her a cup of tea laced with brandy.

Once she seemed calmer, Father asked her what had happened.

"I don't rightly know," she said with a shake of her head. "I was taking your steward his dinner when someone hit me hard on the back. I fell, and someone reached about my neck from behind. I couldn't breathe. Everything turned black. The next thing I knew, I was in the barn with Jo—Mr. Straton."

"You saw nothing? Heard nothing? No reason given for the attack?" Father asked.

She shook her head. "No, sir. One minute I was walking toward the stables. The next, I was on the ground."

I exchanged a glance with Mother over the woman's head, my brows knitted together. We both knew exactly what the woman had experienced after she was struck from behind. While we hadn't blacked out, both of us had gotten close when we'd practiced the hold shown in Mr. Moto's *baritsu* manual. Someone else had been trained in this Japanese form of combat. And was quite willing to use it with force.

Emily shifted about, checking around the chair and then opening the blanket.

"What is it, lo—Miss Emily?" Straton asked. "Are you missing something?"

"My shawl. I know I had it on…"

Mr. Simpson held out a woolen wrap. "Is this it? I found it on the ground. Must've fallen off when we put the blanket around you in the barn."

He passed it to Straton, who held it out to her. As she started to reach for it, he pulled it back. "This isn't yours."

"It belongs to Constance. Mine got wet when I was over there fixing dinner for the children. She loaned me hers to come back tonight."

I opened my mouth, ready to support her story when Mother shook her head ever so slightly. Best not to let Father know I'd been over there. Again.

Another thought, however, snapped my mouth shut. Emily had been wearing Constance's shawl when we returned together to Underbyrne. In the twilight, the older woman could have been mistaken for my friend if the most identifiable item was the shawl. If so, the attacker might have realized the mistake after knocking Emily down and the shawl fell from her head. No one would mistake Emily's dark hair for Constance's red. Perhaps the attacker choked her merely to put her to sleep in order to get away.

If that was the case, what had the attacker planned for Constance?

My breath caught in my throat, and I fought the urge to run out of the house toward the Straton cottage. Somehow, something had put her in danger, and I wanted to warn her. To be on guard for…what? Whom?

Who had something against her strong enough to provoke an attack? The only one I could identify as harboring such animosity toward my friend was…Mycroft. A flare of anger formed in my chest, and I felt its flush travel through my body.

My hands curled into fists at my sides. It made no sense, but the only way to know for sure was to ask him.

Forgetting all social convention, I turned and rushed from the room. Only when I made it to the hallway did I realize I had no idea where my brother might be. He'd been at dinner with us but hadn't followed my parents and me to the stables when Straton appeared. Surely he wouldn't have quietly completed his dinner while the rest of us had seen to Emily's comfort?

From my vantage point in the foyer, I glanced about me. The stairs leading to the bedrooms on the second floor lay on my right. Father's office and library were behind me. The dining room and parlor doors were in front of me. If he hadn't retired to his bedroom, he would most likely be in the parlor. It was the one place he and Miss Meredith would be allowed to be together according to social convention.

I marched across the hall, ready to confront him.

Uncle Ernest turned toward the door as I stepped inside. My rage cooled slightly when I failed to find my target.

"Sherlock old boy," my uncle said, "I considered following the others, but there seemed to be more than enough people checking on her. I had wanted to show something to Herbert—Colonel Williams—but he wasn't in his room. I came in here, but he wasn't here either. How's Emily?"

"Mother says she'll be all right. The poor woman was attacked." I quickly summarized Emily's story and ended with, "I was looking for Mycroft. Have you seen him?"

"He and Miss Meredith were here when I came in." He chuckled. "I'm afraid they didn't appreciate my presence. They left shortly after I arrived."

The idea of the two of them together rekindled my anger, but it was mixed with concern for my brother and the plans discussed earlier in the stables. They'd agreed to wait until tomorrow night. What if, because Mycroft knew they'd been overheard, they'd decided to leave earlier?

"Thank you," I said, my thoughts racing as I played out various scenarios in my head. "If you'll excuse me."

My uncle stood. "You aren't thinking of going out in search of them?"

"Well, I—"

"Your father made it quite clear not to go out after dark

until this whole situation is resolved."

"But Mycroft and Meredith—"

"Are adults," Ernest said. "And are together."

Shifting my weight, I considered my options. As much as I wanted to determine if they hadn't left the premises, I feared having my uncle accompany me. Should the two young people be caught in some attempt to leave for Gretna Green or simply in too deep an embrace, a marriage might be forced to avoid scandal. And that was exactly what I sought to prevent. The best course of action was to at least appear to follow my father's directive.

After a moment, I dropped my head in resignation.

"You're right, Uncle. I'd best stay here. I think I'll check on Trevor. He was awake earlier."

"That's the boy," Ernest said, but rose from his seat. "I haven't seen the lad either. Maybe I'll come up with you."

A sense of dread urged me to distract my uncle and go in search of my brother, but I turned my footsteps toward the stairs instead. As we passed the library door, Mother opened it and peered out at us.

"Sherry, dear, I'd hoped it was you," she said, stepping into the corridor and shutting the door behind her. "Mrs. Simpson will take Emily to her room, and I've told her to rest for a few days. Beyond the fright from the attack, I see no permanent harm to her. Of course, Mr. Holmes has told Straton to fetch the constable in the morning." She turned to her brother. "I need to speak to Sherlock, if you don't mind, Ernest."

He glanced at me and the stairs before focusing on my mother. I was certain I saw relief pass over my uncle's face at not having to ascend to the third floor.

"Not at all. We were going up to visit Trevor. We can do it later. I'll go back to the parlor."

"Thank you. If you wish, I'll send Sherlock to fetch you before he goes to the nursery."

With a nod, my uncle turned on his heel and returned to the parlor. After he'd closed the door, Mother motioned in the direction of the greenhouse. Only when she shut the door to that room did she speak.

"I know you came to the same conclusion I did that the attacker meant to harm Constance. Do you have any idea why someone would wish to do so?"

I stared at the nearest plant, a eucalyptus. From even the few feet away, its scent reached me. Mother often mixed its oil with mint and other herbs and applied it to my temples for headaches. The perfume mix was quite relaxing, and I wished I had some at the moment, for I was anything but calm. I saw no way to share about Mycroft's attitude and treatment of Constance without also describing Meredith's plans for Mycroft.

But perhaps there remained a way to prevent them leaving if they had decided to do so tonight.

"Maybe we should check where Emily was attacked? We might find something."

"An excellent idea. We'll pick up the blankets in the kitchen with the excuse of returning them."

We had no problem finding the spot where Emily had been pushed. The plate she had been carrying still lay on the ground.

"Pity it's so cold," Mother said, turning about with the lantern. "There is nothing much to see in terms of footprints. But the plate…"

We both stepped to the dish. It lay faceup, the contents, a stew, now splattered about it on the ground, the edges already crusting.

"Imagine if you were pushed from behind," she said to me. "Step over there and pretend to carry a plate. Now fall forward as if pushed."

I followed her directions, my imaginary plate flying from my hands.

"It would probably turn over. Scatter the contents in a forward manner."

"And if you dropped it?"

"Land upright. Perhaps a more even distribution about it."

"My thoughts as well. Let's carry the dish back to the kitchen and consider what this suggests."

"Beyond appearing that Emily dropped it?"

"Precisely. I think we needn't be as concerned about Constance's security right now. Let's get these blankets to the barn."

Slightly relieved over my friend, I shifted my thoughts to more pressing concerns—my brother's future. The knot in my stomach returned as we approached the barn for fear of what we would find there. I held my breath as Mother opened the door. All was quiet, however, and after leaving the blankets, we returned to the house. Where was Mycroft, then? And Miss Meredith? Or Colonel Williams? I continued to have my reservations about his integrity — despite my uncle's trust in him.

I considered sharing some of these thoughts, but events overtook me when we entered the kitchen.

"There you are," Miss Simpson said. "Miss Bowen was looking for you. Apparently, Trevor has been asking for you both."

My cousin was sitting up in bed. Some color had returned to his cheeks, but he jiggled one leg without stopping. When my mother and I stepped into the room, a smile broke across his face, but his leg remained in motion.

"You were right," he said. "I do recall the necklace now." He pouted and puckered his forehead. "Or I think I do. I mean it seemed quite real in my dream." He sighed and glanced at us. "Are you cross with me?"

Mother moved to his bedside and placed a hand on his cheek. "Never."

"Why don't you share with us what you do remember, and we'll sort it out together? Sometimes dreams are a way of helping us recall what we've forgotten. It's happened to me."

Another sigh from Trevor. He continued to squeeze his eyebrows together. "I'll try. In my dream I had the necklace in my hand—"

"Do you have any memory of finding it?"

Mother frowned at me from the other side of the nursery bed and shook her head. "Let's let Trevor tell us in his own words."

Her reprimand stung, but I understood her concern. Pushing my cousin might make it more difficult for him to share what he did remember. As much as I wanted to direct his story, I had to keep quiet and let it unfold.

"You had the necklace in your hand..." Mother said, prodding him to return to his tale.

He nodded. "That's right. I had the necklace, and I was running." He closed his eyes. "I don't know who was chasing me, but I was scared. And I knew they wanted the necklace."

I bit my tongue to keep from asking if a woman or man was chasing him. Any harder and I would have drawn blood.

"I was in the stables," he said. "And then I wasn't. I was in...in..." He shook his head. "I'm sorry, but I don't remember any more."

"That's all right," Mother said, giving him a pat on the shoulder. "It will come."

I rose. He had nothing else to share, and I still needed to find Mycroft.

"You aren't leaving, are you?" he asked.

His lower lip poked out, and tears welled in his eyes. Mother gave me a hard stare. I knew she expected me to stay with him for a while. I recalled my vow to be kinder to him, and so I sat again. "I can stay for a bit, if you wish."

A smile stretched across his face. "Very much."

"What would you like to do? A game of chess?"

He shook his head.

I had no idea what other activity to offer. What did the boy like to do? "Or I could read you a story? Or draw?"

The smile returned.

I rose. "Let me get some paper and pencils."

When I returned from the schoolroom, Mother was gone, but a table had been pulled to the side of his bed. I dragged a chair next to it, and he turned to sit on the edge of the bed. We both stared at our papers for a moment, deciding what to sketch.

"What are you going to make?" I asked.

"The same picture I drew last time."

"You mean the one from the other day?"

He nodded, head down as he concentrated on his pencil. He'd only made a few marks when he raised his head to stare at me. "Miss Meredith," he said.

"What about her?"

"I remember now. I was searching for Mummy. To give her the drawing. It was a ship. On the ocean. When I went to the second floor, I was confused about the rooms. I opened one thinking it was Mummy's, but Miss Meredith was in there. She turned around and that's when I saw the necklace. The one you showed me."

Almost afraid to breathe, I asked in a whisper, "And then

what?"

"I-I don't remember." His voice wavered, and I feared he was going to cry.

Reaching out, I placed my hand over his. "It's all right. See? You've already remembered two things. More will come. But I want to share this with Mother. Can you finish your drawing while I do that? I'll send someone to sit with you."

"All right, but not that Emily. I don't like her. She says mean things about Constance."

About to rise, I sat more firmly in my seat and asked, "What sorts of mean things?"

"That she's a wicked girl, trying to act rich when she isn't. I told her that's not true. That she's kind and my friend."

My opinion of Emily shifted on its axis. I had chalked up Constance's criticisms of the maid as exaggerated and based on jealousy. Now, however, I had to consider that Emily was the jealous one.

I had much to share with Mother.

After stopping in Miss Bowen's room to send her to stay with Trevor, I went in search of Mother.

She was in the parlor with my father, Uncle Ernest, and …

Chanda.

They all turned to me when I entered, and my cheeks grew hot from the attention. The shock of seeing the *rajku-mari* left me speechless, and completely forgetting all social convention as well as my original purpose in coming down-stairs, I couldn't even express my relief at the woman's release. I could only stare open-mouthed at her.

Mother, however, saved me.

She rose, stepped toward me, and placed an arm about my shoulder. "Look, Sherry, dear, isn't it wonderful? Miss Chanda has been released from gaol."

"Forgive me, Miss Chanda," I said, finding my voice. "Your presence was rather a shock. I'm truly thrilled to see you've regained your freedom."

"It was rather a shock for me as well," she said, one side of her mouth lifting slightly.

"With the attack on Trevor occurring while she was in gaol," Father said, "Colonel Williams insisted I persuade the constable that she could not be behind the attacks."

"We are all so glad to see you," Mother said to the woman. "I know you will want a bath. It was one of the first things I indulged in when I was freed. I'll speak with Mrs. Simpson about arranging for one."

"You're too kind, Mrs. Holmes," she said, putting her hands together and bowing her head slightly.

"I'll seek out Mrs. Simpson, and she'll let you know when the bath is ready." She turned to me. "And I need to speak with you, Sherry, dear. Why don't you come with me?"

After we had gone a good distance down the hall, she said, "I must say, the last thing I thought would happen today was Chanda's arrival."

"And that Colonel Williams was behind it. Didn't you say you thought he wanted her to stay there? For her own safety?"

"I have no explanation for his change in heart, but I agree, it is odd."

"What does Father say?"

"I'm afraid I haven't had a chance to ask him, but I suspect he'll be as puzzled as we are. Although I also believe he'll see no reason for them to remain here now and will strongly suggest they move on to London, or...wherever."

Her mention of London reminded me of the reason I had sought her out in the first place. "Does Miss Meredith know? That Chanda is here?"

She paused. "You know, that is a good question. I haven't seen her, or Mycroft, in quite a while."

My heart skipped a beat. Again, I remembered Mycroft had committed to leave tomorrow. But what if Meredith knew of Chanda's return and pushed Mycroft to leave tonight? Or was afraid that Trevor might report her having Chanda's necklace?

I gripped Mother's arm. "We need to find Meredith. Trevor remembers seeing her with the *mangala sutra*."

"Is he certain?" she asked. When I nodded, she tapped her lip. "What would her interest be in the necklace? Especially if it belonged to the woman she claimed attacked her?"

The question, although logical, created a dilemma for me. Had Father told her about Meredith's past? That as an orphan, her position in society was compromised? And her true profession was that of spy? I couldn't very well share this information with her without explaining how I'd eavesdropped on my father's interrogation of Colonel Williams.

"I-I'm not sure."

"Let me arrange for the bath, and then I'll search for Miss Meredith. We can use the pretext of informing her that Chanda is here." She shook her head. "Why the colonel would choose to bring Chanda now, under the same roof as her accuser, is beyond me."

After checking both the first and second floor and not finding any sign of either Meredith or Mycroft, we agreed they were most likely together and in one of the outer buildings. When we pulled on coats against the winter wind and stepped out into the dark night, I couldn't decide if I preferred to find them both in the stables and preparing to flee, or in each other's arms in a secret meeting. Either way, Mycroft's fate was most likely sealed. I shuddered to consider Meredith as my sister-in-law.

Mother must have noted my reaction because she said, "It's taken quite a cold turn."

I didn't contradict her.

Mother shone a lantern around the empty barn. I was grateful for the shelter from the wind. It howled through the rafters, and the horses stomped and protested in response. A quick review of the stalls indicated all our stock was present, and I let out a breath I hadn't realized I'd been holding when we opened the door.

Mother glanced around and shrugged. "No one appears to be here. But while we're here, show me where Ernest puts his traps."

Turning, I squinted at her. Uncle Ernest's traps? Why the sudden interest?

In response to my confused look, she put a finger to her lips and then pointed to one of the empty stalls. Who did she think was in there?

Approaching the stall, Mother chatted as if she had no other interest. "I do need to talk to Ernest about these traps. It's one thing to capture the rats and then use them in experiments, but when he doesn't empty them out, it seems rather cruel. They could literally starve to death—"

"All right, Mother," Mycroft said, rising from the stall she had indicated to me. "I know you know I'm here."

She showed no surprise at his sudden appearance. "You mean, 'us,' don't you, dear? Miss Meredith, please come out of there as well."

The woman stood, and Mycroft stepped next to her.

"I suppose I should ask what you're doing—"

He reached out and took Meredith's hand. "It's rather obvious, isn't it? We're in love, Mother. I hope you can accept that."

She rubbed her forehead. Mycroft shifted on his feet, but Meredith straightened her shoulders and stared at my mother. Her lips turned up ever so slightly, as if she found some amusement in the situation—whether at being caught and forcing a marriage or at my mother's discomfort, I wasn't certain.

After another moment's deliberation, Mother sighed and said, "I think it best we all share this with your father and uncle immediately. They are in the parlor."

She motioned to the couple to step out.

"Father and Colonel Williams are together?" he asked as we all headed toward the door.

"They were when I left to look for Miss Meredith," she said without breaking her stride. "To let you know Chanda has been released."

Meredith halted and pulled Mycroft to her side. She clutched his arm. "I-I can't go back there. Not into that house. Not if Chanda is there. What if she attacks me again?"

"Really, Mother," Mycroft said, placing a hand over Meredith's, which continued to grip his arm. "Do you think it's safe?"

"Obviously Miss Meredith's uncle does. He was the one who worked to get her freed."

Meredith blinked her eyes and stared up at him. I was certain she was on the verge of tears. "Please. What am I going to do? I-I can't very well stay in the same house as that…that woman."

"I'll speak to your uncle," Mycroft said, patting the hand that gripped his arm. "I'm certain we can work out an arrangement where you feel safe."

"Shall we go to the house now? I can assure you you're

quite safe," Mother said.

The young woman glanced first at Mycroft and then at our mother. Her shoulders dropped, but her features remained rigid. I considered it not to be from relief of her anxiety or tension, but rather from resignation. Mother gave a little tug on my brother's arm, and we all headed toward the house.

Shortly before entering, Mother turned to the couple. "As I mentioned, your father and uncle are in the parlor. I'll join you there momentarily. I have a necklace that I believe belongs to Miss Chanda. If it is hers, I'm certain she would want it back. Trevor says he remembers seeing it before he was attacked, but unfortunately he has no recollection of how he came upon it."

"Trevor's awake?" Mycroft asked. "How is he doing?"

Mother rubbed the back of her neck. "Physically, he'll be fine with another day or two of bed rest, but I'm afraid he might never recover his memory of the attack or attacker."

Almost involuntarily, I spun to catch Mother's gaze and correct her. Trevor had recalled more than she reported— and we both knew it. Realizing that she *did* know, I also grasped she had shared about the *mangala sutra* on purpose —perhaps to catch the other woman's reaction.

If the knowledge of the discovery of Chanda's missing jewelry concerned Meredith, she hid it well. She entered the house and, with her hand on Mycroft's arm, moved toward the parlor.

The two of us followed them until we reached the stairs. I moved to continue to the parlor. I was anxious to learn how Mycroft's and Meredith's futures would be resolved. With my brother unaware of all the circumstances surrounding the woman, I longed to see his reaction when he learned the truth. Would his total dedication to her disappear or become more resolute? I didn't consider my brother fickle or easily dissuaded, but neither did he like to play the fool. In this case, the revelation might be enough to break any spell the woman appeared to have over him.

Unfortunately, Mother touched my shoulder and indicated I was to follow her upstairs. As we ascended the first step, I glanced over my shoulder and sighed when I saw the couple enter the parlor.

"You know your father would have sent you out," she said, continuing up the staircase. I caught up with her, and she glanced across at me. "Besides, I have a special request for you. I want you to stay with your cousin tonight."

"I do every night. We share the nursery together."

"But I need you to stand guard. For whatever reason, Miss Meredith had the *mangala sutra* in her possession and knows that Trevor saw her with it. She may be worried that he will remember."

"But she showed no interest when you mentioned it just now."

Mother's mouth turned down. "Perhaps its significance has lessened with the importance of Mycroft's attentions. All the same, it is best to be prepared."

While I was quite willing to serve as my cousin's body-guard, I wasn't sure I was the best selection. "Wouldn't it be better if Mr. Straton—"

"Straton's presence might throw off any efforts against Trevor. I plan to keep watch over Chanda tonight after I share with the others about the discovery and return of the necklace. I will also speak to your father—"

"No. I refuse. I will not wait." Meredith's voice rose through the foyer and up the stairwell.

Was she referring to staying at Underbyrne with Chanda? Or had she and Mycroft announced their plans?

Mother must have been as curious as I. She hustled up the stairs to stand at the railing overlooking the corridor below. I followed, stepping into the shadow at one end to gain a view without revealing my presence.

The young woman stomped out of the parlor, the men following behind her.

"Please, Meredith dear. Let's hear them out," Mycroft said, trying to keep up with her as she continued toward the stairs.

She paused at the first step and faced him. "Are you saying you don't love me?"

"Certainly not," my brother said, his voice having a quiver I'd never heard before. Despite his protest, I could hear uncertainty creeping into his voice. "I do see some logic, however, in the year's engagement your uncle and my father suggested. By then, I would have read for the law, and we would be more financially secure to begin our household."

Her reply came in a wavering voice. With her back to me, I couldn't see but detected tears in her voice. "But…but what about our plans? London? The town house—"

"Are you saying you planned to live in the London town house?" Father asked. His face now mimicked my brother's. Truly, they were two peas in a pod, father and son. "I can assure you, should you follow through with this mad scheme, you will be cut off. There'll be no town house for you, boy. Or anything else."

Mycroft faced my father and straightened his back. While the term *boy* most likely stung his pride, I was more certain the reference to his mental state was what locked his spine. No one could accuse my brother of anything that wasn't based on cold calculations, which was why I had never understood his obsession with Miss Meredith from the beginning.

"Do you really think that concerns me?" A sneer tinged his words. "This…this hulking anchor around your neck holds no interest to me. Cut me off, if you wish. I'll make my way without any help from you."

"If you think you can use the Holmes name as a means of continuing your contacts in London or the law, you are mistaken. You marry this woman, and you'll be cut off from all polite society as well."

From my vantage point, I could see the back of my brother's neck deepen to a dark crimson. He fairly ground out his response through clenched teeth. "If you're threatening to spread tales—"

"I'm not threatening," Father said, giving his vest a tug as if to straighten it. He squared his shoulders as he continued to address his son. "I'm stating a fact. This…*girl* will never be accepted into polite society once the truth about her past is known."

Meredith confronted the colonel, who had remained silent during this exchange between my brother and father. Now, it was her cheeks that darkened. "You…you *told* them? I can't believe—"

Before the colonel could answer, Mycroft turned to the woman. I could now see his face. The skin about his eyes sagged. When he spoke, all vinegar had left his voice. "Meredith, …dear, what are they referencing?"

Father's gaze fixed on Meredith. "Williams here is not her uncle. She's an orphan. Lost her parents several years ago."

"But that doesn't mean—" Mycroft stopped as all the pieces of Father's implications finally fell into place. Regardless of the colonel's comportment during any travels with Meredith, the girl's reputation was ruined. Not to mention her having been a spy and served in the field with another man—a younger one at that—who was not her husband or even betrothed. How could the heir of Father's lands and position ever marry such a woman? Not to mention, the deceit on Meredith's part certainly dampened any affections he had developed for her. He spoke to the woman who had now been cast as a quite different person from the one he knew. His tone was now cold, without any hint of emotion—good or bad. "Meredith, is this true?"

She raised her chin. "That I'm an orphan? Yes. But I can assure you the colonel has treated me as a niece, regardless of any blood connection." Her voice carried the same haughty tone she had used since the first night.

"Were it not getting quite late," Colonel Williams said, giving a little cough, "I would suggest we leave immediately. But given the hour and difficulties of finding transportation or other accommodations tonight, I would like to ask you to indulge us one last evening. We will all three be gone in the morning."

Mother inhaled a breath. I knew she was considering the implications of the three of them leaving before we had identified the attacker. Not to mention possibly putting at least one—most likely Chanda—into the hands of a killer.

Father's stare settled on each of the three for a moment before his head bobbed in agreement. "I will allow you to stay, but the first train leaves for London at seven in the morning. Simpson will have the wagon ready to take you at five. Once you are on the train, I don't expect to hear from any of you again."

"Quite right," the colonel said. "I appreciate your hospitality. I do want to have a chance for a proper good-bye to Ernest."

Meredith, however, seemed not quite willing to take her leave from my brother so quickly. She stepped to him and kept her gaze on him until he finally met hers. He blinked several times, and my heart went out to him. All illusions about the woman he had professed to love had been shattered. I bit my lip, worry pressing on me. Instead of the burst of anger I might have anticipated, his features seemed to droop—from exhaustion or regret, I wasn't sure.

"Is that what you want?" she asked when he turned his full attention to her. "For me to leave?"

"I-I want…" His voice trailed off and ended in a sigh. "For things to be as they were. What with all I just learned…I don't know what I truly want."

"Things are only different if you allow them to be. I haven't changed. I'm the same person I was."

"I-I am not sure I am." Another sigh. "I-I can't think right now. Perhaps it would be better if you left. There is nothing that would keep us from renewing our…acquaintance once certain difficulties have been resolved."

The girl scowled at him in response. "Surely I am more than simply an acquaintance? If that is all that I am to you, perhaps it is best to end it now. I wouldn't want you to be burdened by such an inconsequential matter as—as me."

This retort was followed by her storming toward the stairs. Mother grabbed my arm and pulled me toward her sitting room. She had barely enough time to close the door before our guest stomped in the other direction toward her —soon to be mine again—room.

I opened my mouth to ask a question, but Mother put a finger to her lips. She leaned an ear against the door. I had no idea for what—or whom—she was hoping to hear. After an interminable time, she straightened and shook her head.

"No one appears to have followed Meredith up the stairs. Not even the colonel. Why did he not seek to comfort her? There are times I wonder…" Her thought trailed off, and she stared out the window for a moment before focusing on me.

"All the actors are here, and the traps set. I do hope the guilty one will take the bait."

"Colonel Williams, right? I've considered him from the beginning."

"The colonel? Really?" she asked. "I suppose that's possible…" Again, her thoughts seemed to take another path. A moment later, her attention shifted back to the room. "I don't need to tell you how important it is for you to remain vigilant over your cousin tonight."

A rock settled in the pit of my stomach. "Do you think I can? Take on anyone who might harm him?"

"Of course," she said, setting her shoulders. "You are a highly trained combatant, and I know there is no one who would defend your cousin with more heart than you."

I glanced away from her, my cheeks burning. While I appreciated my mother's confidence, I worried it might be misplaced. A "highly-trained combatant" suggested more than a few months of *baritsu* training. But she was correct about one thing. After all I'd been through with my cousin in the past few days, I knew I would make every effort to keep him safe.

CHAPTER TWELVE

Once again, I found myself waiting in the dark for someone to appear. At least this time it was inside and warm, which made it a little more difficult to remain awake. Add to that Trevor's rhythmic breathing, and I had to fight to keep alert. I dug my fingernails into my palms, bit the inside of my mouth, and completed complex mathematical equations to maintain my alertness. Despite all these efforts, as the foyer clock struck one, my eyelids drooped, and my thoughts drifted from the square root of some quite large number to the soft, warm cocoon I could form in my bed.

With lethargy weighing my limbs and my mind contemplating the comforts of sleep, I forced myself to rise from a dark corner at the far end of the room where I'd kept vigil and slip to the schoolroom next door. My body required some movement.

No sooner had I entered the room than I heard footsteps coming near. My stomach roiled at the sound, and I suppressed the urge to slap my forehead. Had I just put my young cousin in danger by leaving his side?

Taking a deep breath, I tiptoed back through the corridor and peered through the still half-opened door. Despite the quite dark night, I recognized my brother's bulk immediately.

"Mycroft," I said in a harsh whisper through the crack. "What are you doing here?"

The large shadow spun about to face me and responded in a similar whisper.

"Looking for…" His voice trailed off for a second. "You. I was searching for you. You *are* sleeping here?"

I waved a hand, although he probably couldn't see it in the dark. "Come out here. Let's talk in the classroom."

After closing the door, I considered lighting a candle, but feared I might alert someone coming onto the floor. Instead, I turned to him and kept my voice low. "You weren't checking on me. Who was your true interest? Meredith?"

"She seems to have disappeared." He hesitated as if listening for something.

My ears ached as I searched the silence for whatever he'd heard. After several heartbeats, I opened my mouth to tell him he was hearing things but shut it when I detected it too. The step was soft, dampened to the point of almost no sound. My brother crept to the door and cracked it open. After a pause, he stepped out and a slight struggle ensued. When quiet returned, Mycroft escorted Colonel Williams into the schoolroom and shut the door.

In the dark, I allowed myself a secret smile. My suspicions had been correct. The colonel was the one behind the attacks, and he had come to finish Trevor. Before I could congratulate my brother on his capture, the colonel spoke to Mycroft.

"Have you seen her?"

Mycroft waved a hand in my direction. "We are not alone, sir."

"What? Oh, I see," he said.

"At this point," Mycroft said, "I don't believe there's a need to keep things a secret from my brother. In fact, it might be worthwhile to bring him in on our charade. I believe he and my parents might be working at cross-purposes to our own efforts."

I was quite glad darkness cloaked us. Social convention would have censured my staring open-mouthed at the two men, but that was all I could do. My brother and our guest seemed to be working together. Which of us had been duped? Mycroft or I?

My brother answered that thought with his next breath.

"We don't have time to go into all the particulars," Mycroft said, "but suffice it to know that my attraction to Miss Meredith has been a ruse. The colonel pulled me into his confidence shortly after our arrival when she seemed to have fixed her attentions on me."

"You're not in love with her?" I asked, a flood of relief passing through me even as anger at his deception rose. At least I didn't have to worry anymore about the woman becoming my future sister-in-law.

"I became aware of some odd behavior by Meredith on our journey from India," the colonel said. "Once we arrived in port, she disappeared for several hours. She reported having identified some agents of Chanda's father and that is why we decided to seek refuge. Your uncle came to mind."

"Only with Father and Mother now pushing them from Underbyrne," Mycroft said, "her plans appear to have changed. If they had allowed me to run off with her, we might have found out her true intentions. Instead, she may have escaped without any indication of her full plans."

All this information required me to reassess what I had observed or overheard to that point. My brother wasn't besotted with the woman as Mother and I had feared. The girl was manipulating, but also being manipulated. But there remained the issue of…

"Chanda," I whispered.

"She is as we have presented her. A loyal subject of the crown. Who risked her life to bring vital information to our attention," the colonel said.

"That's where Meredith might be," I said. "Chanda has something that Meredith covets."

The colonel's shadow motioned to the door. "Go. Make

certain she's all right. I'll stay here to ensure your cousin is safe."

The two men stepped into the hallway, but I hesitated. I had already abandoned Trevor once this evening, now I was being encouraged to do so again. And leave him in the hands of a man whose identity was not clear from the beginning. The only thing that persuaded me to follow my brother was Mycroft's and Ernest's trust in the man. I only prayed it was not misplaced. I silently pledged to return to Trevor's bedroom as soon as I established Chanda's safety.

The servants' area was eerily quiet. Of course, the times I had spent there packing Mr. Moto's room and helping Mother search and straighten Chanda's occurred during the day. While the area itself might be devoid of people, their bustle in the kitchen and other areas below traveled up the stairwell. Now, only their rhythmic breathing, interrupted by snores, passed under their closed doors.

Outside Chanda's room, we paused, and I searched the dark for Mother. She had planned to keep watch over the Indian woman, but the area around her room offered no space to hide. Chanda's room offered the only alternative. Mycroft placed a hand on the knob and leaned against it, as if checking for movement.

His shadow raised its hand and rapped on the door.

We waited. Once again, I held my breath as my hearing sought any indication of movement from the other side of the partition.

Nothing.

The second knock was louder, but not so forceful as to wake those behind the other doors.

Still nothing.

He turned the knob, and the door swung open.

I focused my attention first on the unusual condition of the unlocked door.

A moment later the continued quiet in the room raised the hairs on the back of my neck. My concern rising, I pushed past my brother and into the room. With my second step, I hit something soft and nearly fell on top of whatever blocked my path.

My eyes already adjusted to the darkness, I could make out a heap on the floor. I reached down. The form was warm and covered in a woolen fabric. I turned to my brother.

"We need some light," I whispered.

"But—"

"Find a candle and light it. But be careful. I think I just found Mother."

Mycroft disappeared and returned with a light.

"What's going on?" a woman asked from the hallway.

Mycroft spun about, illuminating one of the maids. She must have been awakened by our movements. Her hand flew to her mouth to stifle a squeak.

The three of us turned our attention back to the room. Mother lay sprawled facedown on the floor. Chanda lay in her bed with her head hanging off the side. The covers were scattered at the floor at the foot of the bed, as if she had kicked them off.

"Good lord," the maid said. "What happened here?"

"Meredith," Mycroft said and glanced over his shoulder at the maid. "Find some smelling salts and bring them here."

The woman ran off, making little whimpering noises that I was certain would draw some of the other servants from their rooms. He turned Mother over. My throat constricted when I saw her ashen face. When he placed a hand near her nose, my mouth dried to the point I could barely scratch out my question. "Is she—?"

He rocked back on his heels. "She's breathing. Just unconscious."

When he rose and turned to attend to Chanda, I knelt beside my mother. Color now pinked her cheeks, and my own breathing returned to a more normal rhythm. I ran my hand over the back of her head, checking for lumps or any other indication of how she had been attacked. I could find no marks on her until I happened to see her hand. The nail of the middle finger on her right hand was torn. The index finger's nail was bloody. She must have fought her attacker.

A second later, she drew in a deep breath, and her eyes fluttered open.

"Sherry, dear, what are you—?" She raised herself on her elbows and searched the room. "Chanda. Is she—?"

"She's fine, Mother," Mycroft said from behind us. "Just passed out, but her color is returning."

Mother's eyes widened. "Trevor. Did you leave him alone?"

"Colonel Williams is with him," I said, placing a hand on her shoulder. She grabbed my hand, her eyes now quite round.

"Get back to him. Now. He's in grave danger." She turned to Mycroft. "I'll see to Chanda. Go. Both of you."

The urgency in her voice propelled me out of the room and up the servants' stairs to the nursery. No longer concerned with stealth, I ran up the stairs, the pounding of my footsteps reverberating off the stairwell's walls. I could hear Mycroft huffing behind me as I took the steps two at a time.

I paused at the nursery door and scanned the darkened room. Besides Trevor's form in the bed, I could make out another shape on the floor by the foot of the bed. I dashed over and turned the colonel over to check him. He was still breathing. Before I could check on Trevor, a hand landed on my shoulder, and I yelped before I could stop myself.

"Hush, you fool," Mycroft whispered.

But it was too late.

Quick footsteps neared. From the threshold, Miss Bowen raised a candle, revealing the scene.

"Oh no," she said and rushed to Trevor's bed, throwing back the covers.

What I had thought in the dark was my cousin, I realized now was a pillow placed to appear as if he were in the bed. The colonel had been unable to fend off the attacker, and now Trevor was gone.

Mycroft addressed the governess. "You make certain Trevor isn't hiding here in the nursery. Sherlock and I will start the search for him elsewhere."

"What about the colonel?" she asked.

Based on Mother's and Chanda's responses, I said, "He should be all right and awaken shortly."

Mycroft signaled me to rise and follow him. Along the way, I snagged a candle and lit it from Miss Bowen's.

Once in the hallway, I circled about but saw nothing out of the ordinary.

"She can't have gone far," Mycroft said in a low voice when I faced him again.

I paused to consider her options. "The schoolroom?"

We rushed to the next room and threw back the door. The room appeared empty.

Until we stepped in.

Once inside, the door shut behind us.

I spun around too fast with the candle and extinguished the flame. The image I saw before the room darkened, however, seared into my brain. Meredith held my cousin in her grasp, her arm around his throat as we had seen in Mr. Moto's *baritsu* manual. He made no sound, but his rounded eyes let me know he was conscious. The hold had to be the same one she'd used to take out my mother, Chanda, and the colonel. From what Mother and I learned from our practice of the move, it would not take much to make anyone faint. A longer hold would result in the victim's death.

My brain spun. I had to get her to release Trevor before he passed out—or worse.

"Meredith," Mycroft said in a soothing tone I didn't believe I'd ever heard him use, "I've been searching for you."

"I wager you have," she said, the sneer evident even without any light.

"I thought…we were leaving tonight."

"I know, my dearest. All I needed to do was to tidy up a few things, but"—she stopped as her voice cracked—"it didn't work out as I planned. Nothing has."

"We can forget it all. Leave it all. Make a new life. The two of us."

His voice was farther from me, and I guessed he was making his way toward her.

"I-I can't forget it." Her response reached higher tones, sounding more like Aunt Iris during her hysterics. "He was in love with me. I know it. We'd worked so well together as a couple. He said so when we'd pretended to be married. Then, he met her, and she…she *stole* it all from me."

Somehow, I knew she was referring to Chanda. Before I could stop myself, I said, "The man in the barn. He married Chanda. So you hatched a plan to rob her of everything, including her husband and her freedom. And stole her *mangala sutra.*"

"Your little brother is almost as meddlesome as this boy,"

she said. "The necklace should have been mine. *This* one caught me with it, and I almost fixed it, but *he* found him before it was finished."

"There's no need to complete the task anymore. Release him and let's be gone while there's still time." Mycroft's tone remained coaxing, as if talking to a skittish horse.

She exhaled, ending in a sort of whimper. "I-I can't go through the charade anymore. I don't love you. Never have. I would have left you the moment we got to London. You were simply my ticket to get there."

Silence settled on the room. I strained to hear any indication of the others' movements. Was Mycroft getting closer to her? Nothing indicated the location of the others until Mycroft finally responded. His voice was now the one that cracked with emotion.

"Y-you don't mean that," he said. "What we've shared these past few days. You can't have playacted it."

"I'm afraid I can, dearest." The sneer returned to her voice, only to disappear a moment later. "I had only one true love in my life…and now he's gone. I'll deal with both of you after I deal with your cousin—"

The word ended in a squeal. I could hear struggling but couldn't make out more than dark shapes in the dim room. If only…

I remembered the candle and rushed to the teacher's desk for a match. In the spark that followed, I saw Trevor was now free, but the two others struggled in a sort of wrestling hold.

I caught Trevor's gaze and shouted at him. "Run!"

He seemed frozen, staring first at me and then at the other two. I pointed to the door. "Get help!"

At that command, he sprinted to the door.

When I turned my attention to Mycroft and Meredith, I realized my brother was no match for the woman. She had obviously trained in *baritsu* or a similar art, because she was able to dodge and parry his attempts to seize her. The colonel had said she was a street fighter. While my brother seemed to be holding back, as if he were reluctant to physically overpower her as he might a man, she attacked with the viciousness of a rabid mongrel.

If I didn't help him, I was certain Meredith would overwhelm him.

Searching about for a weapon, my gaze fell on the bookcase at the edge of the candle's reach. I hurried to the case and once again the breeze extinguished the candle. In the darkness, I grabbed the first book my fingers touched and turned to the two struggling forms. Stretching my arms overhead, I held the book high and brought it down on the back of the smaller figure.

The blow must have surprised them both. Meredith let out a gasp. She shifted, turning toward her attacker.

Mycroft sensed the shift in momentum and used it to subdue the woman. Following a rustling noise, I heard him say, "I've got you now."

The next moment, I heard him exhale sharply in pain, as if hit in the stomach. A *thud* followed, and then a stomach-churning bash as she connected with his body, now on the floor. If the first blow had taken his breath away, the second certainly stunned, if not knocked him out.

At that point I realized she could now turn her attention to me. I spun about, hoping to make the door and possibly the safety of those coming in response to Trevor's alarm. I only took a few steps before her arm wrapped around my neck. In that split second, I chastised myself again for not heeding Mr. Moto's admonition to never turn my back on my opponent.

As it had when I had practiced with my mother, the pressure in my head increased. Had the room not been already been dark, black spots would have certainly dimmed my vision.

"I was kind to your mother and Chanda," she whispered in my ear. "I only put them to sleep. But you…". The pressure increased, and the blood pounded in my temples, threatening to block out her voice. "I'm not so sure I won't just finish you. You've been a thorn in my side since you almost caught me in the barn."

My heart drummed in my chest, and I knew I had only seconds before her threats might become real. With great effort, I forced myself to *think*. To recall the countermove I'd found in Moto's book and practiced with Mother.

Something about my legs…

I reached up and grasped her arm. Swinging my leg to reach behind her, I became tangled in her skirt but pushed back against her. Both of us fell, and I landed on top of her.

As soon as we hit the floor, I turned against her forearm and broke free. I rolled to her right and pushed myself to my hands and knees, coughing violently as I gasped for breath.

A swishing sound warned me that Meredith had risen to her feet. Between pants, she said, "You little beast. That meddlesome Moto was no match for me, and neither are you. He might have known some *baritsu*, enough to teach you, but I know some tricks that aren't taught in books. And I've used them quite effectively."

An image flashed through my thoughts. Mr. Moto limp on the greenhouse floor. Bile rose in my throat, and I feared I would retch. I tamped down my panic, chiding myself to act.

I rolled away from Meredith in the hopes she would lose me in the shadows. Instead, I rolled into Mycroft. He grunted slightly. At least I knew he was alive. Before I could do more, she pounced on top of me.

Somehow my *baritsu* training rose to the surface. As her arm went around my neck, I threw my head upward and managed to hit her square on the chin. The blow stunned her long enough for me to roll out from under her. In the time it took for me to draw a breath, I was on my feet, facing her in a crouched position.

I searched about for a weapon—something, anything, to use to defend myself.

At that moment, the door opened, and Trevor stood in the doorway, the *tonfa* I'd given to him for his protection in his hand. She raced toward him, and he raised the stick, preparing to swing it like a club. Just as I had earlier, she failed to protect her back. I tackled her from behind, landing on top of her, and we both fell forward at Trevor's feet.

Before she had time to raise her head, I grabbed the *tonfa* from my cousin's hands and slid the wooden rod under her throat. Grasping the stick on both sides, I pulled it tight. She took one choked gasp before bucking against me as I sat on her torso. Her arms flailed backward, trying to reach my arms or head, but she was unable to gain a hold before her body slumped forward in my arms.

Despite her slipping into unconsciousness, I continued the pressure on her throat until a small, white hand covered mine.

"Cousin Sherlock," Trevor said. "Stop. She's asleep. She can't hurt us now."

I stared up at him. Confused by his compassion. This woman had tried to kill him. And succeeded with at least two others. "But—"

"He's right," Mycroft said in a raspy voice. "We've had enough death in this house."

Footsteps pounded up the stairs and toward us as I let Meredith's limp body drop to the floor.

CHAPTER THIRTEEN

The foyer clock had just struck eight the next morning when Constable Gibbons took his leave from our house. Meredith had been taken away hours before by one of his deputies. Despite our lack of sleep, the family, Colonel Williams, and Chanda assembled about the breakfast table. Only Aunt Iris and Miss Bowen were absent.

My mother clasped her hands together and rested her elbows on the table, forming a sort of tent over her plate, her gaze set on Chanda. "What are your plans now?" she asked.

The woman shifted in her seat, glanced at the colonel, and gave a small cough. "We truly haven't had time to discuss it. I only know I can't go back to India."

"I know Mr. Holmes's original request was that you

leave today, or rather quite early this morning, but I'm not sure the urgency remains."

Father raised his head at the mention of his name and opened his mouth as if he planned to comment on the change in circumstances.

Mother, however, continued without a glance in his direction, and he snapped his mouth shut. "Why not stay through the festivities?"

During the next silence while Chanda and the colonel exchanged glances, and then both readjusted themselves on the chairs, I clamped my teeth together to keep my mouth from dropping open as my father's had. I knew Mother well enough to suspect she had an ulterior motive, but her purpose was beyond me. We had more than enough guests without them.

My next thought brought me up straight in my chair. I glanced at Trevor, who was beaming at me and had already figured out what I had just concluded. With Chanda's true identity no longer a secret, she could not be expected to remain in the servants' quarters. Even if she wasn't given Miss Meredith's—*my*—room, someone would have to occupy it, and my only option was to remain in the nursery, along with Trevor.

Oddly, I found the prospect less disturbing than I had when I first took up residence on the third floor. Instead of a nuisance, I now viewed my young cousin as more insightful in some respects than I. His enthusiasm for the holidays gave a fresh appeal to all the activities that would be occurring over the next weeks. At that moment, I determined that even if the colonel and his charge decided to leave, I would request to remain in the nursery with Trevor during his visit.

When I returned my attention to the discussion around the breakfast table, I perceived a slight battle of the wills playing out.

I caught only part of Chanda's response. "…couldn't possibly impose any more. We've created enough chaos."

"But where will you go?" Ernest asked.

Mother's gaze shifted between her brother, his friend, and Chanda, and I thought I understood her interest in keeping our guests here awhile longer. With the arrival of his friend, my uncle had been more animated and open than I had ever known him. I knew his time in India had changed him because my mother explained his sometimes-odd silences and tinkering in his workshop stemmed from that experience. She must have seen something of the brother she had known long ago in his interactions with the colonel, and perhaps was loath to lose it too soon.

The colonel gave a final pause before answering. "We do have connections in London. That was where we were to go when we arrived. There's no danger for us to do so, as we had been led to believe."

"Meredith was truly diabolical in her approach, wasn't she?" Mycroft said.

Williams shook his head. "I'm afraid so. I had no idea learning of Captain Rodgers's marriage to Chanda would unhinge her. She hid it quite well, concealing it on our voyage as she developed her plan. She was the one who reported that Chanda had been followed. I grew suspicious when Rogers shared he'd heard no such reports. I only got confirmation after we arrived here."

I drew in my breath. "The advertisement from St. Barrens."

"Mycroft confronted me about it," he said with a nod. "That's when I drew him into my confidence and asked him to keep close to Meredith."

"I'm afraid not close enough." Mycroft frowned. "Mr. Moto would still be alive, otherwise."

"He left the library that first night and caught Meredith returning through the greenhouse. I'm afraid he was quite mercenary. He'd sent a note to Meredith to meet him in hopes of extorting something from her. She then used it to lure Chanda to the workshop and eliminate two threats with one blow. During her convalescence after her 'attack,' she managed to sneak out of her room that first night when Mycroft and the maid had fallen asleep. She searched Moto's room for the evidence he said he had. But she found nothing."

We all fell silent at that point—some to recall the losses we'd experienced that night, and Mycroft, most likely, his inability to stop Meredith. After a moment, I felt the need to shift the mood settling over the table.

"I have to agree with Mother," I said before I lost my nerve. All heads turned in my direction, but I plunged on before anyone could interrupt me. "You must stay.

Constance and I have worked hard on our pieces, and we need an audience."

"I would, I think, enjoy that very much," Chanda said, dropping her gaze to her plate. "I have read about your English Christmas. I wouldn't want to miss an opportunity to experience it."

"It is settled, then," Mother said, buttering a piece of toast. "We'll discuss changing the rooms about this afternoon."

Out of the corner of my eye, I watched Uncle Ernest steal a glance at Chanda. Just how long would social convention allow the two to remain at Underbyrne? For those with large estates, it was not unusual for guests to remain for a summer or winter, but ours was not so grand. All the same, if the pair's presence remained therapeutic for her brother, I felt Mother might extend the invitation indefinitely.

Before anyone could dispute Mother's conclusion, a knock at the door caused us all to turn toward the front of the house.

"Who could that be?" Father asked. "It's too early for Rose. She said they would be taking the evening train."

A moment later, Mrs. Simpson entered the breakfast room and said in a low voice, "There's a man here to see you, Mrs. Holmes. A *China*man."

If Mother was as puzzled by the ethnicity of her visitor as I was, she didn't show it. She raised one eyebrow and said, "How interesting. Please show him to the parlor and let him know I'll be there in a moment."

Mother stifled a yawn and stood. "Mr. Holmes, will you be so kind as to accompany me? I think Sherlock also."

Once in the foyer, I asked, "Do you know who it is?"

"My speculation is that someone has come in response to my telegram to the Japanese embassy and sent someone to collect Mr. Moto's things."

A thin Asian man in a suit, a bowler in hand, rose from his seat as we entered the parlor. He was young but old enough for a thin mustache. He bowed from his waist and then spoke with only a slight accent in his voice.

"I thank you for seeing me, Mrs. Holmes. My name is Yamana Tokikane, and I am a student here. I received a request from the Foreign Ministry in Japan to collect some items left by a Mr. Takahashi Fusamoto."

My heart skipped at the name and glanced at Mother. While we had been instructed to refer to him as Mr. Moto, I recognized the full name of our *baritsu* master. Her letter to the British consulate had produced a response—much quicker than I had anticipated.

"Yes, of course, Mr. Tokikane. Mr. Mo—Fusamoto's trunk and other items have been stored away. I'll see about having them brought down." After introducing my father and me, she pointed toward a settee. "Please have a seat while I make those arrangements and call for some tea."

The man gave another bow and perched himself on the edge of the couch. He sat erect, his hat on his knees.

Father and I took seats opposite him. After settling in the chair, Father asked, "Did they also provide instructions concerning Moto's…remains? That will require a trip to the coroner's. I can accompany you, if desired."

"A very kind offer," the student said. "I'm afraid I was only told to request his personal items…for his family."

Until that moment, I hadn't considered the final fate for Mr. Moto. What were the customs in Japan? As much as they might wish for his return, the long ocean voyage would prohibit doing so. He might have even been interred already, although I doubted it.

At once, a mixture of feelings, melancholy being the most prevalent, swept over me. It gave me no joy to think of him buried in the pauper's graveyard, but at the same time, he'd deceived all of us and committed treacheries against my uncle as well as Miss Meredith.

Mother stepped back into the room and broke into my thoughts. She smiled at Mr. Tokikane. "The trunk and other items will be down shortly. I must say I hadn't expected someone to come for them, but rather simply provide an address where to ship them."

"I cannot elucidate on my government's decision for requesting me to come to collect them in person. My studies here have been supported by the empire and are now ending," the man said. "I am only responding to their appeal for assistance to include them with my things as I return to my country."

"Of course," she said and flashed another smile.

A clatter of footfalls echoed outside the room, followed by a heavy *thump*. All of us started at the noise, but Mr. Tokikane leaped from his seat. "I would assume the trunk has arrived."

"Would you like to check out the items?" Mother asked, rising as well.

Heaviness pressed upon me once again as I contemplated Mr. Moto's things leaving our house. The image of the man lying on the greenhouse floor rose unbidden to my mind. He had saved my life in a way. Trevor's use of his *tonfa* had interrupted Miss Meredith's effort to strangle me enough to allow me to break free.

"This is all?" the man asked, studying the large and small trunk now in the middle of the foyer.

Mr. Simpson and Mr. Straton stood back by the door. Simpson nodded to my mother, although the information wasn't necessary because she and I had packed them.

Without a word, our visitor opened the larger trunk and inspected the items inside, lifting the things on top to check what lay below. He did a similar review of the smaller trunk. "It appears that all is in order." He glanced at the front door. "I have a wagon outside and can take them to the station now."

"You wouldn't care for some refreshment before you leave? The tea should be here shortly."

"No, thank you. I have a long journey ahead of me, and I would prefer to continue it as soon as possible."

"Of course," Mother said and directed the two men to carry the items outside.

The men stepped back to the trunks but paused when Colonel Williams and Chanda appeared from the breakfast room.

"Colonel Williams," Mother said when they moved toward our guest, "allow me to introduce you to Mr.—"

"Tokikane," the colonel finished for her. He turned to our guest. "What are you doing here?"

"My government asked me to retrieve Mr. Fusamoto's effects and return them to Japan."

"He's a student," Mother said. "Or rather was. He just completed his studies."

Williams stared at the man, but our guest remained poised, as if such scrutiny wasn't occurring. In the end, the colonel said in a cool tone, "He's no student."

Father's gaze moved from one man to the other as he considered the information. "Are you saying…?"

"Our paths have crossed more than once. He's an agent of the Japanese government. These things will not be returned to Moto's family."

Color rose from my father's neck into his face, flushing his cheeks. "I would suggest you leave. Now."

"As a representative of the Japanese Empire, I have the right to—"

"As a representative of the *British* Empire," Williams said, drawing himself to military attention, "I can confirm you have no rights to be in this house when the owner has revoked his invitation. Furthermore, I am now impounding these items in the name of the queen. If your government wishes them back, I would suggest formal diplomatic channels through the Home Office."

For a brief second, Mr. Tokikane's reserve broke. His eyes narrowed and flashed over thinned lips. I drew in my breath in anticipation of some angry outburst from the man. Instead, he bowed low at his waist. When he rose, the same unreadable expression he'd shown under Williams's scrutiny masked any emotions he might have felt.

"You will be hearing from us," he said.

He might have wanted to say more, but Father waved his hand at Simpson and Straton, and the two stepped to each side of the man. The three turned and left the house together. A moment later, the crunch of wheels on the gravel drive signaled his departure.

When the men returned, Father pointed to the trunks. "Take them back into storage."

"Holmes," Williams said, "would you mind if I had a go at them?"

Father glanced about at those assembled and nodded.

"Did Tokikane examine anything before we arrived?" the colonel asked. After Mother described what she had observed, the man opened the larger trunk and pulled out the articles Tokikane had removed. He pulled something from the trunk and straightened. A *tonfa*.

"That's the mate to the one upstairs in the schoolroom," I said.

My breathing quickened when I recalled using it against my attacker's throat last night.

If he noted my agitation, the colonel said nothing as he turned the weapon about in his hand. After careful examination of the stick, he twisted the end of the handle. Everyone gave a little gasp when it came off in his hand. The handle was hollow. He pulled out the drawings Mother and I had found earlier. "I'll arrange to have these things shipped to London, where they can be more thoroughly examined. He may have collected and hidden more information."

"Do you suspect he came here specifically to steal Ernest's inventions?" Mother asked.

I knew her unasked question. It was the same as mine. Had we been duped by our *baritsu* instructor just as Meredith had hidden her plan for revenge? Had Mother's innocent effort to help develop our defensive skills somehow put her brother's ideas—and perhaps the whole nation—at the mercy of a spy?

"Not specifically, no," Williams said. "The government has been sending over 'students' these past few years—some of them legitimately to study; others to gather information on our country, its strengths and weaknesses. Tokikane was one of the latter, and I suspect Moto as well. They have learned to blend in and observe. Moto was more likely sent to study and observe British country life. Stumbling upon Ernest's creations in the workshop during the *baritsu* lessons was just a lucky happenstance. And also his undoing."

Mother's lips formed a thin line. "You're referring to Meredith."

"She said…" I swallowed past the lump in my throat and began again. "She said he was stronger than she expected, but she knew things—from the streets—he didn't."

"Meredith's love had warped into a sort of obsession that provided a logic allowing her to kill the one she loved and have her rival accused of his murder," Mother said, shaking her head, as if the movement would banish the ideas from her mind.

Engouement.

"She did quite a job of setting Chanda up," Father said with a nod.

The colonel turned to my uncle. "I'm grateful to still be here and able to stop Tokikane from leaving with the plans for the crossbow and possibly others of your inventions. I do think the government will have an interest in the bow, as well as other creations."

"You don't consider them irrelevant?"

"As you noted, if the Japanese government has an interest, shouldn't we?"

The grin that spread across my uncle's face stretched literally from ear to ear. "I do have a few more devices I could show you."

"Don't forget the spectacles," I said, hoping to include one of his more singular inventions to the list. "They're almost like a portable microscope."

Williams drew back his chin. "You don't say. I do think a thorough review of all your tinkering might be in order."

"I'm at your service," Ernest said, bowing slightly at the waist.

Mother, however, was the one who caught one detail in Colonel Williams's remark. "You will be moving on to London, then?"

"I received a communication from my superiors. I have been called home, if you will. But not until after Christmas. It seems now that I will have something to show them when I arrive." He turned to my uncle. "Of course, we'll need to have you come and explain things. I do hope you'll be willing to come to London for some extended stays?"

"Well, I…" Ernest glanced at Chanda and another grin flitted about his lips. "I think it can be arranged."

A FEW DAYS LATER, Constance and I stood in front of a semicircle of two rows of chairs in the parlor. The family, including my Aunt Rose and Uncle Peter and their daughter, Lily—all newly arrived from London—were politely applauding our rendition of "Angels We Have Heard on High." Those standing in the back behind them, however, showed much greater enthusiasm. Mother had invited all the servants to listen to this part of our Christmas celebrations. After all, they knew Constance better than those who were seated. Her singing in French had to impress them as well. She'd done two of the four verses in that language.

Mother stood up from her seat at the pianoforte, and the three of us took our bow.

"I do hope you all enjoyed our little recital," Mother said with a smile. More applause came in response. "Please join us for refreshments in the dining room."

The invitation was only for those seated, the staff knowing to return to their duties. When I turned to follow the others heading to the dining room, I realized Constance hadn't followed me. She shook her head when I turned to check on her.

"I shouldn't go in there," she said, dropping her gaze.

"Don't be silly," I said. "You're here as a guest. My guest."

She shook her head again and blinked several times. "My papa tole me I wasn't to be gettin' airs just cuz you're learnin' me to sing and speak French and Latin and all that."

She glanced at me, but I didn't answer immediately as I pondered an appropriate response. I couldn't very well tell her to go against her father's orders, but then again…

"And who told your father this?" I asked. If *my* father or mother had been the one who spoke to Mr. Straton, then I knew to whom I would direct my request to allow Constance to join us.

"I-I don't know. He just said it weren't proper for me to be thinkin' I'm above my station."

"Will he be in the kitchen? I'll speak to him," I said, stepping past her on my way to confront her father.

"Please don't," she said, pulling on my jacket sleeve.

I turned to her. "I'm not going to argue with him. Just let him know you're invited."

Laughter floated from the dining room into the corridor, and Constance glanced at the door. She blinked again, her features softening and her shoulders drooping. I saw in her stance a longing that I was beginning to understand in her. She wanted to be in that room with us but was held back by social conventions. With a sigh, she let go of my jacket.

"I promise," I said, laying a hand on her arm, "I'll not argue. Just ask permission."

She bit her lower lip but nodded.

The staff all turned when we stepped into the kitchen. I realized I had disrupted their own celebration. The scent of spices, apples, and warm bread surrounded me and reminded me I hadn't eaten before the recital. I was too nervous about missing notes in my accompaniment of Constance's singing to do so.

"Master Sherlock," Mrs. Simpson said, "may we help you?"

"Is Mr. Straton here? I wanted to speak to him."

The woman ran her hands down her skirt before she answered. "He's gone back to the barn. I could send a boy to fetch him, but—"

"Yes, please."

I shifted on my feet and observed the others go about

sipping from their cups and nibbling at the food from the plates on the kitchen table. The laughter and conversation we'd heard in the passageway had disappeared when I'd entered. While they did speak, it was in low voices and only after a glance in my direction.

The sigh of relief from the assembled was almost audible when the pounding of boots echoed from the back entrance. Mr. Straton stepped into the room, his cap held in both hands in front of him. "You sent for me, Master Sherlock?"

"Yes, I wanted to ask your permission to allow Constance to join us in the dining room. Just for a little bit."

The man pulled on his collar. "Well…"

He drew out the vowel and glanced to his right. Emily straightened her spine as his attention rested on her. One might almost have missed the slight shake of her head, the signal was so subtle. I knew then who had given Straton his directions, and I prepared additional reasons for the man.

Before he could respond, however, the door opened, and Mother joined us. "Sherry, dear, there you are. Everyone has been asking for you…and you, Constance."

"I came down to ask Mr. Straton's permission—"

"'T ain't right, ma'am." Straton's gaze slid in Emily's direction and back before he added, "Constance needs to know her place."

Straton's glance didn't escape Mother. She considered the maid before her also. Emily lifted her chin.

"I would warn you not to take your direction on

etiquette from Emily," she said, turning her gaze to Mr. Straton. "The woman is quite deceitful."

Emily glared at my mother, her lips sealed tight and straight.

Mother retuned the stare and continued without breaking eye contact with the servant. "Miss Meredith has been interrogated about all the attacks occurring the past few weeks. She denied attacking Emily that night outside the barn."

Scarlet crept into the maid's cheeks and her voice took on a sharp edge. "I have the lump to prove it. How do you explain that?"

"I don't deny your injury," Mother said. "Only how it was inflicted. The woman did it to herself. Just as Meredith did."

I jerked my head toward my mother and then surveyed the others in the room. All were staring at her, and more than one with an open mouth. This bit of news shocked me as much as any of them. Once I accepted this fact, my next question was...

"She confessed this too?" I asked before I even realized the words had escaped my mouth.

Mother nodded. "Although I suspected as much at the time."

"How?" Again, the word slipped out before I could stop it.

"Their symptoms were too severe for the injury," she said with a matter-of-fact tone. "I have seen more than one person with a head injury, and one or two have lost consciousness, but not when hit where those women were. Meredith had at least the good sense to appear to have a brain commotion. But Emily—"

"Was back to work the next day," Straton finished for her.

"This is getting all twisted around," Emily said, stepping toward him. "I-I only wanted you to realize how much you truly cared for me. I'd taken care of your children, fixed you meals, b-but you never *looked* at me the way you did when you spoke of your dead wife."

Tears now ran down her face, and she reached out to Constance's father. He stepped back and raised his hands as if to warn her off.

"Joseph, please. I *love* you. When I saw how Mr. Mycroft was so kind to that woman after her attack in the workshop, I knew that i-if something like that happened to me, you'd be the same. And that night, in the barn, for the first time you did *look* at me that way."

She covered her face with her hands and sobbed into them. I almost felt sorry for her. Her pain appeared quite real. A glance at Constance, however, told me she had no sympathy for the woman. She stared at Emily, her head high.

Apparently, her father had a similar reaction. He pointed his finger at her and then at the door. "You—you viper. Get out of my sight."

The maid stood where she was, her lower lip trembling, before lifting her skirt and running to the back door.

Mother turned her attention to Mrs. Simpson. "She's run off without a wrap. Send someone to fetch her back and escort her to her room. I'll expect her gone in the morning." She turned as if to leave and then turned back to the house-keeper. "Give her two months' wages and a decent recom-mendation. Her actions weren't honorable, but they were not criminal."

At the door, Mother turned to me and Constance. "The guests will be wondering where we've gone off to. Come along."

Only after we were in the hallway, with Mother several strides ahead of us, did I glance at Constance. I'd expected her to be quite pleased with what had occurred, but instead found her mouth and her eyes turned down.

She caught my gaze and shook her head. "She truly cared for my papa. Only he loved my mama too much to replace her so soon. I should've seen that. Maybe told her. Of course, she might'n of not listened. Would've thought I was too jealous of her tryin' to take my mama's place. And I was."

I nodded, recalling her anger the night I'd visited her cottage and helped her bring water into the house. I also considered her observation of how emotion had tempered her judgment. Had I not acted similarly with Trevor? Instead of jealousy, annoyance had made me push him away, and it almost cost him his life. How did one avoid such errors?

Then there was my assessment of Colonel Williams, Mycroft, and Miss Meredith. I was certain the colonel had committed the murders and Meredith had besotted my brother. Beyond Mycroft's acting abilities—which had not manifested themselves to such a degree until this holiday—I had allowed myself to accept and reject data based on my own prejudices. I promised myself not to disregard information in the future simply because it didn't seem to fit some hypothesis.

I reached across and gave Constance's shoulder a quick squeeze. "We can all be blinded at times."

From the passage, I heard the family singing a carol, and when we entered, they all continued but raised their glasses in our direction. Trevor brought me a glass of punch, and I accepted it before joining in the last chorus of the song. The genuine affection on display in the room forced me to blink away the tears forming unbidden.

CHAPTER FOURTEEN

W ithin two days following the New Year celebration, our guests packed and left for their homes. While I regretted Trevor's departure, my greater regret and trepidation involved my imminent return to Eton. The very thought created a spasm that shook my body. While I had known my return was inevitable, I also had been able to consider it something that was a while away.

I could no longer fool myself when I stepped into my newly reclaimed bedroom and found my trunk in the middle of it, ready to accept my uniforms and other school clothing.

The few weeks I'd experienced before being called home when my mother had been accused of murder had been true torture. Most of the other boys—particularly Charles

Fitzsimmons—expressed resentment at my ability to breeze through lessons with little effort.

I would, however, return slightly changed. I doubted any of the other boys at school had been involved in solving more than one murder, having their life threatened more than once, or saving the life of their younger cousin.

Poor Trevor, he'd clung to me and cried when he left, and only my promises to visit him in London over the summer had gotten him to board the carriage with his parents. I planned to use the same promise for myself to get through the next school term. All the same, summer appeared a long way off.

THE HOUSE SEEMED QUITE empty the day after everyone took their leave, and my footsteps' echo in the corridor on the way to the dining room only reinforced the return of our family's solitude. As I had regretted my loss of silence and privacy—especially my bedroom—at our guests' arrival, their departure had created a sort of void in my life.

My thoughts were deep enough that when I entered the dining room, the exclamations of "Surprise!" made me fairly leap in my boots. On the table were my favorite foods and a chocolate cake. Everyone, including Mycroft, was wearing paper hats and a small pile of presents was set next to my plate.

My parents stepped forward, Mother to give me a kiss

and Father, a slap on the back. Even Mycroft and Uncle Ernest pumped my hand.

"B-but my birthday's not until next week," I said, more than slightly confused as I glanced at those circled about.

"It was your mother's idea," Father said, giving a nod in her direction.

She smiled. "Trevor's actually. He said it was a pity you would be in school for your birthday. He made me promise to give you a party before you left. We wanted to have it while he was here, but your Aunt Iris was in too much of a hurry to get back to London. He did make you this."

I took the handmade card she held out to me. He'd drawn what I first thought was a dog, but given the long hair on the neck, I determined it was a horse. Lace edged the image—a little too neatly, and so I assumed someone older had helped with that part. The scrawl inside, however, was purely his writing:

Happy birthday, Cousin Sherlock.
Thank you for being my friend.
Your loving cousin,
Trevor

"I'll write him a thank-you note." I blinked several times to clear my vision and closed the card.

"Can we eat now?" Mycroft asked. "I've been inhaling the aroma of the shepherd's pie for half an hour while Sherlock took his time coming down to dinner. He's not the only one who enjoys Cook's creation."

Father and Mother both gave him a stern look, but I laughed at his outburst. My brother's reaction was not only typical for him but would not have been far off from my own in a similar situation. The difference, of course, was he announced it out loud.

After dinner, I opened the presents in the parlor, which included a book, a new penknife, and a new pen to take to school. When I'd thanked everyone, Mrs. Simpson stepped into the parlor.

"Might Master Sherlock come to the kitchen for a moment?" she asked.

I followed her, expecting the servants to perhaps have prepared a similar display for me there. When I found everyone bustling about as always as they cleaned up after our meal, I stopped inside the entrance, unable to determine why, then, I'd been called down there.

Mrs. Simpson pointed to the back door. "She's waiting for you there."

I entered the boot closet and found Constance dressed in a coat and shawl. Her cheeks were pink from the cold, and she held her hands behind her back.

"Constance, why didn't Mrs. Simpson have you come to the parlor?" I asked, afraid there had been another dispute about her presence among the family.

"I tole her to bring you here," she said, her cheeks

reddening even deeper than from the cold. "I brung you a present."

She now brought her hands in front. A puppy, a bow around its neck, was cradled in them. The dog had a spaniel's shaggy coat and floppy ears but a different snout. It snored contentedly in her arms.

I ran a finger between its ears. The fur was like silk. It cracked its eyes open long enough for me to see the deep brown in them before snoozing again. "It's lovely," I said.

When I raised my gaze, she smiled at me. I recognized the glint of pride in her eyes and knew she was pleased with my response to her gift. How was I going to reject it without hurting her feelings?

"You know," I said, picking my words carefully, "I'm going to school in a week."

"Of course I do, silly." She shook her head as if I were daft. "I figured I'd keep it for you and have it trained. My papa said Mr. Benson was sayin' how he needed some new huntin' dogs. When you come back this summer, he'll be all ready for you."

She lifted the puppy to her face and rubbed her cheek against it. "I thought if I gave it to you now, it'd be kind of like me havin' a part of you here while you was at school."

I held out my hands, and she handed it over to me. As it curled up in my arms, I smiled at her. "It's the best birthday present. Ever."

She studied her shoes a moment and said without lifting her head. "I've been harsh with you lately, and I'm sorry."

The next bit came out in a rush, as if she couldn't stop the emotion that flowed out with it. "I know you're above me. I've always known it. But when I seed all the ladies visitin' lately, how dif'rent they was from me, I knew we couldn't be friends forever. That made me sad, but also…mad."

She raised her head now, her eyes shimmering. "I figured if I was to make you mad too, it wouldn't hurt so much when you left."

"I'll be coming back. It's not forever."

She shook her head. "It won't be the same. It can't be."

As much as I wanted to assure her that Eton wouldn't change me, my recollections of Mycroft following his first year at Eton held me back. While he had never been particularly demonstrative of any emotion other than annoyance, I found him even less tolerant when he returned.

"I will miss you terribly at school. You're my first true friend outside of my family. That makes you special. No matter what. You need to promise you'll work on your letters and music."

"I will." She stroked the puppy's head. "I'd better take him back before he messes your clothes."

"I'll come by later to see you, and… Does he have a name?"

"Toby," she said with a broad smile. "He 'sembles my Uncle Toby. Those big eyes."

I nodded. "Take good care of Toby. I promise to write to both of you."

"Just don't use big words." She lifted the dog from my

arms, and it snuggled into hers with a contented sigh. "Toby's still learnin,' and he don't understand them big ones."

"Nothing more than five letters long," I said, crossing my chest.

I gazed at Constance. Color rose in her cheeks again, fading the freckles there a little, and she gave me a half-smile in return. "I'm really glad I met you that day you killed the pig. You've changed my life."

"Well, it wasn't only me—"

"But you were the one that asked your father to bring me back here and give me the boots. Cuz of that, I learned to sing, I got my papa back, and that ole Emily lost her hold on him. I will never forget you or ever stop bein' grateful. I'm goin' to learn hard so's I can make somethin' of myself."

"I have no doubt, Constance, that you can do whatever you set your mind to. I—" A steady dripping stopped me in midthought.

"No, Toby. Bad dog," she said and held the puppy away from her. The direction in which she thrust him, however, gave him perfect aim at my chest. The spot was warm but quickly cooled.

She sucked in her breath, and her face now flamed bright scarlet. "Oh, I'm so sorry."

Her panicked face produced a bubble of laughter that burst from my lips, and soon we were both cackling. I wiped a tear from my cheek when we finally subsided. "I'd better go and change before I return to the parlor. What about your clothes?"

"I'll be fine. I'll just return Toby to his mother on the way."

She pressed her lips to my cheek quickly and stepped outside, the puppy under her coat to protect him from the cold.

I stared at the door for a moment, and my hand drifted to the spot where her lips had touched. Turning on my heel, I headed upstairs to change before someone came searching for me. I felt as if I held a secret that might be guessed should I linger too long at the back door. On my journey to my newly reclaimed bedroom, I considered all the changes this holiday had brought in addition to more public knowledge of Constance's skills: my uncle's acquaintance with the daughter of a lost love, the government's interest in some of his inventions, and Mycroft's new connections of his own with the government through Colonel Williams. Perhaps changes had occurred at Eton as well?

Regardless, I knew that whatever was sent my way while there, I'd been through worse and survived.

ACKNOWLEDGMENTS

Many eyes viewed earlier versions of this manuscript, and I am grateful to all their comments, remarks, and corrections. I would like to especially thank the following: Nancy Alvey, Richard Schmidt, Sally Sugarman, Liz Lipperman, and Claudia Rose. In addition, I received comments from various anonymous reviewers in contests where I entered the manuscript as well as from agents and editors who shared their views on earlier drafts. Finally, a special thanks to Alicia at iProofread and More for her content editing and Gretchen Stetler for her final edits. Any errors that remain are my own.

ABOUT THE AUTHOR

 **_Liese Sherwood-Fabre_** knew she was destined to write when she got an A+ in the second grade for her story about Dick, Jane, and Sally's ruined picnic. After obtaining her PhD from Indiana University, she joined the federal government and had the opportunity to work and live internationally for more than fifteen years. After returning to the states, she seriously pursued her writing career. She is currently a member of The Crew of the Barque Lone Star and the Studious Scarlets Society scions and contributes regularly to Sherlockian newsletters across the world. You can follow her upcoming releases and other events by joining her newsletter at: www.liesesherwoodfabre.com

ALSO BY LIESE SHERWOOD-FABRE

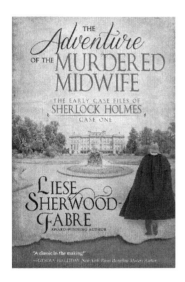

Before Sherlock Holmes became the world's greatest consulting detective, scandal rocked the Holmes family.

Only weeks into his first year at Eton, Sherlock's father calls him and his brother back to Underbyrne, the ancestral estate. The village midwife has been found with a pitchfork in her back in the estate's garden, and Mrs. Holmes has been accused of the murder. Can Sherlock find the true killer in time to save her from the gallows?

Available at all major bookstores.

THE ADVENTURE OF THE DECEASED SCHOLAR

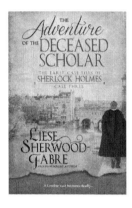

Before Sherlock Holmes became the world's greatest consulting detective, the discovery of two bodies disrupted the 1868 Oxford-Cambridge boat race.

When Mycroft Holmes identifies the body of a drowning victim, the Holmes family is drawn into a scandal that could destroy not only the deceased's name, but their reputation as well. Sherlock and his family have only a few days before the coroner's inquest to explain Lord Surminster's demise. If it is ruled a suicide, his family's assets will be returned to the Crown, leaving his survivors destitute. Should that happen, the victim's sister has threatened to drag Mycroft's good name through the mire as well. Will Sherlock be able determine what happened before more than one family is destroyed?

Available at all major bookstores.

THE ADVENTURE OF THE DECEASED SCHOLAR
EXCERPT

I wrinkled my nose at the Thames' murky waters and shuddered. Anything could be lurking in its fetid waters. Tugging on my collar, I glanced up at the sun's white disk. Despite the day being on the cool side, the crush of people around me blocked any breeze. We were in a green area near the Old Ship pub and had managed to get spaces right by the stone wall protecting the public from dropping onto the river's silt and sand slowly disappearing with the incoming tide. The Oxford-Cambridge boat race was timed to use the rising tide to assist the rowers, and those along the route were expecting it to begin at any moment.

The sunlight sparkled off the water, and, shielding my eyes from the glare, I studied a similar crowd gathered along the opposite bank. No empty space could be seen along that stone wall, either. So many people. All to catch a glimpse of the boat crews as they rowed past.

Rising on my toes, I leaned over the wall, checking downstream to my left for either boat appearing around the river's bend.

"Quit fidgeting," Mycroft said out of the side of his mouth.

I opened my own mouth to protest, but Mother rebuked him first.

"Really, Mycroft." She fanned herself, although I

doubted it did much to cool her. "You can't blame him. If this race doesn't start soon, Sherlock and I are leaving. I'll not have either of us collapsing because of the lack of oxygen in this crowd."

My brother crossed his arms over his chest and gave a little snort. I could almost hear the protests swirling around in his brain. *He* hadn't been the one to decide to come to London for the second part of the season. *Or* suggest we attend the annual Oxford-Cambridge boat race. *Or* insist it was time for him to begin attending some of the season's balls and parties as a country squire's first son. After all, Father had remained at Underbyrne to attend to business affairs for the estate, and we could have too.

Before he could actually express any of these or other sentiments out loud, a far-off shout sent a wave of excited chatter among those surrounding us. Finally, the boat race had begun. Cheers and shouts of encouragement moved up the bank as the boats passed the spectators. Those about us jostled and pushed on all sides, making me feel a little like the flotsam bobbing along in the waters below.

Mycroft bounced on the balls of his feet. While his idea of exercise consisted almost exclusively of strolling between buildings at Oxford—from his rooms to the dining hall, the room over a tavern he and some friends had rented for the Diogenes Society meetings, or to the occasional lecture—I was impressed with both his interest in the race and the exertion he expended in this display of enthusiasm.

"How long will it be before we can see them?" I asked, glancing down the river again.

"The whole race is about twenty minutes," my brother said without taking his eyes from the same spot where I focused. "We're about halfway along the course, so I would estimate eight to ten minutes before they appear."

Ten more minutes of strangers' elbows in my ribs? I wasn't sure anything was worth such torture.

"Excuse me, Mr. Mycroft Holmes?"

The feminine voice made us turn to face a pair of women who had somehow managed to push through the press to our position. They were obviously mother and daughter. Both had the same straight-backed-chin-raised bearing, light brown hair and tipped-up noses. The older woman wore a dark dress that, while fashionable, lacked any flourishes, indicating the final stages of mourning—not yet ready to leave her weeds completely behind. The younger woman, however, wore a pale lavender dress with a matching parasol and a jaunty hat on top of a pile of curls.

Mycroft stared at the two, a hesitation broken by my mother's cough. I coughed as well, but to cover my amusement. That these two ladies seemed to know my brother and had shocked him into silence gave me a certain delight. Only the opposite sex ever seemed to ruffle my brother—my mother being, of course, the exception.

At my mother's cue, he appeared to shake himself free of whatever had stunned him into silence and bowed at the waist. "Forgive me," he said when he straightened. "We've only been introduced once, Lady Surminster, Miss Phillips. Allow me to introduce my mother, Violette Holmes, and my brother, Sherlock. This is Lord Surminster's mother and sister."

"Lady Surminster, how wonderful to meet you," Mother said. "You too, Miss Phillips."

The older woman glanced at her daughter before saying, "We recognized you as one of Vernon's classmates and were hoping—"

The younger woman seemed unable to restrain herself. "Vernon is missing." She turned to Mycroft. "Have you seen him?"

My brother pulled back his chin and dropped his mouth open. A second later, he snapped it shut and shook his head vigorously. "I'm afraid I've been here all weekend. With my family."

"But here lies our concern," Lady Surminster said. "He was supposed to meet us here in London as well. We've been in contact with some of his other classmates, and none has reported seeing him since Thursday. We were hoping he might have been staying with a friend."

Mother placed a hand on the other woman's arm. "I'm sure he's simply enjoying the sights of London. He may even be back home by now."

She shook her head and glanced away, as if to avoid us seeing the worry creasing the corners of her eyes. "We would have heard. I insisted a servant find us immediately if he appeared."

Her daughter's mouth drew down, and a line appeared between her eyebrows. "Which is why we came here. We thought he might perhaps be viewing the race. And why we sought you out, Mr. Holmes."

"Mycroft can make some enquiries for you among his classmates. I'm sure we'll have word soon enough."

"Our address in town is Saint Abel Lane. Number Seventy-four. Please, if you learn anything, let us know."

"Of course. I would suggest it best to go home and wait. Young men in spring often enjoy kicking up their heels a bit."

Before either could reply, the crowd's shouts had us all turn to watch the first boat pass in front of where we stood.

"That's Oxford. I told you we'd win." Mycroft shifted his gaze in the direction they'd just come. "Cambridge is just now passing the bend."

I couldn't help but feel a bit of pride for Oxford. Because my father's plan involved me attending the same university as Mycroft, I already felt a certain affinity for the school. While I still hadn't completed my first year at Eton and, at fourteen, had five years before I would enter university, I couldn't suppress a smug grin at the much-less-enthusiastic cheers flowing through the crowd as the "Light Blues" of Cambridge rowed by.

Another shout downstream followed after the second boat moved on. My breath caught in my throat when I realized the crowd's emotion was different. Instead of cheers, screams punctuated the rumbling.

Made in the USA
Las Vegas, NV
21 September 2022

55701370R00201